SMALL COMFORT

Sara Mac Key

Ia Genberg (born 1967) began her writing career as a journalist and published her debut novel *Sweet Friday* in 2012. She went on to write *Belated Farewell* (2013), *Small Comfort* (2018) and *The Details* (2022) – all widely praised by critics and frequently featured on Swedish bestseller lists.

The Details, shortlisted for the 2024 International Booker Prize and winner of the August Prize 2022, has since sold in thirty-nine territories around the world.

The English translation of *Small Comfort* publishes in 2026.

Kira Josefsson is a writer and literary translator working between Swedish and English. In her translation, Ia Genberg's *The Details* was shortlisted for the International Booker Prize, Judith Kiros's *O* was a finalist for the Barrios Book in Translation Prize and Johanna Hedman's *The Trio* was on the shortlist for the Bernard Shaw Prize. She lives in New York City, where she writes on US issues in the Swedish press and organises with the National Writers Union.

Praise for *Small Comfort*

'A delightful and exquisitely executed literary mini-study that brings to mind Joan Didion'
Expressen

'I haven't read anything better this year'
Sydsvenskan

'Genberg has a joy in language and precision in expression'
Göteborgs-Posten

'The sharpness of Genberg's powers of observation, her humour and delight in language make the stories crackle with life'
Svenska Dagbladet

Praise for *The Details*

'Textured insights into human nature'
New Yorker

'The miraculous sort of novel that fuses with our personal memories and becomes part of us'
Hernan Diaz, author of *Trust*

'A compelling, uncannily precise meditation on transience'
Hephzibah Anderson, *Observer*

'I've underlined half of the book. I wish I could write like this'
Fredrik Backman, author of *A Man Called Ove*

'Brief and penetrating . . . Genberg's marvellous prose is also a kind of fever, mesmerizing and hot to the touch'
Catherine Lacey, *New York Times*

'Emotionally nuanced and formally innovative'
Susannah Dickey, author of *Tennis Lesson*

'I won't forget this beautiful book'
Jenna Clake, author of *Disturbance*

'Genberg's prose is a feat of characterization, a triumph of lending language and profundity to observations of daily life.'
Eliza Smith, *Literary Hub*

'With [Genberg's] latest novel, the curiosity for humans shines through.'
Aftonbladet Literary Prize Jury, Sweden

'In this highly perceptive feel for the small details, an entire world comes alive.'
August Prize Jury, Sweden

SMALL COMFORT

Ia Genberg

Translated from Swedish by Kira Josefsson

Copyright © 2018 Ia Genberg

English translation copyright © 2026 Kira Josefsson

The right of Ia Genberg to be identified as the Author of the Work has been asserted by her in accordance with the Copyright, Designs and Patents Act 1988.

Originally published as *Klen Tröst* in Sweden in 2022 by Weyler förlag.
Published by agreement with Salomonsson Agency.

First published in English translation in paperback in 2026 by Wildfire
An imprint of Headline Publishing Group Limited

9

Apart from any use permitted under UK copyright law, this publication may only be reproduced, stored, or transmitted, in any form, or by any means, with prior permission in writing of the publishers or, in the case of reprographic production, in accordance with the terms of licences issued by the Copyright Licensing Agency.

All characters in this publication are fictitious and any resemblance to real persons, living or dead, is purely coincidental.

Cataloguing in Publication Data is available from the British Library

Paperback ISBN 978 1 0354 3394 0

Typeset in 10.69/16.5pt CentSchbook BT by Six Red Marbles UK,
Thetford, Norfolk

Printed and bound in Great Britain by Clays Ltd, Elcograf S.p.A.

Headline's policy is to use papers that are natural, renewable and recyclable products and made from wood grown in well-managed forests and other controlled sources. The logging and manufacturing processes are expected to conform to the environmental regulations of the country of origin.

Headline Publishing Group Limited
An Hachette UK Company
Carmelite House
50 Victoria Embankment
London EC4Y 0DZ

The authorised representative in the EEA is Hachette Ireland,
8 Castlecourt Centre, Dublin 15, D15 XTP3, Ireland (email: info@hbgi.ie)

www.headline.co.uk
www.hachette.co.uk

Contents

1. Success Greger 1
2. Penance 107
3. Speech at a Wedding 151
4. The Loser's Claustrophobia 173
5. Small Comfort 253

Large parts of the research described in chapter four are based on work done by social psychologist Paul Piff at University of California, Berkeley.

1
Success Greger

First print-out

Ia Genberg: Well, the light is green now.

Greger Johnson: Maybe double-check?

IG: No, I think it's working. All right, Greger Johnson. You spell it with one s, huh?

GJ: Yep. Took out an 's' and added an 'h'. It sounds better somehow, kind of American.

IG: American?

GJ: Yeah. Names that end with 'son', spelled with just one 's', they sound American. Easy to pronounce in English. Couldn't tell you why, but it's true. A name is important, a marker you should finesse if you can. Ia . . . is that short for something?

IG: No, that's my real name.

GJ: Not much to finesse there. Kinda short.

IG: Indeed.

GJ: But easy to remember.

IG: Yep. So how about we get started?

GJ: It's the same with Greger. Nobody my age is named Greger. Nobody born in the seventies is named Greger. That's why it's a hell of a good name if you want people to remember you. And then of course I look like this too.

IG: Like this?

GJ: Yeah, I mean, you can see it with your own eyes. People meet me once and they never forget. I live in their memory forever. For better or worse, of course. For better or worse.

IG: Right. So, listen, why don't we dive right in.

GJ: Of course. Who else did you talk to?

IG: Everyone. Everyone who's alive. Pippi, Emil, Mio, Junior and Karlson, Rusky and Jonatan, Lotta, Ronia the Robber's Daughter and Birk. Tjorven. The whole gang. Plus a bunch of directors. You're the last one out the gate.

GJ: And this is for a book?

IG: A small run, a local publication printed in her memory. There will be other texts in there too, someone else is writing those. And a load of photos from her life. A literary historian is doing something. My job is to interview the child actors, the child actors who are now adults.

GJ: And what do you get?

IG: What do you mean?

GJ: You're a freelance journalist. I assume

you charge something. That you'll be sending an invoice.

IG: Yes. Of course.

GJ: Okay, how much do you take home?

IG: I don't think that discussion is relevant for the interview.

GJ: Who cares if it's relevant or not?

IG: They're giving me thirty thousand kronor. Though that's before social fees and taxes. I keep a bit over half of that.

GJ: So you'll make more writing about me than I got to act in that movie.

IG: Hmm.

GJ: I'm just saying. Just noting.

IG: Those were different times. Plus there's been quite a bit of inflation since.

GJ: It's just something to note. Considering how many people saw and appreciated the movie, how famous it made some of the adult actors. How well things turned out for them.

IG: So you're unhappy with your reward?

GJ: You fucking bet I'm unhappy with it. Are you going to put that in the text?

IG: I don't think so. These pieces are meant to have a pleasant tone. They're meant to be a nice retrospective with pictures from the film shoots, that kind of thing. The publication is meant to help people remember, and also to provide a personal touch, add something new. Can we begin?

GJ: Sure.

IG: Why don't you start by telling me how you got the role.

GJ: My pops sent me to a tryout. Audition, or whatever they call it.

IG: Audition, yes.

GJ: That's what I said.

IG: Sure. Audition. The 'au' doesn't have a diphthong. Audition.

GJ: Diphthong?

IG: Forget it.

GJ: I went to the tryout. There was an ad in the paper. They were looking for a fast-talking boy between eight and ten with a mop of blond hair. I was pretty much made for the role, you know. When I got there, this woman touched my hair to check if it was real or if I'd dipped it in yellow paint. Then she made me stand in front of a camera to answer some questions and talk freely about whatever I wanted. Next they gave me a piece of paper with a few lines I had to read as naturally as possible without looking into the camera. Then I left. They called the next day.

IG: What do you remember from that moment, when you heard their decision?

GJ: It was Pops they talked to. He came to my bedroom, slapped my back and told me I was about to become a national celebrity.

IG: That's what he said?

GJ: Word for word.

IG: Were you excited? Did you scream? Did you run around? What was your reaction like?

GJ: I assume I was excited. I think I called Grandma. I can't quite remember.

IG: You must already have read the book. Did you read it again after that?

GJ: What book?

IG: Uh . . . I mean, the book. The book the film is based on.

GJ: There's a book? I thought it was a movie?

IG: Umm – well . . .

GJ: What? Is there a problem?

IG: Ah. I guess . . . I don't know what . . .

GJ: Haha.

IG: You're laughing?

GJ: Hahaha. You fell for it, didn't you? Haha.

IG: I'm sorry?

GJ: For a second you thought I was an idiot, didn't you?

IG: No, no.

GJ: An illiterate dumdum, just because I was raised in the poorer suburbs by a single, working-class dad, a car mechanic to boot. Out of all the fucking jobs. Audition-audition, diphthong or no diphthong, you tell me it doesn't matter, but of course it does, it always matters. And in your imagination there was no bookcase in our home, right? No, wait, there was a bookcase, filled with ceramic figurines and a couple of Donald Duck Christmas comics, that sad edition with every other spread in colour and every other in black and white. I'm right, aren't I? There was no Mayakovsky like you had growing up. No Göran Tunström, no Selma Lagerlöf, not even Astrid Lindgren. Right? For a moment you thought you'd have to inform me that the film I starred in is in fact based on an enormously famous book by an enormously famous author. Isn't that true?

IG: I wouldn't say that, no.

GJ: Okay, let me tell you what it was like. My old man spent twenty years submitting his poems to Bonnier. Fantastic poems, if I may say so.

IG: Oh?

GJ: And, finally, they decided to publish him. It came in the mail, a personal letter from one of those bearded, bespectacled types who sit all day in their swivel chairs and decide things. A letter with a signature in real ink. It said they were impressed, that it was a raw collection of poems written in a modern, yet personal tone, that they'd tried to call him and asked him to call them back, with a number and name at the end. I still remember it.

IG: The name?

GJ: Yes. And the number. Because I called that number, eventually. And I spoke with that bearded man for a long time. And he asked what we had in our bookcase, and I walked down the shelves and told him everything we had in there, and the bearded man made some good guesses about some of the foreign names I hadn't heard about. How about Gregory Corso, he asked, and I walked over to C and found two of his books. That was after the funeral, when I was putting everything in boxes.

IG: The funeral?

GJ: Pops died two days before the letter came from Bonnier. Cancer in the large intestine. Those tumours just exploded in him. It didn't even take three months.

IG: So there was no book, then?

GJ: No. They had a meeting and retracted their offer.

IG: Ah.

GJ: And our bookcase contained most of what should be in a bookcase. I read Mayakovsky at fifteen, just like you did. But I read him from below. You get what I'm saying? The way he wrote.

IG: None of this has anything to do with our

interview, and I don't know why you sound so angry. If you believe that I came here with a bunch of ideas about who you are, you're probably right. But they might not be what you think. And you shouldn't be so sure that you know everything about me, either. I read Mayakovsky from below too. Though I was about twenty.

GJ: What are your ideas about me, then?

IG: You've been to prison, for instance. Things like that do paint a certain picture, at least for me.

GJ: Like what?

IG: I mean, it's not necessarily negative.

GJ: And why is that?

IG: You haven't been convicted of any violent crime. Violent crime is scary: killing, fighting, unpredictable people. Your crimes are – I don't know, harmless. You tried and failed to take things that weren't yours. Fraud, forgeries.

GJ: And?

IG: I don't know.

GJ: You're saying I'm a loser?

IG: Not at all. Not at all.

GJ: No?

IG: And, anyway, that was a while ago, right? It's sort of past the statute of limitations by now.

GJ: A prison sentence never expires. It follows you for the rest of your life, no matter how short your time, no matter how insignificant the crime. Every prison sentence is for life, by definition. You go to prison and try to land a job afterwards and you'll see how easy it is. Or a flat.

IG: You work now, though, don't you?

GJ: Work? I'm self-made.

IG: Self-made?

GJ: An entrepreneur. You know: Jacob Wallenberg, Antonia Ax:son Johnsson. Only I'm Greger Johnson. I'm an entrepreneur; I own a company.

IG: In what industry?

GJ: The treasure-hunting industry.

IG: Okay.

GJ: Though lately I've been thinking of quitting.

IG: You've found the treasure, then?

GJ: Yes. I wouldn't be lying if I said as much.

IG: Anything that'll put you back in touch with the justice system?

GJ: Hardly.

IG: I've got a source who works as a cop. Called him before this. Turns out you're implicated in an open investigation.

GJ: A small car loan, yes. The other day. Pure self-defence.

IG: Self-defence?

GJ: Protection against the cold. It was minus ten. If not more.

IG: Can you tell me about it?

GJ: Are you going to write about it?

IG: Of course not. I'm just curious. My source said it was an odd affair.

GJ: Okay. So I was out on a walk.

IG: Yesterday? In minus ten?

GJ: Could have been minus twenty. If not more. It was the day before yesterday. I wasn't wearing appropriate clothing.

IG: Why not?

GJ: My girlfriend had thrown me out.

IG: Ah.

GJ: We'd had a fight. It's her flat – I just live there. Like I said: you go to prison and try landing a flat afterwards. I live with her, but sometimes she gets sick of me and then she'll throw me out. She's a pretty dynamic person. She'll turn on a dime about loving me or not, about loving someone else, what I need to do in order for her to love me. She explodes at regular intervals and when that happens I'll go for a walk in the neighbourhood until she cools off. Sometimes I'll take a half-hour to sit outside the basement office door and smoke.

IG: Like Emil in Julle's workshop.

GJ: Right, though that's a different movie. This time the basement was locked, so I had to take a hike. She lives next to a flush neighbourhood and I like to stroll around there, check out the homes. They're huge, you know. Some of them have a pool, patio, a two-car garage. Just the toys scattered on the lawns have a combined value that exceeds my annual income. But this evening was dark and snowy and really fucking cold. A cold you can't even imagine. I normally enjoy walking around there, but not this time. Way too cold.

IG: You normally enjoy looking at toys whose combined value exceeds your annual income?

GJ: Yeah, because at some point it's going to be my turn. Right? That's got to be what everyone thinks when they see rich people, when they find themselves with their nose pressed to the bulging wallets of other people: I'll show them. It's gonna be my turn one day.

IG: I'm not so sure about that.

GJ: You don't think that way? You can't be too rich yourself.

IG: Not too rich, no.

GJ: You're not drowning in jobs, and they don't pay that well. Am I wrong?

IG: No.

GJ: Well, then I'm convinced that you're thinking: Soon enough, you arseholes. Just you wait. It's going to be me soon, driving one of those fucking four-wheel-drive land yachts, and I'm not going to stop when you're at the pedestrian crossing.

IG: I have to say that I almost never think that way.

GJ: You're happy with your lot in life, then?

IG: I don't know if I experience any particular lot in life. I don't think I've been handed a lot to be happy or unhappy with.

GJ: That's precisely what sets the lower class apart from the upper classes. We experience our lot in life. The rest of you don't. You think you've decided to be a little bit poor, don't you?

IG: I wouldn't say that I'm poor, exactly. Or rather, the financial stuff, I don't know if that's the most important thing. That it matters all that much.

GJ: Exactly.

IG: I'm sorry?

GJ: That unwillingness to make any sort of analysis. But if you did, as I do almost daily, even several times a day, you'd immediately realise that things could be different, and that you want to get back, claw back. You'd realise that it has to be your turn at some point.

IG: Revenge?

GJ: No. A righteous reset.

IG: Ah.

GJ: A little bit of success.

IG: I see.

GJ: I don't think you do. Not in any sort of real

way. But, in any case, that is the feeling I have whenever I amble down those leafy streets lined with villas.

IG: Okay, but if you're always thinking about revenge—

GJ: I'm not.

IG: Call it taking back, getting even. It's got to be hard to walk through life with that feeling?

GJ: Tons of people walk through life with that feeling. Anyone who's ever experienced the *'in'* of *in*justice walks through life with that feeling. They all live in that sensation; they've made a home inside it.

IG: Okay. Let's get back to your story.

GJ: Are we in a rush?

IG: No. I was just checking the time.

GJ: It's not often you see a wristwatch these days.

IG: I know. Impossible to find someone who'll repair it. All they do is tell me to get a new one. But yeah – no, we're not in a rush, I just wanted to check the time. Keep going.

GJ: Where was I?

IG: In a swanky neighbourhood, knee-deep in your usual desire to rectify things.

GJ: Right. And there it is. It's minus ten with a sprinkling of snow, it's windy, the spit on my lips is transforming into fucking ice, the foreskin is cracking inside my underwear, my toes are long gone, my fingers and nose – I am, to put it simply, succumbing to the cold. And, all of a sudden, there it is.

IG: What is?

GJ: The car. With the engine on. A BMW, I don't know which model, but the colour is that heartfelt shade of golden yellow, as if the enamel had been tuned. A BMW is an extreme car in many ways – you have to agree with that.

IG: I don't know. I don't know anything about cars.

GJ: Didn't you make a movie about cars? About drivers' licences or something?

IG: It was about people. Did you google me?

GJ: Of course I did.

IG: Fine. I know a bit about cars, but I'm not exactly passionate about models and stuff like that. Keep going.

GJ: With a BMW, you don't get into your seat the way you would in a regular car. You sink into it. You let it hold you like another body. It's organic in a way no other car can even approximate. As close to a mammal as a car can be without ceasing to be a car.

IG: I see. Keep going.

GJ: The varnish gleams, there's no snow on it, it looks brand new. It just stands there, engine humming, a purring little animal, ready to embrace me and take off. The only way to understand this situation is as a kind of offering, right?

IG: An offering?

GJ: Here I am, about to freeze my ass off. I've been told to hit the road and it's going to be several hours before I can go home again. I've got nothing on me other than an empty wallet and two smokes, I'm wearing a suede blazer, a button-down shirt and a pair of jeans without long johns underneath. Ice is forming on my lips and I've got no hat on. No hat, no car, no friends who are home and willing to let me in, barely even a girlfriend at this point. No car, no food, no booze. No car. Especially no car. And there it is: a kind of offering. The door is unlocked, the engine is on, the key is in the ignition. Don't tell me you wouldn't have got in.

IG: I don't think I would.

GJ: Not even for a spin?

IG: Never. No matter how poor or cold I was. I'm too much of a chicken.

GJ: It's not about being bold. It's about desperation. Your degree of desperation.

IG: Some kind of courage is necessary. There's a line there I can't cross. I don't want to cross it. And I can't.

GJ: You've never had to cross it.

IG: Perhaps.

GJ: You're sighing.

IG: Yes.

GJ: You're looking at your watch.

IG: I am?

GJ: What time is it?

IG: I don't know. Did I look?

GJ: I'll continue. The car is there, its engine is humming, it's calling my name with an offer I don't refuse. I don't even think of it as theft, not exactly. It's more as if I was suddenly given a chance to protect myself against the cold. And the feeling of getting inside that car... It's indescribable. Pale leather seats, armrests that fold down. A compact, powerful gearshift. A dashboard that looks like it was carved out of a single piece of wood. It doesn't even look like a dashboard, with technical controls, but like something else, a living thing. The car itself looks as if it has a heart, and I can almost hear it beating. Then there's the fact that it's golden yellow. It's just too much. Do you get it?

IG: I don't.

GJ: I shift into first gear and we roll off. I don't even need to think.

IG: But your plan was to warm up a bit?

GJ: I don't know what the plan was. I got inside and suddenly it was the most natural thing in the world to take off. There it was, so warm.

IG: Where did you go?

GJ: Not far.

IG: Where were you planning to go?

GJ: Initially, I was just going to take it for a spin.

IG: A spin?

GJ: An easy spin. I turned on the radio, took off my blazer, adjusted the temperature. Mozart's Sixth Symphony. I changed the station. Deep Purple, that eighties record. What's it called again?

IG: *Strangers* something. Their best.

GJ: By far. I drove south, towards the city, coasting. Turned wherever I felt like it, was planning to park it somewhere, have a smoke, then take the subway home.

IG: But?

GJ: Yeah, then I realised it wouldn't be so hard to pass it on. That goddamn car could be out of the country in forty-five minutes as long as I got hold of the right people.

IG: Oh?

GJ: You don't know much about this stuff, do you?

IG: No. I know very little about this stuff. I've gathered that there are ships in Frihamnen that move goods to the Baltic countries.

GJ: The Baltics and beyond. They've got auto paint technicians working on board, one of the best painting gigs you'll find in this country. My yellow pearl would dock as a green emerald. Or a red kiss.

IG: Okay. You went to Frihamnen?

GJ: That's where my troubles began. When I started to make plans. It's always where the troubles begin. I got my phone out, trying to get hold of the right person for this kind of undertaking. Made a bunch of calls while navigating the roundabouts to the city. Red lights. People were looking. I was getting nervous. I was starting to feel rushed. You understand.

IG: Not exactly.

GJ: I was agitated, anxious. I felt pursued.

IG: I heard you drove straight into a snowdrift and were seen running off.

GJ: Who says that?

IG: The police report. Like I said, I read it.

GJ: I was seen running off? Period?

IG: You were seen running off.

GJ: That's all?

IG: What's all?

GJ: Running off. Nothing else?

IG: What would that be?

GJ: Oh, I don't know.

IG: Is there something else? This story feels kind of incomplete somehow.

GJ: That's because you're a journalist. You guys

arrange stories that way, as if everything is finished with a bow tied on top. But the real world isn't whole like that. It's totally fucking half. Unfinished, like your name.

IG: That's too kind of you.

GJ: No offence.

IG: My question is why you're smiling in that – how can I put it? – triumphant way.

GJ: I'm not smiling. Why would I be smiling? The cops showed up and nabbed me the next day, so why would I be smiling?

IG: You smiled. I asked why.

GJ: To summarise: I hit the snowdrift, got knocked by the steering wheel, couldn't get out of the drift. I peaced out. Took the subway home, knocked on my girlfriend's door, bled a little, she let me in. All is well on God's earth. The next day – yesterday – the cops rang my doorbell and brought me to the precinct for questioning. They let me go, but there's a small charge waiting for me. I assume probation, and in the meantime I'll lay low. Ulrika and I have made up again.

IG: Ulrika?

GJ: My girlfriend.

IG: I'm glad.

GJ: And, since the car barely even had a scratch, it was able to return to its owner the next day, after a brief stay at the repair shop. It was the shortest of thefts, more like a little loan.

IG: What's so funny?

GJ: It's just crazy, all of it.

IG: What, specifically?

GJ: I'll tell you some other time. Another time. Later.

IG: Okay.

GJ: I'm gonna take a leak.

IG: To the right, in the hall.

GJ: Thanks.

IG: Hi, honey. No, not yet, it's going to be a while. Are you home already? Was there any mail for me? I see. Okay. No, he's a total loser. It's just nasty. No, he's in the bathroom. No, I've got no idea how I'm going to produce a piece about him. The others have normal lives. This guy – I don't know. No, I don't think drugs, but a load of crimes. Prison and stuff. He's confrontational, keeps arguing with me, trying to put me in place somehow. A total loser. No, that's too hard. I've asked Paul again. I think he'll do it. It's not like he's got anything else going on. I'm going to call him now. See you. Kisses.

Paul, hi, did you get my message about the transcription? Great. I'd guess it's about two hours, a bit more. No, there's no huge rush. Sometime next week would be swell. I'll send you the file when I'm done. Great, talk soon.

GJ: I took some more coffee.

IG: Good. Shall we?

GJ: And a cinnamon bun. Did you bake?

IG: No. My colleague did.

GJ: It's a co-working space, this. Small.

IG: Yes.

GJ: You don't have a private office?

IG: No. Space is at a premium in this city.

GJ: See? You've got financial circumstances too. But you don't have the correct analysis.

IG: I'm not sure what there is to analyse. I rent a space with a few friends, and before that I was working from home. This feels like luxury to me.

GJ: And Percy Barnevik?

IG: What about Barnevik?

GJ: Does it feel like luxury to him? Or Niklas Zennström, Filippa Knutsson, Fredrik Eklund, all those CEOs? Would this feel like luxury to them?

IG: I don't imagine so, no. But I don't compare myself to them.

GJ: Why wouldn't you?

IG: Well, why would I?

GJ: Because you're all humans. You and Niklas Zennström, for instance, are born the same year.

IG: You really did google me.

GJ: In the same suburb, even. Do you know each other?

IG: No, not at all.

GJ: Have you met?

IG: No.

GJ: But you could have been friends, right? You could have been neighbours, your parents could have socialised, been co-workers, attended each other's Christmas cocktails. You could have been in the same school and year, gone to each other's graduation parties, maybe kissed each other outside a cinema on Storgatan some late night. Right?

IG: What are you trying to get at?

GJ: You could have been him. There's no reason you didn't become him. Don't you think?

IG: Absolutely not. He's a genius. I was a goalie for my football team and set a new district record for number of missed saves in a game. Twenty-two.

GJ: That's not what makes the two of you different.

IG: No. There's a whole host of other things too.

GJ: What makes you different from one another is luck. Pure chance. The tiniest little things with enormous consequences. And we only look at the consequences when we try to determine how different we are from each other. Otherwise, we wouldn't be able to bear it.

IG: I don't know what you're talking about. It sounds interesting, but I think we've got kind of off track.

GJ: And the track is?

IG: You could tell me a bit more about the film shoot, for instance. Was Astrid there?

GJ: Astrid who?

IG: Har har.

GJ: Yes, in fact. She crouched down and didn't touch my hair. I was so used to everyone touching my hair when I was little. Everyone would come and tug and pet and tousle, but she didn't even look at it. We talked for a good while.

IG: About what?

GJ: No idea. But I remember that I understood how she was able to write those books. She saw things from below. It's not about the stories, but the perspective.

IG: Right.

GJ: The pen's position. Where it's writing from.

IG: Right.

GJ: Take yourself, for instance. You'll write this from above.

IG: That's what you think?

GJ: Because it's the only way it can be written. Because this kind of thing is always written that way. It's in the nature of the thing. I'm sure it will be empathetic, thoughtful, sensitive, spot-on, with a few zingers. But from the above. It's inevitable.

IG: I guess I'd prefer it if you read the piece before judging it.

GJ: I don't need to read it to assess it. If white has thirteen pawns left and black has two, everyone already knows the result. Isn't that right? Nobody needs to see that game.

IG: I'd want to know how it went. How black lost its pawns.

GJ: That's the thing. The game starts that way, with that distribution.

IG: Oh God.

GJ: What time?

IG: Two thirty.

GJ: What are you doing after this?

IG: I need to pick up my kids.

GJ: Daycare?

IG: After-school.

GJ: A drag?

IG: A drag, and fun.

GJ: That's what you're obligated to say, right? Add that word. Fun.

IG: I don't think anyone is obligated to do anything. It is fun.

GJ: Sometimes?

IG: Most of the time.

GJ: And hard, most of the time?

IG: It's both. It comes with the annoying parts. It comes with the fun parts. Can we get back on track? You were telling me about the film shoot: Astrid came to visit.

GJ: Yeah. She came up to me before she talked to any of the others, including the director. I thought she wanted to touch my hair, but no. She just sat down in front of me and asked for my name, if I was in school, how I felt about the shoot, the adults, if I was homesick. That kind of thing. She didn't look at my hair at all, and not at my body either. I had already started to look like this, you know.

IG: Like what?

GJ: Like a hunchback. Kyphosis paired with scoliosis and progressive spondylolisthesis. Inexorably congenital. As if my spine was about to make a loop and had a change of heart halfway through. But she didn't look at me in that way, and it was a relief. I mean, I didn't think of it as a relief back then – kids don't. I just experienced it. I was inside of it for a few minutes, a few hours. I wasn't analysing. All of a sudden, it was easier to breathe, and I didn't know why. I thought of her as an old woman, but now I understand that she was still pretty young at the time. Of course she did become an actual old woman, an old lady. But she still had that thing. It was obvious. The way she looked at the children.

IG: Would you say that your encounter with Astrid—

GJ: Would I say what? That it changed me?

IG: That it meant something.

GJ: Right, now you're looking for a headline. An angle. The encounter with Astrid changed his life. The respect in her eyes, blah-blah-blah. Just lay off it.

IG: Why?

GJ: Why you gotta be like that? You journalists? Why are you always on the lookout for these twists, these resolutions, these clever little angles on everything? Why do you bend reality to suit you? It's as if you can't live otherwise.

IG: Okay, so the whole thing about writing a text for a magazine or a book is that you have an angle, a throughline, a beginning and an end of some sort. And since this publication is meant to add to her memory for the celebration of her life, it needs to have a positive spin. It's meant to be cheerful and happy overall. Which is why it would have been great if the encounter with Astrid gave you something, but

Small Comfort

I can't put that in if it didn't. People want to read about cheerful things. At least in this type of publication.

GJ: What did you do before this piece? What was the last article you published?

IG: Something for an in-flight magazine. The kind you'll find in the seat pocket on an aeroplane. I often do interviews for them. Businessmen, actors, international celebrities, entrepreneurs.

GJ: Cheerful stuff.

IG: Articles in the in-flight magazine are meant to be positive. That's the nature of things.

GJ: Right. So people don't have to think about death and starvation, wars. All those goddamn massacres of innocent children who are just trying to get to school on a Tuesday morning. The oil crisis, the rain forests, the plastic that fills the ocean.

IG: That's the idea, yeah. Long, substantial pieces, but nothing that makes people unduly distressed.

GH: And this little thing we're doing here, how did you describe it? Light and cheerful?

IG: Exactly. There's a target audience, which is everyone who joins or reads about the local celebration of this world-famous children's-book author. It's meant to be a pleasant reading experience. They want to remember something they've forgotten, learn something new, feel happy and revived.

GJ: So you write about happy things in a sad world.

IG: Perhaps. Though that's not how I would put it.

GJ: And what if that happiness isn't real? Or if it's not enough? What if Greger Johnson, the lead character who was promised a bright future full of success and riches, the incredible child actor with the crooked physique, what if his success never came? What if there is a Greger-shaped hole in that successful future, a hole nobody saw unless their attention was drawn to it? What if all that talk about success was, in fact, a little push in the opposite direction? What would you write if that were true?

IG: I don't know. I guess that's what I'm sort of pondering here.

GJ: Fine. I'm sure you'll find an angle. A positive angle. A jack-of-all-trades, he's often still recognised thanks to his unusual looks. And he has never forgotten his encounter with Astrid.

IG: Something like that, probably. Sounds about right.

GJ: Jack-of-all-trades is a great description in situations like this. Whenever someone is jobless, in jail, dissolves in various psychiatric states of emergency for prolonged periods of time, turns into an anxious shut-in, drinks too much, goes digging for gold in Australia, sets sail on the oceans: voilà! You just call him a jack-of-all-trades.

IG: Australia? Are you talking about yourself here?

GJ: Yep. Found a nugget. It's at home. Nobody wants to buy it. Too small. What a tiny bit of success, so minuscule that it was too small to be anything but itself. It's exactly how some types of achievements work.

IG: How come you went digging for gold in Australia?

GJ: There's your angle, isn't it?

IG: No. More like a story.

GJ: Journos and their goddamn stories. These packages, these sad little packages. But, yes, I did go to Australia. I tagged along with a buddy who was going to look for gold. People find a brook and then they pan from five in the morning till seven at night when they return to their cabin to drink beer and count the nuggets they might have found. Gold seekers are intimate with their own naked desire for fourteen hours a day, several weeks on end. This greed that they find in themselves and others, in the eyes. Everyone wants to find that nugget, the one people talk about, the rumours that spread and the stories, the gossip. Spots like that – they're wholly mythical. Overrun by stories of wealth. At night, everyone dreams of gold. In the daytime, we sift the sands.

IG: How long were you there for?

GJ: Three months.

IG: Wow.

GJ: Yep. Most people hold out for a week or two. I was going to head home, but then I met someone who'd just found something – or more likely I met a story about someone who'd just found something – and then there was a guy who'd been there for a year without any luck until he panned this big fucking hunk. So that kept me for another week, and then another. And at this point I start to have these hunches, like off by that rock and to the right, if I walk over there, I'll find something. And I seek out spots I think nobody else has tried. I'm out in the wilderness where no person has ever set foot before and I can feel it, this is it, nobody has tried this spot before and I'll dig for days until I find a cigarette butt shoved into the ground next to a half-empty can of white beans. That's a pretty good description of human life, right there.

IG: And what does that description look like?

GJ: Let's see. Greedy, oblivious.

IG: Not very optimistic.

GJ: Ah, you were looking for optimism? Sorry, no

can do. It's against my nature, against my lived experience.

IG: Fine. But it's still an adventure, right? Panning for gold in Australia.

GJ: On paper, sure. Absolutely. A lot of stuff looks like an adventure on paper. You could write that, why not. Greger Johnson: gold-digger, adventurer, jack-of-all-trades. A seeker. That's another good word. Seeker.

IG: Are you? A seeker?

GJ: Sure, I was searching. Obviously. Passionately. Searching for gold.

IG: That's not what I meant.

GJ: I know, I know. You were looking for something deeper. Something you can write about.

IG: I was just asking. So far you've told me quite a lot of things I can't write about. And I do have to file something.

GJ: They pay you by the word?

IG: They're paying for the whole job. Interviews with all the actors, the main characters. It will be obvious if someone is missing.

GJ: A Greger-shaped hole in the publication?

IG: Something like that.

GJ: Everyone's going to notice?

IG: I don't know what people notice. But I assume some will realise, yeah.

GJ: Which means that it's actually better to not participate. If you want to be seen. It's easier to see what's been left out.

IG: I'm not so sure about that. I think it's probably best to be seen if you want to be seen. Most likely.

GJ: But you're not entirely sure?

IG: I'm pretty sure. I know it makes the whole better.

GJ: What are the other stories like? You said I'm the last one out the gate.

IG: Well. Some of them have become real actors, as you know. Others are engineers, advertising creatives, teachers, all kinds of things.

GJ: Nobody like me?

IG: Nobody like you, no.

GJ: They've done well for themselves? They're successful?

IG: Depends on how you define success, I suppose.

GJ: Money.

IG: They appear to be successful in their chosen lines of work.

GJ: Do they have money? That's what I mean by success.

IG: I don't know. And I don't think that's how people in general think about success.

GJ: It definitely is. They just don't know it.

Small Comfort

Money is at the top of the list, and it's at the very top for people who think they don't care about it. Because there it's invisible.

IG: Hmm.

GJ: That's why I can ask you. You absolutely know if they've got money or not. You're the type of person who always does a quick income assessment. It's not something you do consciously, but later on, when you say goodbye after spending time with someone, you always have a sense of how much they make, if they've got wealth, and so on. Stuff like that registers for you way before the rest of it.

IG: What's the rest of it?

GJ: IQ, ethnicity, shoe size, sexuality, where they live, how they drink.

IG: I don't know about that.

GJ: Am I wrong?

IG: I honestly don't know. But I probably have a sense, yes. I guess so.

GJ: Okay, so answer my question. Do they have money?

IG: Two of them do. One seems to have been rich from the beginning. Two of them don't.

GJ: See?

IG: Fine. But of course there are many ways to be rich.

GJ: There's only one way where the rich person is actually rich. One original.

IG: I don't know if that's true.

GJ: I need a smoke.

IG: Sure. Toss the butt in the pot by the door when you're done. The neighbours flip out otherwise.

IG: Hi, it's me again. No, it's dragging on. Do you think you could pick them up? Great. Their PE bags too. Thank you, seriously. No, it's rubbish. Not a gangster, no. Small-time at the most. A tiny Smurf gangster. Yeah. No, I'll get groceries on the way home. We can do some kind of pasta. He's back. I'll call you when I'm on my way. Okay, bye.

GJ: So you were telling me about the others?

IG: Do you all hang out?

GJ: Never. I was invited to some kind of event once. A reception, soon after her death. I'm sure some of the others were there.

IG: But not you?

GJ: I was in the slammer.

IG: Ah.

GJ: The evening papers made a little thing of it. Me being in jail. They tried to paint my life as tragic, calling what I did petty crime – not in the extenuating sense, but in a belittling way. Petty financial crime, fencing, double-dealing, conspiracy to commit fraud. Basically, there's nothing below conspiracy to commit fraud. I wasn't even able to commit minor fraud; it began and ended with the attempt itself. I tried without success and that's when they got me. I tried to defraud someone and all my plans were for naught.

IG: What happened?

GJ: I took the money and ran. Like so many times before. It's the simplest of all financial crimes, the one that offers itself up to you. You take the money, you run.

IG: How is that fraud? Running away with someone's money is theft.

GJ: Depends on how the prosecutor decides to spin it. I ran. Technically speaking, I ran. Before that, I'd lied a little. The accounting was in a rubbish bin in the garden of my summer house, and of course they found it.

IG: Pretty sloppy.

GJ: I thought I had the concept all figured out, but it didn't hold water.

IG: Just like with the car the other day.

GJ: Just like with the car. But it's not the same thing.

IG: Why not?

GJ: Success requires luck. Despite it all, this

particular event had a few things speaking for it in that department.

IG: What department?

GJ: The department of luck. I found myself under the sign of luck.

IG: Seems to me you found yourself in a snowdrift.

GJ: That too. But not only that.

IG: All right. This is taking longer than planned. Could we pick up the thread again?

GJ: Sure. You were telling me about the others. Someone is rich, another isn't, they're all relatively successful in their chosen lines of work. They've probably designed their paths with great care.

IG: That's all I know. This publication isn't meant to deal with their adult lives other than on the periphery, as an enlivening detail. It's going to focus on the film shoots, memories from it, the way you remember Astrid and your relationship to her books. Light fare, upbeat. You and I have spent a bunch of time talking about other things, and that's good because it gives me a broader picture of you. But the piece won't focus a great deal on any of that.

GJ: So what will it focus a great deal on?

IG: The film shoot, for instance. Could you tell me about it?

GJ: It took place in the summer, as you know, but

Small Comfort

we started filming before school was out, so I missed the end of the semester. That must have been where the others learned how to be friendly and polite, and presumably also algebra and the rest of the shit I never learned. We spent a whole day travelling into the back of beyond somewhere for the shoot. We stayed at a hotel. I shared a room with one of the actors. One night, I woke up and realised he was jacking off while watching me.

IG: Are you serious?

GJ: Yes. Come here, he said. But I just turned round and closed my eyes and waited for him to finish, and when he fell asleep I went outside and walked around the village.

IG: Did you talk to anyone about this?

GJ: Who would I have talked to?

IG: I don't know, the director?

GJ: This actor was buddy-buddy with everyone. I asked to change rooms, though. I told them I'd heard a rat and that I was scared of rats.

IG: And they let you?

GJ: Yes. But everyone laughed. The actor laughed too, came up to me and sniffed and made rat sounds.

IG: Oh my God.

GJ: That was just one episode, though. Filming was fun. I decided that I wanted to become an actor and everyone said there was no reason I shouldn't, that I had the requisite talent. Now, in hindsight, I understand it was just something they said to make me perform better, so that I would pull myself together in front of the camera, but at the time I believed it. I really did. After we finished shooting, I was an actor. At least that's what I thought. I'd experienced something my classmates hadn't, something absolutely unique. A hatch had opened right next to my head and I'd be able to climb out. That's how it felt.

IG: And what happened?

GJ: I went back to school after summer break. My classmates didn't care all that much, the excitement from the spring semester had faded, things were back to normal. Then the film premiered and the excitement returned, but only briefly. The whole thing melded with everything else that was going on. It was shown in cinemas for a while and then it went away. I thought I'd become a celebrity and somehow take revenge.

IG: How did you feel watching the movie?

GJ: It was in a small screening room with Pops and some of the actors. The rat man was there too. He smiled at me and greeted Pops politely. Shook his hand, said I was talented. Then the movie started, and it was weird to see yourself on screen like that. When it was over, everyone told me I looked so natural, but all I could see was a hunchback moving about stiffly. The camera kept finding all these weird angles, hunchback angles. And I thought, okay, it was the back they wanted. And the hair. And the mouth with all those teeth. And the way I talk so fast that people almost can't hear what I'm saying. Clearly it was only the details that counted. The attributes, the accessories, the little idiosyncrasies. Not me.

IG: Is that what you think?

GJ: If you saw the movie, which I assume you did somewhat recently—

IG: Yesterday.

GJ: Well, what did you see? What did you see when you looked at me?

IG: I saw a child on an adventure, played by you.

GJ: No. That's not what you saw. You saw a weird child, played by a child with weird tendencies. And what you remember is that weirdness – that's what stands out, that's why it's me in front of the camera. But it's not me. Do you see what I'm saying?

IG: Okay, but those attributes you're talking about.

GJ: Yes. The hair, the talking, the teeth. The back, especially.

IG: They're a part of you, aren't they? That's what it's like for all actors. Mikael Persbrandt has his fair share of attributes too, right? His voice. His height.

GJ: His arse.

IG: Sure, why not?

GJ: That comparison would make sense if his arse had a tail. But his arse doesn't have a tail, right? His arse is attractive. Am I wrong?

IG: What are you getting at?

GJ: You know what I'm getting at. And you're just trying to be kind. I appreciate it – don't get me wrong. The thing is, I could see through that already when I was nine, sitting there in the cinema. And I saw it in my old man's eyes. I could see he saw what I saw. It was painful for him. I heard him crying later that night. He cried in the kitchen after I'd gone to bed.

IG: Did you feel like they'd taken advantage of you?

GJ: Not at all. The shoot was fun. It was a chance to do something different. I probably could have become an actor if I wanted. Mikael Persbrandt with a tail, I'm sure they need those on a stage somewhere. Or in a movie somewhere.

IG: Did you try to become an actor?

GJ: When I was ten, I joined a theatre club at school, and I auditioned for a lot of other roles, but it never happened.

IG: Why not?

GJ: I don't know. I used to dream of a comeback where I was the world's best actor, where I'd tread the boards on the nation's biggest stages, shoot with Scorsese and be so in demand that I didn't even bother to respond to every invitation. It would only be fair – that's how I felt. I basically thought it was my right, that it would be my turn. That it wasn't even a question.

IG: Don't all kids dream of revenge?

GJ: They do. And all adults too.

IG: So what happened?

GJ: I didn't get any roles. The theatre club dissolved after one production. *Hamlet*, of all the fucking plays. I was a ghost and also handled the curtain. Ophelia sold tickets. It was a goddamn joke. I didn't become an actor. I wanted to, but I never did. A million kids wanted to be Zlatan and only Zlatan became Zlatan. Everyone else didn't. They became highway or water engineers, homeless, PR consultants, prematurely retired. They live quiet lives. They remember their dreams with some sense of embarrassment. They don't like to talk about them. Our lives unfold forever in the shadow of our past dreams.

IG: Honestly, I think most people are just living their lives.

GJ: No, they're not. There's way too much going on in here, inside their skulls, a glut of parallel lives, regrets and choices rehashed, complaints and wallowing, nonstop chatter.

IG: Hmm.

GJ: It's just true.

IG: Okay. Could you tell me a little bit more about your life after the shoot? You wanted to be an actor, but it didn't happen.

GJ: Nope. That opportunity never showed.

IG: So what did you do? Did you go to college?

GJ: You know how I make a living, don't you? I got the impression that you've done your research.

IG: You're in estate sales.

GJ: Yep.

IG: I assume that's not what you studied in college.

GJ: I double-majored in social sciences and arts in high school. I dropped out, did military training, met some people, started trading.

IG: Trading?

GJ: Buy, sell. You know. Like Monopoly.

IG: Real estate?

GJ: Electronics, machines, stuff. And papers. The right document to the right guy at the right time. With the right signature. I might not have followed the letter of the law in each and every situation, but I lived. I was waiting for an invitation to do something bigger, trying to stay hungry. But my looks might have been detrimental. I was way too visible.

IG: Yeah?

Small Comfort

GJ: So a few years ago I started a company that buys up estates. Entirely legal, for the most part. I specialise in the more idiosyncratic estates, given my connections in the more idiosyncratic industries.

IG: What industries?

GJ: Are you going to put this in the piece?

IG: Depends. I'm mostly curious.

GJ: The arms industry, for one. Old weapons with an illegal past. Strange cheques, cash that needs to be moved, goods that have been stolen or need to be stolen, goods that should have been stolen long ago and need to turn up in a different part of the country, submitted in good faith by an anonymous customer who suddenly disappears. But the lion's share is legal, old ladies who kick the bucket and their sons and daughters who want to be rid of all of it, who are relieved that I'm able to show up with a truck and three junkies ready to cart it all off. That I can empty the home so they can sell the flat and move on. They do get a bit of cash in hand, but that's a secondary concern. It's all those boxes, the old paintings, that dresser nobody wants to inherit, their bad conscience – that's what I pack up and drive off in my truck. The mothballed dresses, the furs, the shoes, the slippers. The bathrobes with hardened tissues in the pockets. I'll take it all. I take the garbage and the silver, the paintings with a signature they don't recognise, the toiletry bag with the wedding band in a forgotten pocket. I take it all, pass the junkies I've hired a few hundreds and then I start rooting around. I pick through every little object, scrutinise and evaluate, make some calls to collectors and check the web for artists I've never heard of. Kévork Zabounian, for instance. You ever heard of him?

IG: No.

GJ: Two weeks ago, I found a watercolour in a cracked glass frame, this small, in the bottom of a box full of trash. A hundred K.

IG: Wow. And the owners?

GJ: I am the owner.

IG: I mean the previous owners.

GJ: They've sold it to me, the whole kit and caboodle. The trash and the tissue stiff with dried mucus in the bathrobe, the watercolours by Kévork Zabounian. There's a blind aspect to this process: they close their eyes when they sell and I close mine when I buy. They have no idea that they own a hundred-thousand-kronor watercolour. Or that there's a 1973 LEGO fire station in unopened original packaging in one of the boxes with toys. It's too much. They can't be bothered to know, to find out.

IG: LEGO?

GJ: Five K online, the next day. Or old teddy

Small Comfort

bears. There's a teddy-bear appraiser a few blocks from here. I probably call him once a month. Cups and glasses, of course. Not a ton of furniture. The details, that's what people tend to forget.

IG: The wedding ring in the toiletry bag?

GJ: Yep. The money in the mattress, or the pillowcase – that's even more common with old people. And crumpled thousand-kronor bills in the bag of sugar. Which they've forgotten about.

IG: You never return anything?

GJ: I've bought the whole lot. All-inclusive.

IG: Okay, and then what do you do?

GJ: I rummage, call, text, google, haul. Drive to the dump. Drive to appraisers. Everything needs to be transformed into money. Takes a week most of the time. The Red Cross picks up what is left. Though, of course, they do call sometimes. It happens.

IG: Who?

GJ: The sellers of the estate. When they remember that there might have been a couple of thousand-kronor bills in the pillowcase. When someone tells them that Great-Grandma kept her money in the sugar in the pantry.

IG: And?

GJ: And what? What do you think?

IG: I think you tell them that the pantry is the first to go in the trash. And those pillowcases, they've long since been deposited at the dump. Very sorry, in other words.

GJ: That's right.

IG: You tell them they're most welcome to come look for more money in what remains, if they want.

GJ: Yes. But they never do. They just sigh, picturing a couple of thousand burning at the dump and feel – I don't know. Panic, probably, a claustrophobic little jolt of panic. Money you could've had, there's nothing worse. I get it. The thought of money. The thought of money lost, money that could have been there. Money they could have got their hands on.

IG: Would you say it's a good job?

GJ: Job?

IG: Yes, buying and selling estates. Do you enjoy it? Would you say it's a good job?

GJ: It's not a job.

IG: No?

GJ: No, no. It's not a job. Not in the sense you mean by job. In this business, we don't have jobs. Not like you lot. You've got a job, right?

IG: Yes. As you know. I write articles and stuff like that.

GJ: And it's working out well for you.

IG: Decently.

GJ: Which is to say, you're able to feed your body, keep it alive by selling your time to someone.

Small Comfort

IG: Yes. Even if I decide what and when and how much myself.

GJ: It's a sort of exchange.

IG: That's the set-up. In work, in society.

GJ: I'm on the outside of that system. I go straight to the source, the money. I search for valuables, buy cheap and sell expensively. I am society's revolving door, the nave where goods turn into money. The centre. Everything you see will ultimately end up in my hands, where it is assessed and sold or trashed. You see a dresser, your grandma's dresser where she kept her jewellery and stationery. I see money. All I see is that dresser's value. Or, rather, I find a hidden compartment that only Granny knew about, where she kept her real diamonds. And when I find them? I see money. There's a price for everything. People don't realise that, but you can put a price on everything. Everything can be transformed into money.

IG: I think people do know that.

GJ: No. They hang on to their belief that certain things are priceless. But I can put a price on anything. I can tell you the exact value of your entire outfit.

IG: Oh yeah?

GJ: You've got a pair of fake Converse. Worth one or two kronor. The jacket, however.

IG: Inherited.

GJ: And the shirt.

IG: What about it?

GJ: You've got expensive clothes, carelessly worn. I like your style. It's this carelessness carefully curated. I can tell a lot about you just by looking at your clothes.

IG: Fine, though we might note that this conversation isn't meant to be about me.

GJ: We might note that.

IG: Your job. Which isn't a job. How would you define it? What can I write?

GJ: My work involves buying things and transforming them into more money than they cost me to buy. As well as making some discoveries. The surprise aspect is important, that undefined variable.

IG: The thousand-kronor bill in the bag of sugar.

GJ: Exactly. Every time I open an old suitcase that's been rotting in some old man's attic. That thrill. That's why this is not a job. Working with money is not a job. It's something else.

IG: And what is that?

GJ: It's the origin of everything. The way boxing and running are the most foundational sports.

IG: Are they?

GJ: Yes. Think about it. Look at boxers, runners. They're just human beings. Timeless, without tools, systems, or complicated rules. Boxing is the first sport. Take a human and peel off everything else, all the culture, manners, and social mores, everything that's been taught, and you'll be left with boxing as the only sport. Running, perhaps, but boxing is first. It's the same with buying and selling. Wherever you go in this world, whatever backwater it may be, there you'll find three things: a whore, someone who sells intoxicants, and someone who is prepared to buy your shoes or your grandma's dresser. It's the very basis, the heart of human life.

IG: I understand.

GJ: But you don't agree?

IG: Of course not.

GJ: Of course not. Not you, oh no, you're just too good. Too left-wing, too liberal. But it's the truth. I'm not saying it's good. It's just the truth. Those three. And I'm one of them.

IG: You're saying it's your job to be one of them?

GJ: Oh, it's not a job. You think Muhammad Ali called his sport a job?

IG: I imagine not.

GJ: Well, it's the same thing.

IG: He spent many tremulous years with brain damage as a result of his activities in what you're calling the heart of it. Before he died.

GJ: The heart of the man-made world. I can tell you're mad about it. You might be a bit too left-wing for your own good. I'm going to go piss and then smoke.

IG: Stop making all these assumptions about me. I'm not very left-wing at all. I just think that the things you're talking about – prostitution, substance abuse and the market economy – are part of a system created by human beings, good or bad, oppressive or not. But it's still a made-up system. Humans have invented it and it's evolved and changed over time. It's not primordial in any way; it's got nothing to do with the heart of the man-made world, with human nature. Plus, I think you're using – or shall we say abusing – this flimsy ideology to legitimise your own shady activities, your own lack of responsibility; perhaps, in fact, your absolute inability to be responsible. So, yes, it does frustrate me. Boxing has nothing to do with the origin of man. The first sport. What do you mean, the first sport?

GJ: What are you mumbling about?
   IG: Nothing. Just testing the recorder. The sound levels.
    GJ: Is it working?
    IG: Works fine.
    GJ: Where were we?
    IG: You were beginning to tell me about the shoot.

GJ: Was I?

IG: No. But it would be great if you could. For instance: how long were you shooting for?

GJ: It was all during the summer and started before school was over, like I said. And the semester began pretty soon afterwards. So it was a summer, a whole summer with that steamroller.

IG: You mean—

GJ: Yes.

IG: He was a steamroller already back then?

GJ: All you have to do is watch the movie. He takes up the whole frame. People like him devour other people. The rest of us dissolve between his maws.

IG: He's a good actor. People like him.

GJ: He comes across as charismatic, but it's just a personality intended to camouflage other people, making them part of the décor. So that he's alone in it. Everyone else fades. He's the only living being on earth no matter where he finds himself. That's why he seems so alive. It's pure aggression. I've studied him.

IG: At the theatre?

GJ: Oh, come on now. What do you think?

IG: I don't think anything.

GJ: No, I've watched his movies. As well as everything he's done on TV. A load of shows.

IG: What was he like during filming? What do you remember? Anything positive you can say?

GJ: Positive. Let me think.

IG: Yeah, give it a think. I'll go use the bathroom in the meanwhile.

GJ: Positive. All right. His thirteen arms had sixteen hands each that found a way to slip in everywhere, under skirts and blouses on every girl, one by one. Even the location manager. I remember that. I remember her. She was a grown adult woman. Her uncomfortable face. What could she say to him? He's basically a king. What can she say to the king? That was one little episode.

IG: Did you think of anything?

GJ: Yeah. Whenever there was downtime, one of the adult actors would come and explain to me that this is how it goes on a movie set. A film shoot is made up of endless waits. It's something you need to get used to if you want to be an actor. They all came and told me this, sort of lectured me: this is just how it goes. Everyone, except for him.

IG: Hmm.

GJ: And I have to say, it made him look good.

IG: Oh yeah?

GJ: He didn't talk to me at all.

Small Comfort

IG: No?

GJ: Other than this one time.

GJ: Yes?

GJ: I gotta say, makes him look good. The way he didn't give a single shit about me. The way he didn't come down to my level to put a hand on my shoulder to tell me what a film shoot is like.

IG: Okay. I understand. And what did he say?

GJ: Say?

IG: You told me he did talk to you once.

GJ: I was granted an audience in his trailer. He gestured like this with his index finger and I went. We sat in his trailer and chatted.

IG: What did you talk about? What did he say?

GJ: Oh, I can't be expected to remember that. How could I? It was ages ago, two decades. Three, goddammit. Three decades. Lord, time flies. Do you feel that way?

IG: Yes. Okay, come on, tell me.

GJ: He asked me stuff. He asked about my exact height. How long my back had been bothering me. If the doctors had tried to do something about it. He asked about my prognosis, if the curve was expected to correct itself or evolve into a full-blown hunchback.

IG: Full-blown hunchback?

GJ: That is an exact quote. He asked about my grades, if I was in a special class.

IG: Why would you be?

GJ: I don't know. But the fact that he asked. You're nine years old. You're talking to an actor who's a national celebrity. Everyone knows who he is.

IG: Yes. Jesus.

GJ: He asked where I'd learned to speak so fast. If my hair was dyed. He touched it for a long time. Like this, with his fingers in my neck and at the bangs. Tugged it, as if he wanted to check that it wouldn't come off.

IG: Okay, and then?

GJ: That's all. He said he enjoyed the chat. It was time for lunch and we walked over together, to the table with all the sandwiches. But he went and sat down with some other people.

IG: And this was the only time he talked to you?

GJ: Aside from the lines we had in the script. Though nobody can actually perform a dialogue with him. It's sort of like tossing grains of salt at a stone wall. Something you might not want to write.

IG: I do need to mention him, of course. He's a legend. I can't write about the shoot without mentioning him.

GJ: The man, the myth, the legend. It's how he works.

IG: What do you mean?

GJ: Wherever he is, he can't be ignored. His

presence somewhere is an event in and of itself. Even thirty years after the fact. Are you going to interview him too?

IG: I already have.

GJ: I see . . . What did he say?

IG: He acted in several of the films made from her books. We discussed them as one unit, a chapter in his career. When he played dad, gangster, priest, and whatever else it was in these children's movies. A king.

GJ: And what did he say about me?

IG: About you? Nothing. He didn't mention any other actors. Didn't mention anyone else at all. Astrid, maybe.

GJ: See? He wasn't there. His name was there. His star power.

IG: Whatever the case may be, his work in these roles is widely praised.

GJ: I like this use of passive voice when you express an opinion you don't want to own. Is widely praised. Who praises?

IG: Everyone.

GJ: Do you think he's good?

IG: What I think is entirely irrelevant.

GJ: But do you think so? That he's good? That he's making an invaluable contribution?

IG: He's doing his job, I guess.

GJ: I'll never get you to say anything else, will I?

IG: I don't want to sit here and appraise actors. Actors I'm writing about. It would be unprofessional.

GJ: Okay, then let me tell you what you think of him. For the record. And you don't need to respond. You think he's an utter dickhead. You hate his drinking, his womanising, the society circles he moves in. In fact, he represents everything you dislike. And you're glad to have your impression that he's a scumbag confirmed by me, by what I saw and just shared with you. You're glad to know what he said to me, what a fucking jerk he turned out to be. You'll tell your friends – not tomorrow maybe, but later. In confidence, in the category of things you've heard about this guy and that. You like to hate on men his age, men with his background and success, and when you listen to this tape again you'll rewind – or whatever it is you do with that digital thing – you'll rewind and listen back again, and you'll think, man, what a fucking dickhead. And you'll commit the details of my story to mind, store them in there so you can trot out an anecdote at a children's birthday party when the adults are in the kitchen gossiping about actors, or you'll share it with a friend when you go see a movie he's in, or a play – something I imagine you do every now and then, even if it's only for appearance's sake – and he happens to be on that stage. The stories you'll be able to tell others in the intermission after this interview – that's pure gold. So even if I didn't give you anything on this actor that you can use in your piece, what I am giving you is pure gold. Go on, you can sigh and roll your eyes. But I know I'm right. And it will be a few years from now, three or four, after you've shared ten, twenty times this gossip I've gifted you – a piece of gossip you don't feel bad about sharing even though you usually hate gossip, or at least you say that you do, but this you don't feel bad about since it's clearly a sexist man you're slandering, and it's open season on sexist men because they are evil, successful and evil, big and disgusting, rich and greedy – but in a few years from now, two, maybe three, you'll ask yourself for the first time, perhaps mid-sentence, if it's actually true. Or if that petty criminal hunchback was lying to you. When it came to juicy gossip about the celebrated actor you were ready to believe anything that confirmed your idea.

IG: So it's not true?

GJ: It's one hundred per cent true. But I'm not talking about me. I'm talking about you.

IG: Okay, so it's sort of a stipulation for our conversation here that you tell me the truth. You've got a whole host of opinions and theories about me.

GJ: About everything.

IG: Yes, about everything. You really talk a lot. But all I want is to collect enough information to be able to put together a text about this movie.

GJ: And you haven't done that?

IG: No. Not even close. All you've given me is a bunch of stuff I can't write about. Perhaps what you've told me about this actor is true. Perhaps it isn't. It's impossible for me to know. I want you to tell me things that are true and that I can include in this article. Do you understand? When I've finished writing this piece, I won't think about this actor again until I see him somewhere. And I won't think about you, or Astrid, or anyone else. It's a job. Do you understand? I'm here for work, and when we're done I'm going to go to the grocery store, then I'll go home to make dinner and help my kids with their homework. Then I'll go to bed. And I won't be thinking about you, I won't be thinking about the actor – none of that. Do you understand?

GJ: I think you're full of shit right now. I think you'll be walking down that grocery store aisle, pondering that wacky hunchback you met. You'll be looking for organic yoghurt in the dairy aisle while contemplating what he told you about the actor. And you'll smile to yourself. You'll think about the BMW, wondering why it was standing there with the engine on, and you'll decide to call that cop you know to see if you can find out who owned the car and what happened after. And you'll go home and make dinner and you'll make up your own story about this child actor whose life took a couple of wrong turns, a story that's not necessarily based on what I've said or what you've read, but what you imagine a good story sounds like. There's a musical key for those, a rhythm. And you're skilled at finding them – I know that. But nothing you've ever written or filmed has been true in a true way. It's been true in a deceitful way. Which is to say, true in a beautiful way. Right?

IG: No. I get what you mean, but I don't agree. Of course not.

GJ: On your deathbed you will agree.

IG: Okay. I'm so glad you're able to give me a preview of my deathbed. The things I'll be thinking there.

GJ: I mean, it's just my guess, but that guess is as good as anyone's, right? You're the kind of person who defends herself with witty sarcasm. That's fine. I still dig you. Your style, your clothes, this chill vibe you've got. You do believe that what you do is true, that you're dealing in truth. You believe in the true story. You believe that you're working for something other than money. I dig it, it's beautiful.

IG: Sure.

GJ: Yes.

IG: And, speaking of truth, I don't know which of us should be talking about truth, but I still wonder if you could say something true about the film shoot. About the other actors, for instance. There will be pictures of them, of some of them, and it would be great if you could give us some memories we can use for the captions. For instance: I remember Sif Ruud as very warm. She took her role as an ogre really seriously. I still remember her laughter.

GJ: Sif Ruud. She was exceptional. Highly professional.

IG: She wasn't even in the same movie as you.

GJ: She wasn't?

IG: That was just an example.

GJ: Ah, and yet I had such a strong memory of her laughter echoing in between the takes, her sitting by my side, warm and kind-hearted, when I felt a little lost. Those are memories anyone could have of Sif Ruud, don't you think? We've got a collective idea of her, like those photos from Hawaii you've seen so many times that they've basically become your own. Who among us hasn't strolled down Waikiki Beach at sunset? Who among us hasn't sat by Sif Ruud's side, feeling her warm kindness? Who among us didn't fight in the Vietnam War? This collective stuff – it's like a shortcut. We no longer need to live. We don't need to experience anything on our own.

Small Comfort

It's all in the bank, one big joint account. That's what I mean when I tell you I remember Sif Ruud's laughter between the takes. Her astonishing warmth. It's got its own place inside me, regardless. But it's not true, I have in fact been to Waikiki Beach. Not a nice place at all.

IG: I know. It's horrible.

GJ: You can't even see the sunset.

IG: I know.

GJ: All that fog and smog. Produced by idiots who are there to confirm their own fantasy of the place.

IG: Sand fleas.

GJ: That's right. Regular sand-flea infestations. Regular human infestations. New-moneyed youngsters drunk off their hats. That place had enough of itself long ago. But, either way, Sif Ruud is an exceptional actor. Everyone can know that, even without meeting her.

IG: Yes.

GJ: You know, it's really all about divesting from the collective and making your own life. That's all we can do. And nobody does it.

IG: Other than you, of course.

GJ: Ah, that clumsy sarcasm. I love it.

IG: So you're saying we should stop having opinions? Stop with the presumptions?

GJ: Is that what you think I'm saying?

IG: What are you saying? Sincerely.

GJ: I'm saying that you can live two kinds of life. One in the general muck of things. And another that's true. It's not that one of them is better or happier than the other, that it somehow gives you more points, but one of them is true. The other is not. If you live your life in the general muck of things, you'll remember Hawaii whether or not you've been there. You get nostalgic when you hear "Hotel California" even though you weren't even born when it was recorded. You vote left, or right, because your parents did. You've got this position that you . . . I don't know, that you're stuck in. Entirely out of your free will. You're used to it. You keep plodding along, treading around in it. You'd never get into a car that's purring with the keys in the ignition. Right? And drive off. You'd never do that when the opportunity presents itself, just to see what might happen.

IG: The reason I'd never take a car is that I don't steal. I don't want to commit crimes. And that's not because I'm conventional – though I'm sure I am – but partly because I've been taught not to take other people's things, and also because I've understood that I might get punished. Fines, jail, stuff like that. So I don't have that impulse. I guess it's a decision I've made. And that's not because I'm stuck in the general muck of things. Moreover, I think you're getting a whole load of things confused. I'm not at all convinced that everyone has a postcard of Hawaii in their mind. Or that they're nostalgic about things they never experienced.

GJ: The number of people who claim they were at Woodstock is four times bigger than the actual number of attendees. It's become an event outside the real event. Were you there?

IG: Of course not.

GJ: Almost feels like you could have been there, though, doesn't it? You almost remember Janis Joplin preaching on stage.

IG: I've seen pictures from her concert, obviously.

GJ: That's not what I'm saying. I'm saying that you're able to recall it as if you were there. You can easily picture the guy you slept with later that night, the wine you drank, those funky pills you were offered and turned down. Or maybe you can reminisce about the fire you sat around, the grass underneath your bare feet. You recall exactly what it felt like and what the moon looked like. You remember the next day, when Bob Dylan and Joan Baez played together.

IG: Really? Were they there?

GJ: I doubt it. But they very well could have been, and in between two songs in the middle of their set Dylan would have taken forever to tune his guitar, and everyone would have found him charming, and Joan Baez would have sung somewhat out of tune but commandingly, and after the final encore a quiet rain would have put an end to the whole spectacle. Isn't that true?

IG: No. I mean, I don't know.

GJ: What I'm saying is that you can choose to live your life in that region. With the collective truth about everything. Or you can go your own way.

IG: This spiel is some kind of critique of the collective, an interrogation of habits and received truths?

GJ: What I'm talking about here is how to live a true life.

IG: It's not like you're the first person to have these thoughts. The history of philosophy is chockfull of people who talk about casting off the collective cloak of the masses to live as themselves.

GJ: Sure. The difference being that they're not living my life.

IG: That's right. We can assume they're living their own lives.

GJ: What I'm saying is that they don't have a hunchback. They don't have hair like this, eyes like this. They don't look like me, haven't lived my life. They're theoreticians, in the first place.

IG: And you are?

Small Comfort

GJ: A practician.

IG: Yeah, sure. You steal a car, you're caught when you crash into a snowdrift and you make up a theory about it.

GJ: No, no. You've misunderstood everything.

IG: Ah.

GJ: That car. It was something entirely singular. You can't even understand the way it was purring, the way only a BMW can purr. The way a car like that has a mood, a feeling. The things it can exude.

IG: Wealth.

GJ: That too. Wealth, of course, since it costs money, since the leather seats smell of leather the way only leather smells in really nice cars. But it's something else. It's wealth plus another thing, something that goes beyond wealth. In fact, I sat in that front seat for quite a while once I'd crashed into the snowdrift, thinking about it, the feeling that car offers its owner. It's a kind of calm. A stillness, a feeling that you're planted steadily on the ground in your own life. When you were a child and couldn't quite swim, the way the bottom felt against your feet then, do you remember that feeling?

IG: Absolutely.

GJ: Kind of like that. It's not a sensation produced outside the car, by the mere thought or sight of it. You have to be on the inside.

IG: And you have to own it too?

GJ: I assume so. I assume that the full satisfaction appears only then. But the feeling exists for everyone. I tried the back seat too. I sat there and imagined that a driver had just closed the door for me and was about to drive off. Rich people can look out of the window from the back seat of their car in a particular way, with a sort of ownership of the world. And from that vantage point, the instruments and the gear shift, the hand brake – all of it – appears cast and whittled by hand. The gauges, the way they move, that quiet: so alert and exact. It's as if other cars are made clumsy on purpose so that cars like this can appear more fully realised. Every single detail is perfect, and I still don't really understand where that feeling comes from.

IG: That sense of your feet finding the ground?

GJ: Yeah. It's how I imagine life is for really attractive people. Their lives might be going to shit, but they can always look at themselves in the mirror and think: at least I'm hot. At least I've got my looks. That too is your feet finding the ground.

IG: You think this is how attractive people think?

GJ: Of course they do.

IG: Attractive is a totally vague term, though. Flexible.

GJ: No.

Small Comfort

IG: No?

GJ: No, it isn't. Yet another misconception from your odd little world of relativity. Everyone knows who is attractive and who isn't. I'm not talking about ugly-cute or personal taste. For instance, some people might find you attractive. I'm sure there are people who are attracted to you. But you're definitely not attractive in that way. You could never find the ground like that when you're standing in front of the mirror.

IG: I doubt anyone can.

GJ: Attractive people can. They do. I promise you. Just ask someone who's attractive. Look at them when they check their own reflection. I promise. So, yeah, that is the feeling of utmost security that I believe this car conveys. And I'm sure what you're thinking now is that this makes it a compensation for something, right?

IG: Yep.

GJ: But that's not the case. It's just true. It's as true as the security inherent in being attractive. Like finally touching the bottom with your toes. Just as genuine. With the difference that a BMW can be bought with money, and if you lose it you can buy another one. That's wealth, being able to purchase a genuine feeling.

IG: How about stealing?

GJ: What do you mean?

IG: Can you steal it? The feeling. If you steal the car.

GJ: When I steal the car in question, I am borrowing the feeling for a moment. It hits me. I realise what it is that I'm hungry for. I understand what I want.

IG: That car.

GJ: No, the feeling the car grants me.

IG: The feeling granted by money?

GJ: The feeling granted by unlimited money. By money as far as the eye can see, money that stretches across generations, buttressing families and clans the way an ocean buttresses groups of islands. When there's a horizon. But that stuff can't be stolen.

IG: No?

GJ: No. It was already stolen. It's possible to take it back, though.

IG: By you? You could take it back?

GJ: Ah, so you agree, then.

IG: About what? It being stolen?

GJ: Yes.

IG: I don't know. Property is theft. I don't know. Maybe it is, in a way. Though it's a pretty silly thing to say. It doesn't mean anything.

Small Comfort

GJ: Hahaha.

IG: I also don't think it is your or my job to repatriate anything by theft. You can't steal things and make up a theory to defend your actions.

GJ: What can I do, then?

IG: I don't know. Change the social distribution of wealth. That kind of thing.

GJ: The feeling a person has in the BMW – that feeling of finding the bottom with your feet, of having earned something that can't ever disappear – that feeling can't be redistributed away.

IG: But you did have that feeling when you stole the car. A little splinter of it.

GJ: A splinter, exactly. I could imagine it. And there's a difference between stealing and owning. To steal, that's something very active. To steal a BMW, that's one of the most active experiences a thief can have. To sit there in the aroma of leather and think about your childhood, your pops's hands and the cuticles that remained blackened even after four weeks of holiday.

IG: So it was worth it?

GJ: Probation. Court-ordered supervision at the most. No doubt. Honestly, more worth it than you can imagine.

IG: Evidently. You're smiling?

GJ: Yes. I'm smiling. And now I'm going to go out for a smoke.

IG: Hey. No, I'm still here. I won't have time to get groceries. I was thinking lasagne. Sure, with carrots. Yeah. Ah. No, I can't deal with them coming today. You'll have to make something up. Tell them someone has a fever. Yes. Rain check for next week. I need to work on this shit. No, not a sensible word. Yes, that's him. I know, as a child – so cute. Strange and sort of cute. But as an adult, I don't know, everything is twisted. No, we won't have any pictures – he didn't want that. Plus he's a criminal. Stole a car last weekend that he's orating about. Plus he— No, he drove it into a snowdrift and left it there. Yeah, you can imagine the type. And completely impossible to interview. I've got a lily-white notepad in front of me. No, I've got the recorder too, but there's nothing of interest yet. All these hours and he's said zero things I can use. No, I don't know. I guess it will be a brief item. Say, fifty words. Make them all different lengths. I'll have to discuss with Staffan. Okay, here he is again. Bye. Yes. I'll call. Bye.

GJ: Dark outside already. It's winter. And you, biking.

IG: How do you know that?

Small Comfort

GJ: Your bike is outside. Am I wrong?

IG: Yes. It's mine.

GJ: You see. I'm a connoisseur.

IG: Of bikes.

GJ: Of people. A rack over the front wheel with a box affixed. And a back wheel guard for when you drive the kids. You're a bohemian who can't quite shake convention. Or a conventional parent who can't quite shake the idea of herself as a bohemian. You've got a super expensive bike from Denmark that you painted to make it look like it's from the home improvement shop. Why not just buy one from there instead? It's just like your clothes. Creased and slouchy but posh brands.

IG: The home improvement shop bikes break. The gears break. They're not safe.

GJ: And why paint it?

IG: Nice bikes are sold and shipped off. The ugly bikes, the janky-looking bikes, those get to stay where they're locked up. The nice ones find themselves on a ship in Frihamnen before the sun is up. A process you might know a thing or two about, come to think of it.

GJ: I would never steal a bike.

IG: No?

GJ: Stealing a bike is deeply amoral.

IG: You think so? But that BMW, the one you did

steal, it had an owner, did it not? Who was feeling sad as a result, don't you think?

GJ: I think the owner was shocked. Insulted, perhaps. Offended, pissed off. But he wasn't sad.

IG: Could've been a she.

GJ: Likely a he. Losing your bike, that makes you sad. But a millionaire who loses his car isn't sad. Millionaires aren't sad about losing things. They've got some other feeling. What it is, I don't know. But they're not sad, because they can't lose things, not actually. Since their feet find the ground from the very start. They're solid, in every way.

IG: You have a lot of knowledge about millionaires for someone who isn't one.

GJ: I could be one. You don't know – you're not a connoisseur.

IG: I don't think you'd buy and sell estates and sift through dead men's bags of sugar if you were already a millionaire.

GJ: Dead women's bags of sugar. The dead men never hide money in the sugar. You've clearly misunderstood.

IG: So where do the old men hide their money?

GJ: Desk drawers. In glass jars at the top of their cabinets. Books, if they lean that way. A month ago, I found ten thousand in a Strindberg. Unread, by the way, brand new. I never find any money in poetry, only novels.

IG: How come?

GJ: So they're standing in front of their bookcase, and they have to pick a book. There they are, bills in hand, scanning the spines. It won't be the Bible or the Quran. It won't be poetry. Money doesn't work that way. I don't know why, but it's always in some famous novel that every home has but nobody has bothered to read. Or else some thick volume about World War Two.

IG: I find it hard to believe that people would be that strategic.

GJ: They're not. It's totally random. And yet, and yet. It's not any old pieces of paper we're discussing here. Though you might feel differently, since you like to pretend you don't care about money.

IG: Oh, is that what I pretend?

GJ: You and everyone else your age and station. It's as if you have all left the money behind to work on other values. You walk past that car in the fat-cat suburb and the fact that you could get inside isn't even a thought in your mind. Instead, you think about the structures that have put the car there. You think you know a thing or two about those; you've crafted a load of theories about the car owner's successful life. You look at the car, make an aesthetic judgement, perhaps: it's handsome, it's golden yellow, it has leather details. You lot keep the world at a distance; you focus on the analysis. There's the car, engine on, you see how shiny it is, how attractive it is in the glow of the streetlight when all the other cars on the street are covered by snow and frost. You stop and look, perhaps you think a few different things. You're captivated. You commit the scene to memory so you can share it when you get home. You don't get in the car – in fact, it doesn't even cross your mind that you could get in the car. You don't yearn for it. You believe that the owner deserves to own that car, or maybe that they don't deserve it, but you don't see yourself as a person who could get in that car and drive off.

IG: Because I'm not a thief. Exactly.

GJ: Would you say that this is the difference between us? I'm a thief, and you're not?

IG: Among other things. Perhaps.

GJ: It's wrong, though. I am someone who sees things.

IG: Ah.

GJ: And acts.

IG: Okay.

GJ: You merely see.

IG: Jesus Christ.

Small Comfort

GJ: What is it that I do when I get in the car?

IG: You seize the chance to steal a car.

GJ: I restore some kind of balance. We've already discussed this, Ia.

IG: Yes, Greger. We have already discussed this. So why don't we talk about something else? How about discussing the film shoot? You agreed to do this interview. You knew what it was about. Right? You agreed.

GJ: I didn't want to do it at first.

IG: No, but you changed your mind.

GJ: Yes. And I think this is a very interesting conversation we're having. So I don't regret anything in that regard. I'm glad I agreed to talk. This is fun. You'll think it's fun too.

IG: Oh?

GJ: Again. You'll walk down the supermarket aisle thinking about the car. About the revolution. What the revolution might look like now that the poor no longer think about each other or those who are even worse off than themselves. When they think of themselves and themselves only. When thoughts, ideas, dreams about the future, when everything needs to be transformed into money. Since that's the only currency. Since this is where we are now.

IG: When I walk down the supermarket aisle

later, I'll have the same thoughts I always have when I walk down the supermarket aisle.

GJ: Sugar and other toxins.

IG: Among other things. I didn't know you have kids too.

GJ: I don't, but I read the paper, you know. I live in this city. I listen to your conversations. Sugar – it's all parents talk about.

GJ: I wouldn't say it's all they talk about.

GJ: Sugar is unique in that it's able to reach the brain both as chemical substance and as topic of conversation. Sugar and gold.

IG: Gold?

GJ: Same obsession. You ever watch a gambler at a casino? Someone who is doing a little too well? Bets big on black and wins, starts having hunches about things. His eyes are drawn to certain numbers – five, twenty-six – he shuts his eyes to focus: aren't those whispering voices trying to tell him something? Fifteen? Is it fifteen? Or twenty-five? He looks at the ball, at the wheel, he yields to a last-minute impulse: yes, or no. In that moment there's only money on his brain. Pure money, pure winning. It's a highly evolved form of human life that gets re-created at that roulette table.

IG: I see.

GJ: Like the sugar at a children's birthday party.

Small Comfort

Same thing. More, more, more. Once you get a taste of it you can't stop. The guy at the roulette table won't stop until he's forced to leave, when the money dries up or someone comes and carts him off.

IG: Okay.

GJ: I've worked at a casino. I know.

IG: When did you do that?

GJ: Early nineties. Macau.

IG: As a croupier?

GJ: Do you really think so?

IG: I don't know. Sure, why not?

GJ: Can you picture me, in a suit, manning that roulette table?

IG: Sure. I don't know.

GJ: No, you can't. I was a pickpocket. I stole tokens and money from visitors.

IG: I see. A successful enterprise?

GJ: Very. I drew a monthly salary of four thousand dollars. It was a lot at the time.

IG: You stole four thousand dollars a month?

GJ: No. I stole much more than that. I was employed by the casino owner, who paid my salary.

IG: I don't understand.

GJ: My primary task was to keep the wrong people out. Plebs who were there to watch the wealthy. Poor people love watching rich people, right? It's never the other way around. Rich people never look at poor people – they avoid looking at poor people. They don't want to know that poor people exist. My job was to uphold that order. People who didn't have a lot of money and who'd come to the casino primarily to watch rich people gamble: that's who I stole from, so they had to leave. And so they wouldn't want to return. Because obviously nobody wants to visit a casino that's got thieves, that's got pickpockets. Right?

IG: Why not just kick them out?

GJ: And ban people? No casino owner wants to have that reputation.

IG: No?

GJ: Rich people prefer places where everyone is welcome but only rich people go. They don't want to be seen by anyone but other rich people, though they like the idea of others being able to come, the idea that it's open. So there's no point in actually banning poor people – it needs to seem voluntary. It's supposed to appear like an expression of taste and preference, as if they're the only ones who've found their way there.

IG: Which requires a pickpocket.

GJ: Nope. Several. There were three of us.

IG: How long did you work there for?

GJ: Six months. It was good money, fun. But that employment thing, it's not really me.

Small Comfort

IG: Did you gamble?

GJ: Never. I'd never do that.

IG: Why not?

GJ: Because nobody makes money gambling. Rich people don't go to the casino to win money. They go there to play with their coins, watch them roll about. You know, money is highly visible at the casino in a way it never is otherwise. Normally, it's just numbers on a sheet of paper or screen. But here those numbers are allowed to come out and play.

IG: You weren't even tempted? Since you're so interested in getting rich.

GJ: I'm an intelligent person. Rational. I know how people get rich. There are only two ways, and gambling isn't one of them.

IG: Okay, tell me, then: how do people get rich?

GJ: You already know the answer. You'd know if you'd only think about it, but you never do. You're also intelligent, rational, but you focus on the wrong things.

IG: I see.

GJ: You believe there are values. Other values.

IG: There are other values.

GJ: Yeah, sure, but they're all connected to money in one way or another. Money is the common denominator for everything. It's the only variable.

IG: I have to say I absolutely disagree. But okay, go on.

GJ: Say you're in a cab. As an example.

IG: Just get to the point, please.

GJ: The only place you can look is the taximeter. You're a member of the group that looks nowhere but at those ticking numbers.

IG: I don't think that's necessarily true.

GJ: With a growing stomach-ache. Unless someone else is paying, of course. Then you'll look out the window. But in any case.

IG: Yes?

GJ: A person is either born rich—. That's the only way. The best way. And when I really think about it . . .

IG: Yes?

GJ: It's the only real way. That machine sounds really strange right now.

IG: Yeah, I don't know what's happening. The light is still on.

GJ: It was flashing, though.

IG: It was?

GJ: Yes. Like a glitch of some sort. An irregular blinking.

IG: Okay, so, listen, I'd love to talk some more about the shoot. You described your meeting with Astrid.

Small Comfort

GJ: Yep.

IG: Could you say something about what it was like to collaborate with the director? Brandt.

GJ: Right. This was the only movie he made.

IG: Exactly.

GJ: And he was widely celebrated for it. Well deserved, if you ask me. He was very talented. I remember him as nice – pleasant – though later on I realised that he'd given me some pretty unflattering angles. With my back and everything. But he had this warm demeanour to him, he really did.

IG: How did you react to his death?

GJ: I was at the funeral, you know.

IG: Any memories from there?

GJ: Lots of people. Lots of alcohol. Lots of actors.

IG: Anything else?

GJ: I mean, I remember it as a great disappointment. Of course I knew he was ill, but I'd hoped he wouldn't die since he had promised to give me more roles. He was my connection, the one link I had. And then he went and died. It was as if everything went up in smoke. I guess I wasn't the only person who felt that way. I wasn't the only person whose future was buried with him. He had a stable of actors that were sort of his own. They all disappeared with him. Their careers ended.

IG: You think that's what people thought? That's what the actors he worked with thought?

GJ: I don't think anything. I know. What did you think, that they were sad for his sake? For his family?

IG: For instance, yes.

GJ: Hahaha. I have to laugh.

IG: You don't think very highly of people.

GJ: Nor do you, though you like to pretend otherwise. And that's nice – beautiful, even. You can afford it. You can afford to pretend it's true.

IG: Afford?

GJ: Look, it's flashing again.

IG: Can you say anything else about the other actors?

GJ: Aside from Sif Ruud? Yes.

IG: Like what?

GJ: They simply demolished the buffet at the premiere.

IG: Nothing else? Nothing significant? Nothing from the film shoot, like a story from one of the takes or in between the takes? Something someone said, or some prank?

GJ: What would that be?

IG: I don't know, but you've got to have some kind of memory from the shoot. You already told me about your co-star. In vivid terms, lots of details.

GJ: I did?

Small Comfort

IG: Jesus Christ.
GJ: It's flashing again.
IG: Yeah, I saw. Goddammit.
GJ: It's making a sound too. Is it old?
IG: Brand new. Purchased for this proj—

Second print-out

GJ: Wait, this is the same machine.
IG: This one is new.
GJ: The brand is the same, though.
IG: I returned the other one, the warranty was still in effect. It was a factory error. They gave me a new one. Factory error – I'm not sure what the right word is. Some kind of error, in any case.
GJ: And the interview?
IG: No problem. I have it. It's been transcribed.
GJ: By you?
IG: By a guy I know.
GJ: That stuff takes time.
IG: He's quick.
GJ: Did you read it?
IG: Once.
GJ: Will it do?

Small Comfort

IG: No, but never mind. You called me. You wanted to see me again.

GJ: Yes. I don't know . . . you're kind of an outsider.

IG: An outsider?

GJ: You've got nothing to do with any of it.

IG: Nothing to do with what? I don't understand.

GJ: I just had to talk to someone on the outside. In case something happens. And we'd just met. Plus you're not [inaudible].

IG: Could you please tell me what this is about? I'm so confused. And you seem really anxious. Why don't you start by sitting down?

GJ: I'm not sure that thing should be on [inaudible].

IG: Sit down. Thank you. Now, what happened?

GJ: The car.

IG: The car. What car?

GJ: The BMW.

IG: Oh, that car. Did justice catch up with you? A trial?

GJ: No, it's probably going to be a while. And, like I said, I'm not at all worried about the trial.

IG: Okay, could you tell me what's going on? Please sit down again. Hey. Are you leaving?

GJ: [inaudible] door locked?

IG: It's locked. It locks automatically. You open from the inside and slam it shut. Is that a problem?

GJ: And your colleagues? Couldn't they come barging in whenever?

IG: They're not here. It's a Sunday. Nobody else is here, and nobody will come.

GJ: I mean, they could show up and open the door. And if someone would like to enter, now would be a great time.

IG: Who are you saying would be entering? Are you running from someone?

GJ: For fuck's sake.

IG: What now?

GJ: Look. It's wide open.

IG: It's a ventilation window. It's not possible to enter that way, but feel free to close it if you want.

GJ: Do you have other open windows here? Wide-open windows that invite the world to come inside?

IG: No. And I want you to take a seat and tell me. This is pointless. Okay, good.

GJ: I'm seated.

IG: Thank you. Let's get into it. Why don't you start by telling me what happened. What did you do to your face? Your arm?

GJ: They had a little baseball bat. Not quite a baseball bat, but smaller and spikey. He slapped my arm with it. Just held it very lightly, like this, but there was immense power in it. Goddammit, the pain. These huge bumps, like it broke the flesh without tearing the skin.

IG: And who did this? I don't understand.

GJ: And the face. A knife.

IG: Who?

GJ: They got in through a window just like that one. Street-level flats shouldn't have shitty little windows like that. I'm just saying. Close it and let it stay shut. It's the easiest thing to enter that way. You just stick your arm in and open another window. Do you have an alarm in here?

IG: Yes. There's a lot of computers, film equipment, stuff like that. The insurance company requires us to have an alarm.

GJ: Mind activating it?

IG: That alarm goes off as soon as someone moves. Why do you want me to activate it? Who's on your tail? It would be great if you could start from the beginning.

GJ: A bit of coffee, perhaps?

IG: No problem. Milk?

GJ: Yes, please. And sugar.

IG: Give me five. Wait here.

GJ: Fuck, fuck, fuck. Hey, this is Greger Johnson again. How's it going? No? It doesn't matter. Yes, look again, please. Yeah, that's fine. Via Bangkok is great. Try booking that. I'll get back to you. Thanks.

IG: Here you go.

GJ: Thank you. I mean it.

IG: I need you to tell me what's going on. You call me this morning – you want to meet up again. You have something to tell me.

GJ: I didn't know who to call. I had the idea of calling you. A journalist. You're on the outside. A witness of sorts.

IG: Someone's after you. They've cut your face and mangled your arm with a baseball bat.

GJ: Some kind of special tool. This small.

IG: In any case. Some gangsters are trying to get at you for some reason. And you call me?

GJ: Yes.

IG: Why not call the police?

GJ: Are you stupid? The cops?

IG: Yes, the cops.

GJ: Impossible. Too much leakage there.

IG: Leakage? I don't follow.

GJ: I'm not calling the cops. Period. You might call them if your ex-boyfriend is stalking you – that's a good idea – but I don't. It all depends on who's pursuing you.

IG: And who's pursuing you? And why? You mentioned the car, the one you stole.

GJ: The car's owners, that's who's after me. The owners' representatives.

IG: And why are they doing that?

GJ: I don't know. I guess they're mad.

IG: You told me that wealthy people don't get upset – they'll just buy a new one – and either way the car came back.

GJ: Yes. But they're angry anyway. Furious, crazy. Like rabid dogs.

IG: Why? There's something you're not telling me here.

GJ: I'm telling you what I want to tell you. What's important is that you're meeting with me now, that you hear that I'm being pursued, that this is something you know. That you can testify to it.

IG: What about your girlfriend? She couldn't testify?

GJ: My girlfriend. What girlfriend?

IG: I thought you had a girlfriend. The one who showed you the door and left you out in the cold that night you took the car. The woman you live with?

GJ: Oh, no, I'm not seeing anyone. You've misunderstood.

IG: [Inaudible].

GJ: Feel free to sigh all you want, but what I'm telling you now is true. Yesterday morning I was in the bathroom, shaving. It's the bum crack of dawn, I've got a real monster hangover and can't sleep, and whenever that happens I get up, shave, take a shower, wash my hair, go outside for a pizza and then I return to bed to watch some show until I fall asleep again. That way I wake up feeling better. So there I am in front of the mirror with my razor when I hear this sound. I'd been drinking sparkling at home the night before, which gives you a particular kind of drunkenness and a particular kind of hangover. Fluffier somehow, a kind of dimness. So I'm not very alert at all.

IG: Champagne?

GJ: And all of a sudden they're in my face. Two guys, winter jackets, beanies that hide their hair. One begins to pummel me as the other talks. Then the guy who's doing the talking grabs the razor from my hand and does this. They turn the flat upside down. Then they disappear.

IG: Oh my God.

GJ: Yep.

IG: And what are they looking for?

GJ: Looking for?

IG: You said they turned the flat upside down. I assume they were looking for something.

Small Comfort

GJ: I have no idea.

IG: Don't lie. You know what they're looking for. Did they find it?

GJ: No.

IG: So you have something in your possession that belongs to someone else. That's why they're chasing you?

GJ: Could be.

IG: Could you please sit down again? Greger. Sit down. Come on. What makes you think it's related to the car? The BMW?

GJ: A feeling, that's all. And you're my witness.

IG: I don't know about this. You wanted to meet. I have no interest in getting embroiled in some kind of bullshit. All I'm doing is trying to pull together a few pieces for a tribute publication that will be published this summer in time for the celebration. I'm trying to feed my children, pay rent. I've done nine interviews and finished five of the pieces. I'm nearing my deadline. You're the most difficult one – the interview I did with you is unworkable – and then you call me at seven on a Sunday asking to see me again. You sound terrified and talk so fast that it's impossible to understand what you're saying, so of course I'm curious. There might be something here, something I can use for something else. I'm a journalist – I'm always on the lookout for ideas and new stories – but the mafia, violence, men who break into flats and threaten people? No, thanks. When I really think about it: no, thanks.

GJ: What do you mean, no, thanks?

IG: I don't want to be used.

GJ: Nobody knows I'm here.

IG: If that's the case, then why would you keep jumping up to look out the window like that? Drawing the curtains?

GJ: You won't be embroiled in anything. I wanted this meeting, that's all, just in case. In case something were to happen to me.

IG: You're being chased by some people, they're threatening to kill you, and if they're successful in that there'll at least be one person in the world who knows what happened to you. Is that what you're after here?

GJ: Someone who will go to the cops. A decent person, who believes in truth and justice. Who will do the right thing. Who makes sure someone will look for me if I disappear.

IG: And how do I know if you disappear? You want to meet up like this every Sunday?

GJ: I'll be in touch once a month. Postcards, email, texts.

IG: In that case I need to know who is after you. And why. Most of all why.

Small Comfort

GJ: Okay, that thing is going to have to be off.

IG: Why?

GJ: It's not the kind of testimony I want. Durable technical evidence against me.

IG: So you have done something, then?

GJ: Where's the off button?

IG: Something criminal. You know, I almost knew it.

GJ: It's still on.

IG: See, look here, it's off now. The button is red instead of green.

GJ: It's glowing.

IG: That's for standby. Machines like to glow. Remind the world they exist.

GJ: It's off now?

IG: Completely off. So tell me. What did you do? Who's on your tail? What are they looking for?

GJ: Ah. Ooh. Let me just stretch out for a bit. This sofa. Do you sleep on it? Take naps?

IG: Not often, but it happens.

GJ: I'm going to stretch out for a bit if that's all right with you.

IG: Did you take that to the hospital?

GJ: No, for fuck's sake. I patched myself up. No problem.

IG: The arm too?

GJ: Sure. They ask so many questions at the

hospital. Plus they have to report it if it's a certain level of crime. It's some kind of duty they have, those poor automatons.

IG: You're not worried that I'll report it?

GJ: No. Listen, though, what are you up to today? What do families do on Sundays these days?

IG: Spend time together, play, go on outings, hang out with other families. Same as it's always been, I guess.

GJ: And your kids. How old are they?

IG: Fifteen, ten and seven. The fifteen-year-old is only with us every other week.

GJ: My, my. A child of divorce.

IG: That's right. But I don't think we're here to chat about my kids. You show up, all black and blue, with something you wanted to admit.

GJ: Did you know I don't have sperm? Technically, I have a number that's so close to zero that it counts as zero. The concept of no sperm, when the doctor says it, might mean there is sperm, healthy sperm even, but so little of it that it ends up counted as zero. They fall out of their own existence, that's how few they are, how relatively scarce. At one point I was with a woman, and we went to check after a couple of years. She was convinced she was the one with problems, her period, some membrane in there in the wrong place or something. Turned out it was me.

Small Comfort

Twelve sperm, that's how many I had in my balls. They spent half an hour looking for them. Twelve of them. Sluggish, very lonely. A devastatingly lonely place, all things considered. Normally, one ejaculation would contain thirty million, or even more than that. Which means one million is, in the grand scheme of things, almost none. So you can imagine twelve.

IG: Yes.

GJ: Like, theoretically, there's a chance someone could get pregnant by me, but that chance is about the same as getting pregnant in a swimming pool where someone has recently ejaculated. Zero, practically speaking. Practically speaking, zero. Though something else in theory. Which brings up the question: what good is that theory to me? A question I had while speaking to the doctor.

IG: You couldn't take them out and do artificial insemination?

GJ: No. She didn't want that, my girlfriend. These twelve little buggers, when she heard about them I sort of faded before her eyes. Personally, I didn't have anything against them. It seemed to me that twelve was better than zero. For a while I'd chat with them, after she'd left me to look for more suitable pollination. Twelve, such an important number, even though all you need is one to enter the egg. Each and every one of these twelve could lead to fertilisation. But not alone.

IG: Yeah, it's a bit odd.

GJ: One single fucker enters the egg, but needs thirty million others to support him in the project. Thirty million losers. As if success weren't possible without them.

IG: I guess it's a competition of sorts. A race.

GJ: But they're blind and dumb. One should be enough. One successful, accomplished bugger finds his way. Instead, there's all this spillage. Thirty million, which is already an undercount. The doctor told me most men will have a hundred million after two days of no ejaculation.

IG: What happened after that?

GJ: With those twelve? No idea. I assume they're dead, replaced by twelve others. Who knows. It's just something I came to think of. With regards to Sundays.

IG: I see.

GJ: Where were we?

IG: Your arm, your face, these threats you've received. What in the world they were looking for.

GJ: Right, so I was sitting in that snowdrift.

IG: In the car, the stolen BMW?

GJ: The golden-yellow BMW. It had slid in at an angle, so one of the lights lit the snow from inside. I saw it glowing in there. The airbags hadn't inflated. It was snowing, the world was quiet. No cars, no people. An empty bus driving towards the city. And I sat there in the front seat, just sitting. Then I crawled into the back seat. I pretended that I owned the car, that there was a driver up there while I was in the back taking care of business, making calls, reading the paper, drinking a glass of translucent liquor. It's strange, when you think about it, that the owner sits in the back whenever there's a chauffeur. So natural, somehow. They're driven, given a ride.

IG: If you're in the front, you have to talk. Socialise. I always get in the back when I take a cab.

GJ: So you take cabs, then?

IG: Much more often than you can imagine. Continue.

GJ: Yeah, so, in any case, I'm in the back, I put my arm on the folding armrest, squint out the window. I own the car. I stretch my legs. But it turns out I can't.

IG: You can't what?

GJ: I can't stretch my legs. Something is in the way, halfway under the seat.

IG: Oh?

GJ: Just like your hand luggage on an aeroplane. Slid underneath the seat in front of me.

There's something there. On the floor, right at my feet.

IG: What is it?

GJ: A bag. A leather briefcase. Pale brown leather. The code matches the car's registration number.

IG: I'm sorry?

GJ: 485. Times two.

IG: You open the briefcase?

GJ: Yep.

IG: Okay. And?

GJ: Well, what do you think? Crispy and new. Big denominations. Is that thing really off?

IG: It's off.

GJ: I thought it flashed.

IG: It didn't.

GJ: Can't you just shove it somewhere?

IG: I'll put it here. Okay. You find a briefcase that you open. Cash. How much?

GJ: I run.

IG: How much?

GJ: Fast. I run as fast as I can.

IG: How much?

GJ: I run until I get home. Thirty minutes. I run for thirty minutes and it is during that half-hour that I decide to do this interview after all. You'd emailed your request. Very polite, thoughtfully composed. You present the idea. This little publication, the memories, the nostalgia, photographs from Seacrow Island, Emil and his piglet, the cobblestones on Troublemaker Street. Yes, a vibrant summary. And still it was a no-brainer to decline. Obviously. Anyone gets it. This country has great love for people like me, and I have nothing against this country other than that exact proclivity, that great interest in formerly successful flops. Ah, that guy's gone to the dogs, even with all his talent. This enthusiastic interest in me as a person – sure, my abnormal body, of course, and the way I'm still the same, just with everything beautiful gone, that too, of course – but above all what I did and became instead of staying successful. The delight in seeing this child actor, this oddball but oh-so-talented child actor, the one who talked so fast, the one with the hair, that he'd become a loser. For some time everyone knew my name.

IG: They really did, yeah.

GJ: Because then my success turned into setback. Success, setback. Successful, then a failure.

IG: Yes.

GJ: Per a certain currency exchange.

IG: Yes.

GJ: And that's what I hate about this country. There are other things too, of course, if I think about it. The price of beer, for instance. In any case, that's what I was thinking when I received your request. I could sense from your email that you might have guessed I would say no.

IG: I was fairly sure of that, yes.

GJ: You'd done your research.

IG: I knew you'd been to prison, if that's what you mean.

GJ: I thought: oh hell, no. I won't give them that. I won't be in some photo with the rest of them, be lumpy and ugly. I won't say a load of things that'll be printed in some kind of article, lie about this and that, pretend I remember a bunch of stuff. Show that I'm still as fast of a talker. That my hair is still as yellow. And that the hump is the same, only twenty times bigger.

IG: But then you changed your mind.

GJ: Yep, during those thirty minutes when I was running from the car, suddenly everything appeared in a new light. I'm thinking, what the hell do I have to lose? I've already lost everything. There's a briefcase under my arm that's found its way to me by way of merited coincidence.

IG: Merited coincidence?

GJ: Merited coincidence. A balanced achievement that came in the right moment.

IG: You didn't think the cops would come? For instance. Or, say, the briefcase's owner?

GJ: That briefcase became mine in the moment I

found it. So I was its owner, the rightful owner. When I was running, to be clear, during that half-hour.

IG: Okay.

GJ: Money really is life-changing. It's got incredible heft. A heft that cannot be overstated.

IG: Okay, sure, fine. And then you got home. And counted the money?

GJ: I did that in the car. It was easy – they were so neatly stacked and ironed.

IG: And?

GJ: That thing flashed. The red light. You saw it?

IG: No. It's off.

GJ: My theory is that you didn't turn it off. And that it's broken. That this one is faulty too, manufactured for the cost of one dollar somewhere in Asia, put together by a girl who's forced to pee in a plastic bag beneath her work table if she has to go at any time outside of her sole ten-minute-long break. Before it's sold at a three thousand per cent mark-up to freelancing middle-class journalists in the West. Who consider it cheap. Who think it works well. And if she had money . . .

IG: Who?

GJ: The girl. If she could take back even a little bit of what's been stolen from her.

IG: Yes?

GJ: Yeah, well. It would mean this world is

different. But everything is based on the fact that she can't. That she's locked into her position. She too dreams of finding a briefcase. Right? She looks for bills along the side of the road. Once she did find a bill there, some backpacker who was careless with his wallet when he exited his cab and dropped a big bill. It fell on the kerb, seconds before she walked by. Don't you remember what it was like when you were a child and found a coin on the pavement? I can still recall that feeling with great joy. It still makes me happy to think of it.

IG: What are you trying to say?

GJ: That this is the world we're living in. That's all.

IG: Okay, come on. So you run for half an hour.

GJ: That's right.

IG: You change your mind.

GJ: On a number of points. I change my mind on a number of points. That's what money does to you – it will change your life. Nothing else can transform somebody's life as radically as money can. Only love and death are capable of bringing about that kind of change. The next day I call you, among other things. We meet up. It's a nice chat. I take a cab home, I have a bottle of bubbly, I sleep. They show up the following day.

IG: Okay. Could you please just tell me what's going on?

Small Comfort

GJ: Tell you what? What beach I'll spend the rest of my life on? The business I'll build? The life I'll live?

IG: So that's where we're at, is it?

GJ: Yes. That's where we're at. Wait, look at that thing now. It's flashing. And those numbers on the display. Do they tell you anything?

IG: I don't have my glasses. What does it say?

GJ: Let me see. No, it's not numbers. It's letters. Error. It says error.

IG: Whatever. Just tell me. The money. The men.

GJ: Fine, I'll te—

2
Penance

Dear Ms Margit Havne,

The consulate in our capital asked me to share with you some of the details concerning the death of our mutual acquaintance Sebastian Weidar in late March this year. As you are aware, it is presumed that his mangled body has been dumped somewhere in the northern part of the Igna Desert, a wretched place with no permanent residents and barely any visitors other than the bands of outlaws and robbers who claim the area as their territory. At present, the consulate presumes that the crime was committed by one or several members of one of these groups, likely hired by one or several individuals in the corporate structure surrounding Bicks Pharma, as per the anything-but-simple story that is slowly coming to light in the media. Still, I wish to avoid, as far as possible, adding to the speculation around the question of guilt, not least since conjecture will lead nowhere as long as there is no concrete information about the circumstances of his death. After all, there are no witnesses; indeed, not even a body. The following summary is based on meetings I had with Weidar before his disappearance, as well as interviews, interrogation records, internal reports, email exchanges and conversations with people who crossed his path. Furthermore, I have been given access to the journal he kept in the final weeks of his life.

I would like to apologise in advance for the errors that are likely present in the text. The world is but our interpretation of it and, over the course of my work, numerous blind spots appeared on the map I was piecing together, forcing me to make certain assumptions in order to turn this document into a digestible whole. This is particularly true for Sebastian Weidar's inner life. If the case is made public – which is, naturally, an outcome I hope that you, as a civil servant, may contribute to – I am ready to adapt my account of these events to fit the formal requirements of your department. I believe this emailed dispatch will suffice for now.

For the forty-one-year-old Sebastian Weidar, for five years an employee in corporate communications at the drug manufacturer Bicks Pharma, it all began with a closed pharmacy one late evening in early February. A closed pharmacy and an empty pill box, incidentally the brand that his employer sells with runaway success, a mood-stabilising drug that a psychiatrist had prescribed him for daily use following a clinical depression that was preceded by two episodes of hypomania almost a decade earlier. The box was empty of pills, but it still had the insert, and on this evening he took it out for the first time and read the text while seated on the toilet lid, box in his lap. The closed pharmacy led to two days' missed doses, which, in the coming days, turned into three, four and five, after which he decided to abstain from the medication entirely for a while.

One could surmise there were multiple reasons for this choice, but Weidar pointed to the reading of the package insert as the single most important one. He had apparently been popping these pills for almost a decade, and whenever he opened a new box – the design of which had shifted in both colour and font over the years – he would, like most consumers, remove the carefully folded insert and discard it without reading. Not even once did he have the impulse to skim through the text – and wasn't it strange, he came to feel, that a communications strategist in the global corporation that had developed the product, that had researched, modified, and sold it at an enormous profit, would spend ten years unflinchingly consuming this product without even once having the notion that this information might have something to tell him?

Now that he had sat down and absorbed the warnings, what surprised Sebastian Weidar the most was not the number of side-effects listed, but rather how well they corresponded to the state he had long since accepted as the texture of life itself: the itchy rash behind his ears, the tremor in his hands in the mornings, the lack of empathy for other people's suffering, the dead stretch of night between three and five a.m. when he lay awake, even as he felt, as indicated by his own term for this span of time, completely dead.

The tremor was the first to go, along with the rash. The second week marked the return of a type of focus he remembered from his years in college, a honing acuity with a graphite tip; after yet another week his joint pain eased. He was able to touch his toes without bending his knees on the Thursday that Janzon called him to his office, pointed at the briefcase on the visitor's chair and reminded him of the dinner party that evening. Janzon, the pharma company's communications director – I assume you're familiar – who on this morning kept an eye on his laptop while distractedly speaking to Weidar, and who eventually turned the screen to let Weidar see the pictures and read the text: a white miso sauce, with ten-ish ingredients, where the conformity of the components' temperatures was crucial for the outcome.

Small Comfort

The span between 'fridge cold' and 'room temperature' was fascinatingly broad; Janzon scratched the air with index and middle finger as he spoke those words.

That zone was one of emulsions and crises, Weidar learned, one where flavours are coaxed out or silenced forever. A crucial place in time, a sort of gestational state of cooking where results are established, where a felicitous sauce is distinguished from an infelicitous one. A badly tempered egg yolk in a Hollandaise can only result in disaster; I don't think I'm wrong here. And how, Janzon continued, shaking his hand with the palm facing the ceiling, do we live in a world where people pull the swordfish fillet, for which they've paid through the nose, from the fridge and toss it straight into the frying pan? Just to complain that the fish is too dry? That the red meat in the centre is lukewarm?

They'd already gone over the logistics pertaining to the briefcase: *no surprises here*, as Janzon put it. When Weidar began his service at the communications department – perhaps you can picture him, a pallid puppy with sloping shoulders, a vanishing chin and sparse eyebrows, exactly the kind of profile-without-profile that Janzon was looking for – he understood those three words – *no surprises here* – the way most of us would, as a description of a phenomenon that conforms to the basic linear structures of reality. An apple falls downwards from its tree; a ten-year-old turns eleven, then twelve; this is a world where an hour has sixty minutes, and a kilo one thousand grams.

But over time the true meaning of this phrase was revealed. What *no surprises here* actually meant was that the information available to Weidar was strictly limited and that he shouldn't worry about it. Just like everyone else in their department, Weidar came to realise that in everything he did, some part of his own activities would be *terra nullius* for him, a blank spot on the map, sort of like the desert in which it is feared that his body was abandoned and is currently being macerated by the sun. He knew everything and nothing, and the smile in the gap between those two poles was part of the job. It was Janzon's policy to recruit only shapeless matter, and after a few months Weidar could be seen sporting the same disillusioned grin as everyone else in the department, cut and pasted next to his actual self.

At first, his tasks were identical to those listed in the contract: manage procurements, analyse markets, discuss communications strategy with local agents. But as Janzon got a better sense of his new employee and caught a whiff of something, unclear what exactly, Weidar was brought into the smaller circle that dealt with the department's parallel undertakings, which included motivating civil servants, doctors, competitors, scientists and patients to reconsider their priorities, results, opinions, studies and experiences. I can hear your question: what characteristic was it that Janzon picked up on? Malleability, perhaps, a disinterest in consequences, an unwillingness to dig in and get cosy with the gorier details.

The shadows surrounding the tasks he was delegated were offset by his sunny office, Janzon's ebullient dinners and Friday-night socials at the bar. Weidar was happy with his own life – at least per his own definitions of 'happy' and 'life' at the time. He dated women and broke up with them, he took long flights on short vacations and returned with a tan, he stuffed his excess salary into funds that swelled for later use. Gazing at his own reflection, he saw a pale and weightless face, sparse like a clause without a verb, unlined by doubt and concern, and, whenever Janzon asked his direct reports to show up at his office at eight in the morning, Weidar was the only one to get there early. The others tumbled in three, five minutes late, unless they called to inform their boss that they'd been held up by some kind of preschool snack squabble.

Weidar was the star employee. As he climbed the

ranks, he was given his own assistant: Klara, who booked his tickets and managed his calendar. He met and became friendly with Janzon's wife, Helena, a psychoanalyst who, at one dinner party before Christmas, leaned in close and said: 'You're almost too good to be true, aren't you?'

'Too good?'

But she'd already turned and struck up a conversation with somebody else. It was late, the table was full of bottles and Weidar dropped it. But later on, whenever he and Helena greeted each other, he thought he saw her eyes narrow, as if she recalled her previous analysis. Perhaps she discussed Weidar's too-perfect profile with her husband – we can't know, of course – but, in hindsight, Weidar came to see this assertion as a proof of sorts, a prophecy. He was fated to explode, sooner or later.

Since psychotropic medications, if I understand the research correctly, are in fact often implicated in the very mental inadequacies they are intended to cure, Sebastian Weidar had developed a dependency on the drugs he had now stopped taking, a *dependency* in the most biological sense, with symptoms that could scarcely be distinguished from those that once motivated their prescription. It might be difficult for you to picture him in this new state, which he described as at once soaring and drowning. Quitting mood stabilisers in the 2010s is the equivalent of working for the revolution in the 1970s, getting a divorce in the 1980s, quitting your job in the 1930s and seeking a diagnosis in the 2000s. The goal is always the same: to find yourself.

Weidar turned to the internet to read about the methods others used to get clean: they tapered off a milligram at a time, a week at a time, or simply stopped abruptly – cold turkey, they called it – or they skipped their meds for two weeks, after which they picked up again with half the prescribed dose, followed by another, longer period of abstinence. The methods were distinct, but the experience identical across the board: a sensation of having been inside a sticky membrane that suddenly broke and sent its amniotic fluid flooding into the world with the former patient splashing in it, blinking a few times, sneezing, blowing their nose and suddenly gazing upon the world with a ruthless clarity.

It is said that the experience of birth is the same as death, this gathering of the body into a singular leap, and when Weidar left the office in the glass elevator that evening, briefcase in hand, when he looked down at the lobby and the little pond on the ground floor, the carpets with the company logo, and the uniformed guard to whom he nodded before exiting, when he walked up to his car and dug for the keys in his coat pocket, when he turned on the engine and let the wipers brush the windscreen, he didn't feel, for the first time, like a stranger to himself. He was a non-stranger. This is how he tried to explain it to me: You move through life thinking you're awake. And then you wake up and realise you've been dreaming. In the chasm that appears in between your previously experienced – but mistaken – wakefulness and your present authentic wakefulness, a sort of shame appears. That was the type of chasm he had just traversed.

They never found his body. Apparently, there is some evidence indicating that he spent time in a home on the outskirts of the capital, after which he was transported in a car down the coastal highway. Next, the body was allegedly dumped in the desert approximately 160 miles inland, and there are contradictory statements here about fistfights and violent crashes in ditches along the way. We are left to assume that his remains are somewhere in the vast Igna Desert, and at the consulate we are currently considering filing a complaint with the local authorities that the search was ended too quickly. You must understand that we have no resources of our own to conduct an investigation in this dangerous region, and it could be that his death is one of those deaths we just have to live with. If, against all odds, Sebastian Weidar is still alive, he would have good reason to stay away, given the media scandal he has brought on his employer. As he put it, he wanted to toss "maximum shit at the fan" for his employer, and I doubt that he would make himself known again during his own lifetime, even if he were theoretically alive somewhere.

I'm sure you saw the briefcase on TV, stuffed with globally accepted currency, and maybe you were surprised by the *shape* of the bills: the cash, their physicality, their potential rustling. Cash and digital money might be the same, but in actuality they aren't. One is traceable, the other is not – though the real difference is about something else. For instance, the fact that the words for 'cash' are more numerous in most languages than the words for 'darling', and that these two words activate the same area in the amygdala. Or that the effort a person expends on making money can be enhanced by the physical experience of money, e.g. holding it in one's hand, or having one's face being placed in the draught produced by riffling through a wad of notes. Looking at an account statement or a stock exchange chart doesn't have the same effect: no glands are activated, no salivation occurs, no muscles contract. Cash, on the other hand, like a strong scent from one's childhood, takes the fast lane to the human heart. The more digital the world becomes, the more important is the cash-based choreography that constituted the frame of Weidar's work. If you believe it's all zeroes and ones these days, well, then you've never seen the hand an underpaid scientist will place on a fat, unaddressed envelope during a bistro lunch after a few months of lapsed academic integrity.

Was there a subconscious reason he left the briefcase on the floor of that car? Did Weidar, somewhere in his newly reawakened state, want to put that briefcase out of his life, along with everything it represented? He left the office at six thirty for dinner at Janzon's, and by the time he parked on the street outside his boss's mansion and grabbed hold of the handle, the briefcase suddenly felt absolutely foreign, an attribute belonging to someone who wasn't him. He saw now that this was the dutiful accountant's briefcase. It was the very core, the root of all the despicable things in which he had been involved over the past few years, and rather than bring it inside he hid it underneath the driver's seat, locked the car, activated the alarm, and went up the steps, breath billowing from his mouth.

When he rang the doorbell and was met by Janzon's handshake and Helena's brief embrace, his discomfort evaporated. By the time he'd taken the first couple of sips from the glass handed to him, he felt elated again. Like so many others who are recently off their mood-stabilisers, he was dancing inside, skipping towards an open horizon. He greeted the other guests and ended up in the kitchen, conversing with the hosts about the frigid winter that never seemed to end, the traffic and the news-heavy week that was just closing. After topping up his glass with the bag-in-box on the counter, he strolled through the enormous living room, which was technically just an extension of the kitchen and attached to the dining room by two sliding doors. The villa's interiors conveyed a feeling of random and suddenly materialised perfection, the details and the whole in an emulsified balance, quite like the sauce Janzon was in that moment stirring with a balloon whisk in a double-boiler.

If you know Janzon, you'll likely know the rhythm of his dinner parties. Guests arrive late and leave late, which is part of the relaxed international atmosphere he's picked up from the TV shows he and Helena watch on the nights the teens are staying with their other parents. Theirs is a modern family: everyone has their own surname and their own yoghurt tubs in the fridge. This dinner party fell on a week without the kids, and Janzon was alone in the kitchen with a tea towel flung over his shoulder and a dab of sauce on his finger as Helena made another loop round the dining table to adjust the silverware, which was perfectly weighted and very beautiful. Additional guests dropped in and took their seats as beef bulgogi lettuce wraps were served by Janzon himself, tea towel still on his shoulder. The mood in the room quickly brightened as a bowl of chilli flakes passed from hand to hand. Two or three languages were spoken around this table, and glasses were raised with slouchy, innate elegance. Weidar's assistant, Klara, sat to the left of him, pregnant almost to the point of popping. She had promised to drive him home afterwards and park the car in the office garage tomorrow. To his right was Helena, speaking in a taut Oxford accent, and just like Janzon she raised her palm in the air in front of her and wiggled it whenever she sought to underscore some point. Across from Weidar sat two colleagues from the headquarters, as well as a business partner and his wife. Weidar's new mood, this non-stabilised mood, led him to speak faster, his thoughts amassing in clamouring armies before he could quite organise them, and at some point Janzon gave him a searching look from across the table.

'You seem animated today,' he said later on, as they were both clearing the table of the plates from the starter. 'Psyched.'

'The world is so interesting these days,' Weidar replied.

'More interesting than usual?'

'Yes, actually. When I think about our activities, the core of what we're doing.'

'What do you mean?'

Weidar looked into Janzon's eyes and for a few seconds he felt completely naked. But in the next instant Janzon turned to the stove, picked up the saucepan, and raised it triumphantly between them.

'Let's fucking go.'

He put the pan back down, opened a cupboard and took out a gravy boat in stainless steel.

'This product,' he said, 'is about to have a comeback after many decades in obscurity. I just know it. I'll even craft a campaign, goddammit. I'm ready to go all in on this. My gran had a Bavaria, 400 millilitres with both a plate and a lid, but they don't make gravy boats that big any more. The plate is gone, the lid is gone – the entire artfulness around the handle, vanished. I would humbly posit that no young person today even knows what a gravy boat is. What do you think?'

'Might be because sauces don't pour any more. They're spooned.'

'The reign of emulsions, precisely. We might even call it a dictatorship.'

'A reign of terror.'

'That's right. And I, myself, am part of it. I admit

I am defenceless in the face of the many properties of the egg yolk. Sixty-four degrees is a magical temperature. And, despite all this, there are a number of old models coming back into production, a small popular movement I can imagine joining. Import, and then sell to a select number of stores here in the city. There's a lot of interest out there, so I know for a fact that it's happening. A small revolution.'

Janzon rummaged through a drawer and surfaced with a spoon, then looked up at Weidar with a smile and changed the subject.

'Any thoughts on next week?'

'Straightforward, as far as I understand,' Weidar said. 'A local politician needs a little nudge to be receptive to our priorities.'

He was suddenly disgusted by his own wording and looked away.

'And his wife. A journalist,' Janzon said. 'Award-winning.'

Janzon carefully transferred the sauce into the gravy boat, crossed the kitchen to tear off a paper towel from the holder, and wiped the gravy boat's edges.

'Award-winning? Is that relevant?' Weidar asked.

'Not at all. But it's emphasised wherever she's mentioned. Something journalists like to say about each other, about themselves. Award-winning – as if they're part of some kind of competition. When being a good journalist is largely about having the luck to be in the right place at the right time, don't you think? I gather that this woman has had that kind of luck. She's a foreigner, from some European place.'

'And what are my instructions there?'

'Ignore her – focus on him.'

If you have indeed attended a dinner party at Janzon's, you know how they tend to unfold. The way the hours go by as a whole parade of little desserts and desserts on the desserts are served, the way the guests organically split up between the dining-room table and the sofas when it's time for coffee, how some of them will end up on the veranda with a cigar or, as on this evening with its freezing temperatures, clustered around the kitchen-range hood. After a few hours had passed, Weidar took a stroll to the bathroom, steadying himself with a hand on the pale greyish purple tiles as he peed. He looked at the shower curtain, which was in the same shade as the tiles; the six black towels and the little bowl with colourful soaps on the shelf. He didn't feel muddled by the wine he'd drunk, just free and full of clarity, suddenly aware of his own role in everything happening around him.

Perhaps at some point you've come across a person midway through a manic or intensely hypomanic episode. Perhaps neither of you even realised what was going on. If you look at it one way, this state can seem blessed, characterised by the sort of emotional and cognitive flow for which many of us yearn, yielding an apparently endless flood of new ideas and creativity. It's not clear where the frenzied activity comes from – nobody knows the answer to that – but anyone who knows anything at all about art, invention and the history of literary and musical greatness, understands that this state is as old as humankind and not in any way just a private mental-health concern. The symptoms carry our culture; they're human and sometimes superhuman; some of them are indispensable. They might have played a central role when it comes to some of the most providential leaps in the history of our species.

For an individual, however, the symptoms risk wrecking everything at a speed and force best compared to an earthquake. A person can wake up in his regular life at seven in the morning and be relegated to sleeping on the outside of that same life a mere twenty-four hours later. We can't know exactly what happened to Weidar, and between you and me I'll wager that it's probably pointless to spend resources searching for him. He was – and I hope you'll forgive the past tense – an individual under intense chemical pressure, or perhaps liberation, who opened his eyes

Small Comfort

and acted, for the first time, in accordance with his conscience. His new and not very stable mood provided him with the lack of judgement required for the actions he took in the coming weeks. It provided him with enough disloyalty towards his employer and gave him the stamina he needed – even though it might have cost him his life. Still, it would be a mistake to view Weidar's actions as solely the product of a possibly altered – or re-established – chemical imbalance. I sincerely hope that his legacy will be defined by the traits with which he was born and cultivated from childhood on until they were dimmed by his desire for money and medical treatment. He was, in brief, a brave man, Sebastian Weidar. I want us to remember that.

Leaving the bathroom, Weidar ran into Klara, who was coming down the stairs. She had been resting on a sofa in one of the teens' bedrooms upstairs, one of the many naps required by the woman nearing the end of her pregnancy, and now she was sober, tired and eager to go home. Weidar went outside, turned on the car's heater, and brushed the snow off before going to say goodbye to the other guests. He poked his head into the kitchen, where Janzon was standing over a drawer with an unlit cigar hanging from the corner of his mouth, looking for a cigar cutter. They shook hands and exchanged a few words.

Weidar pulled on his coat and stepped outside. He held the door open for Klara, and closed it behind her. She was wearing an enormous down jacket that didn't close over her belly. Weidar turned to look at the street and the car – or, rather, the place where the car had been standing mere minutes earlier. This moment: the empty spot on the street, those square feet of bare tarmac, the air above them that must still have been warm. The wheel tracks in the surrounding snow, soundless and extending into nothingness. The darkness compact and silent around them. The house behind the door he had just closed. The stairs to the garden. The snowflakes. Klara by his side, apparently expecting some kind of action from him.

'Did you move the car?' she asked.

'No,' said Weidar, and remembered the briefcase. He wanted to laugh straight into the dark night.

'But where is it?'

'Yes. Where is it?' Weidar said.

Janzon was still in the kitchen. He'd managed to snip off the end of his cigar and light it and was now standing in a cloud of smoke. Klara sat down on a chair in the hall and called a taxi while Weidar went to the kitchen doorway and told the guests what had happened. In the resulting bedlam, he sidled up to Janzon.

Small Comfort

'The briefcase,' he said once they were right next to each other.

Janzon raised his eyebrows.

'I didn't want to bring it inside.'

Janzon bit his bottom lip, looked at his watch, got his phone out, and began to thumb the screen. It didn't take more than a few hours – during which Weidar took a cab home as the socialising continued in Janzon's villa – for the car to be found, crashed into a snowdrift, by witnesses who were able to provide the police with a description that matched a well-known petty thief. That same individual was brought in for questioning the following day. In the morning, three days later, the briefcase had returned to Janzon's desk, its contents intact, and Weidar traversed the open landscape between his and Janzon's office to fetch it. Janzon was sitting at his computer, studying some detail on his screen, and when Weidar knocked on the cracked door and entered, Janzon immediately turned the screen so he could see the picture.

'Blackberries,' Janzon said.

These appeared to be swimming in a sauce that imperceptibly transformed into a protective dam with a browned, crispy surface. Quite like yellow, fresh-baked snow on a mountainside.

'Meringue?'

He met Janzon's dismayed gaze.

'Korean cheesecake.'

'Of course. Naturally.'

'And these little dots, do you know what those are?'

Weidar peered at the screen.

'No,' he said.

'Vanilla.'

Janzon clicked on a different tab and flipped through the pictures: blackberries in other formations, cloudberries, lingonberries mixed with grated Asian pear.

Weidar cleared his throat. Janzon turned to him with a serious look on his face and began to speak.

'You should never combine vanilla – real vanilla – with any sort of liquor. Not even fortified wine. No alcohol at all. It destroys everything that vanilla can offer a recipe. What you get is a veritable massacre with an easily recognisable aftertaste. Every part affects every other part: a fact people tend to forget when they cook. The whole, the sum. Same thing with kiwi and cream.'

'Kiwi and cream?'

'Actinidine. An enzyme in green kiwi that breaks down the cream's protein in a process that leaves behind an aftertaste of yesterday's sautéed gym socks. And that's not even getting into gelatine and kiwi, which people combine without the slightest hesitation in cakes and all kinds of things. There's enormous ignorance in these matters.'

'I came here to discuss something else,' Weidar responded. 'The cops.'

'Yes?'

'They didn't ask about the briefcase?'

'The cops?'

'You said the cops arrested the guy who stole the car.'

'They sure did. The man was observed fleeing the site and someone called the police, who could easily identify him based on the description. They knew where he lived and were able to pick him up. He didn't deny anything, no problem, the car went into the repair shop, the insurance company is happy, everyone's happy. No surprises here.'

'And the briefcase. It was still there?'

'No. But the police weren't looking for a briefcase, since we'd only reported a stolen car. Unfortunately, the guy who found the car also found the briefcase. So we had to take matters into our own hands. Retrieve it ourselves.'

'Ourselves?'

Janzon lifted one of his hands, wiggled it with the palm to the ceiling, and smiled.

'That's right – no surprises here. There's a man for every job, as my gran used to say.'

Weidar walked towards the door, briefcase in hand.

'By the way,' Janzon said.

Weidar turned.

'Go straight to the hotel. Enjoy the pool and the sun. The meeting is tomorrow.'

'What you're saying is no field trips. Got it.'

'You're there, but you're also not there. Yes?'

'Sure. And our local offices? Or whatever you call them. Our facilities.'

'The test centre. No. Attend the meeting, go for a swim, get on the next flight home.'

Perhaps you have, at some point, tried to reach someone at Bicks Pharma. You might have tried mail, email, text, phone, even an in-person visit? If so, you'll know how complicated it is, how nondescript the email addresses listed on the website are ('reception', 'contact' and 'staff' in various forms followed by the @ sign), how the only phone number provided is a 0771-number, which will take you to someone who thinks of you as solely a customer, provider or staff, and how the void expands when you receive the autoreplies to the emails you send ('We've received your message and will respond as soon as possible.') and you realise that the state of invisibility in which you find yourself might be permanent. Nevertheless, and this is probably a sign of the sender's award-winning luck and competence, an email did reach Weidar on this particular morning. There was a ding as he was about to turn off his computer, causing him to hesitate before he pressed the button anyway. Halfway to the door, briefcase in hand, he changed his mind and fired up the hard drive again.

To Sebastian Weidar, the Communications Department, Bicks Pharma

>Hi there.
>
>I am reaching out with a few questions concerning your company's drug with the preliminary name of Curadal. Bicks Pharma applied for a patent on the active substance two years ago, but the product was recalled this autumn. I have come across several questionable pieces of information about this drug. For instance, it appears that it was tested on humans under the guise of a vaccine programme.
>
>Sebastian, I'm reaching out to you because of your role as communications strategist at Bicks Pharma, but also because you and I know each other. You would know me by my last name, Svensson – Rebecca Svensson – and I believe you'll remember me. I've lived and worked in East Africa for five years now, doing radio journalism for both

local and international media. I work closely with my friend Bertrand Wise, a politician who fights against corruption and other abuses of power. Attitudes and laws in this part of the world make it impossible for Bertrand to live openly as he would like, and in order to ward off rumours and reduce the risk of blackmail he and I have married.

Bertrand has told me that a representative from Bicks Pharma is travelling here for a meeting with him, so I assume it is also in your interest to discuss the matter and get to the bottom of what really happened here.

So, Sebastian. I am asking you, using my most personal voice in this public matter: is there any information about the events surrounding this medication that you can share with me? Like all journalists, I am committed to the anonymity of my sources.

Could we speak, or perhaps meet, in the near future?

My phone number: +254 (0) 733796848

Best wishes,

Rebecca Wise

Weidar read this email twelve times. He heard her voice and saw her lips speak the words. Rebecca and

Small Comfort

Sebastian, Sebastian and Rebecca: indeed, you can almost hear from the harmonious ring of the names spoken together that the two were once a couple. They met seven weeks before her long-anticipated trip to the other side of the planet – literally – and by the time she returned it was all too late.

They were one of those rare couples who had the mutual and authentic sense of *being made for each other*. I don't know if you've been lucky enough to know it yourself. This might not be the forum for a general discussion about love, but, as you have most likely experienced, the common scenario is that one party in the relationship feels that the two are made for each other while the other turns away, and then they swap roles again and again, and on it goes with mounting ambivalence up until the moment when they both look away from each other and are momentarily convinced that they are each made for someone entirely different. Yet another scenario, with which you might also be familiar, is one partner's permanent position as a dog on the other's threshold, scratching at the half-open door, given enough encouragement to stay but still rejected and pushed away so often that it's not long before he's transformed into a difficult, scabbed-over wound nobody can love.

Another common situation – perhaps you know

this one too – is the distracted relationship, a hobby moulded by desire, whose main purpose is to sprinkle a bit of sugar on the week. When Sebastian Weidar thought of this category of relationship – he'd been in several, including with his ex-wife – he saw two partners, all cutesy, rubbing their noses together before one partner left for work in the morning. *Cutesy.* Between you and me: I believe our language has no concept more repulsive than this, and nevertheless it seems as if everyone these days is looking for something cute. Wouldn't you agree? All this empty talk, these orgies of details, and forty-eight mood-stabilising hues of pretentious humbug going in and out of every single human orifice. They lived ensconced in this cutesy world, Weidar and his exwife, they spent eleven childless years in it, bobbing in each other's wake with their minds elsewhere, waiting for her period, which kept arriving with excruciating punctuality, up until the moment when the cute atmosphere – which she sometimes spelled with two or three u's in a text message – pushed Weidar into a state of clinical grief. You might think that a cutesy relationship and the state of grief exist at separate ends of a presumed happiness scale, but, quite like the plaster and the wound, they can, in fact, be viewed as one entity. Every couple that situates itself in this cutesiness knows that it can only lead to death – of the relationship, the individual, mankind.

In hindsight, Weidar couldn't say if his depression had come to save him, whether at its own behest or thanks to divine intervention, or if he had secretly caused it himself, or if it was, in fact, an organic aspect of all that cutesy stuff. Regardless, the break-up was welcomed by all parties. His ex-wife immediately got pregnant with a new man and gave birth the following year to two angry little twins, and when Weidar ran into her downtown one spring day it was clear that the bundles in the enormous stroller had, at least temporarily, forced her to abandon the cutesy atmosphere and enter into something else.

Weidar printed the email and slipped it into his blazer's inner pocket. Then he grabbed the duffel bag with his own belongings and slung it over his shoulder, took Janzon's briefcase and left the office. You're probably familiar with those strange moments of sudden insight when you realise that something you've done hundreds, even thousands of times, is happening for the very last time – a kiss right before it's over, a walk across the floorboards in an emptied flat, the final gaze onto the garden of a house that's been sold, the world's very last drag on a cigarette – and, if so, you might be familiar with the irrational euphoria such moments can produce. I'm talking about how the *Titanic* passengers, when all the lifeboats had been filled and disappeared into the night, went to the bar; how the champagne bubbles must have tickled their throats. His steps between the revolving doors and the taxi – call it nine, maybe ten – the thin-soled leather shoes on fresh, creaking snow. The roads thick with morning traffic, his breath ice-cold through the nostrils, his scalp contracting in the freezing temperature.

Weidar was feverishly wide open, a person who did not waste an ounce of attention, quite like the infant who takes in a brand-new world at every moment, and when he placed the briefcase on the seat next to him, he ignored the seatbelt, met the driver's gaze in the rear-view mirror, said the name of the airport and, with a sudden impulse, one more thing.

'If you were aware of a wrongful circumstance, a sort of crime, what would you do?'

The driver turned and glanced at Weidar with interest. 'A sort of crime? With a murderer?'

'People have died, yes.'

The cab merged with traffic, made an illegal U-turn and steered towards the city. Weidar studied the driver's ID card, which sat in a holder next to the radio. A common name; a dour, patient gaze into the camera; glasses and stubble. A man who spends his

Small Comfort

days driving people to and fro needs a certain kind of patience.

'I'd write a crime novel about it,' the driver said. 'Could you give me the plot in less than six words?'

Weidar and the driver exchanged smiles in the rear-view mirror. The car stopped at a red light which turned to yellow, green and then red again. Traffic was bad, but the driver was in no rush; he let go of the wheel and stretched. There was a cracking sound from his back.

'I don't think so,' Weidar said.

'Try.'

'I don't know. Maybe: *Drugs tested on citizens. People die.* Or how about: *Pharma infiltrates vaccine programme. Shitshow ensues.*'

'Lukewarm. As a thriller, at least.'

'It's real life.'

'Still lukewarm.'

The driver removed his knitted hat, ran the tips of his fingers through the messy dark curls, put the hat back on again and turned to face the back seat. He must have been working all night; deep, dark circles proliferated under his eyes.

'Nobody cares about a real life that isn't interesting,' he said. 'People want cliffhangers.'

'I see.'

'Clarity, well-defined heroes, obvious moral. If

you want your plot to work, you need to introduce interesting details and twists, singular situations that bring the story to a climax. You need a bit of drama to make real life interesting. Come on, six words.'

The congestion eased up once they put the city centre's traffic lights behind them. They left through the tunnels and settled in the motorway's fast lane.

'So you're an author?' Weidar asked.

The driver opened his arms.

'Yes. Technically. But I never land on the right story. That's why I'm here.'

'Disloyal hero uncovers rotten industry, becomes celebrity.'

'That's better. You've got a personal angle with a clearly defined hero. Seven words, though.'

'Or what about: *Confused employee reveals company wrongdoings. Fails.*'

'Could work. But it's better to end on a positive note. Of course, you can stick to the minor key, but it can't be pitch-black. The reader needs something to hold on to. A glimmer of hope that the world will improve. A ray of light, at least. A smidgeon of love.'

Signs for the departure terminals started popping up as enormous airport buses amassed in front of them. They turned off the motorway, drove through a few roundabouts and finally came to a stop across two parking spots by the entrance. Weidar slipped his card and a banknote to the driver, avoiding his eyes. He never knew what expression to take on while tipping, since that little gift, in all its arbitrariness, was a reminder about who set the terms and what the world really looked like underneath its varnish of egalitarian smiles, this world with its servants and masters. A few minutes later, he was in the queue for the check-in counter.

This time: do the right thing.

I assume that as a civil servant you are well versed in the difference between shit-talk and lies. You've probably attended tax-funded workshops with your colleagues on the topic – I imagine book clubs and study circles, years-long email chains discussing how shit-talk can be distinguished from a lie. I picture coffee-break debates on what characterises each category and how to handle people or industries committed to one or the other, as that's part of your job. Am I wrong? You laugh, shaking your head. Are you saying I've got this wrong?

Since Janzon's name has already come up, and since there are plenty of studies on the topic – anthropological, sociological, etymological – we have good reason to delve deeper into the difference between shit-talking and lies. I assume you're aware of the most elementary facts: while the lie is characterised by its relationship to truth, shit-talk is recognised by its rhetorical environment. He who engages in shit-talk has only a passing interest in what is true or not, and the production of shit-talk is not, unlike that of the lie, intended to deliver a false image to a specific recipient. No, the goal of qualified shit-talk is, instead, to bring about a world where the question of truths and lies no longer feels relevant. While the liar must be in control of the truth in order to effectively shoot it down, the shit-talker can easily focus on shaping the reality absorbed by the listener. Nothing is true about the world the shit-talker describes, but not much is false either, as the true purpose of shit-talk is to move away from the dichotomy as a whole. A child learns to lie at age three or four. The first lie tends to be unforgettable and can be thought of as the child's first step towards independence. A lying child is preoccupied with their own integrity and must be respected; the lies that come from their mouth must be shot down in a way that preserves their self-regard. Shit-talk, however, leaves no early memories. We receive it with the water we drink and the air our fellow humans exhale. It rises from the soil, it is a smattering weather that quickly comes to feel normal. Similarly, the panorama inhabited by a shit-talker is never limited. While the liar will sooner or later run into difficulties due to the specificity of the lie, the shit-talker can shit-talk his way through every obstacle by changing tack, shrugging or referring to a general thesis of relativity.

But what sets the liar apart from the shit-talker more than anything else is the degree of success. Systematic liars are rarely effective in the long term. They end up in prison, they are publicly embarrassed, they have their compulsive relationship to truth mocked and scrutinised. They turn into criminals and losers.

Systematic shit-talkers, however, produce the terms that shape the culture; they create a world with no content, only gleaming details, and they can use five loaves of bread to feed five thousand people with nothing but air. Somewhere underneath the shit-talk the listener can sense a promise, which is why we unconsciously gravitate towards the shit-talker and shy away from both the liar and the truth-teller. Moments when we feel familiar and comfortable, when we listen to stories about the world that we like and relate to, when we feel in control – those moments tend to be the ones where we are knee-deep in shit-talk.

You don't agree? What, then, would you call it? Open your eyes: the planet is burning and we're putting in new kitchen tiles, again. We exterminate twenty species every twenty-four hours and sign petitions to save one TV-famous monkey. We open salons that wax buttholes. If you wish to understand Janzon, you first need to understand the essence of shit-talking: there is no calculating focus, no deceitful ideas. Zero ideology – in fact, quite the opposite. It's just a constant blah-blah-blah, or whatever sound you think best captures the opposite of ideology. Shit-talking has its own ideology: one that keeps veering towards something immediately adjacent to the subject at hand, or something different entirely. Or, even better: one that sets up a world anyone could confuse for the real world, a world where the profit motive of pharma companies does *not* make drugs inaccessible to impoverished children. Where we can celebrate our new streaming services in peace, where we feel *true joy* over the tiles, the TV monkey, the waxing salons.

You might be getting to a point in this email when you ask yourself who the sender really is. You turn to the consulate website to get up to speed on the search for the likely mangled body in the Igna Desert. You pause to gaze out over the open office landscape, where most of your colleagues have already left for lunch or gone home, and maybe you realise that you can think of these lines – the fact that they've been written, dispatched and received by your department – as a necessary crack of light, similar to the video

Small Comfort

Weidar recorded of himself in the aeroplane bathroom, which was published yesterday and immediately went viral, with the briefcase and the pills, and the short interview he did with himself about who he was travelling to meet and why.

The crack of light is always a beginning. It is dark, then there is a crack of light and then there's the continuation, the rest of it, which in this case is up to you, and, to some extent, me. Perhaps a hypomanic correspondent is not what a civil servant dreams of when she wakes up on a Wednesday morning, not even with spring approaching and her feeling open and ready for most things. Let me put it this way, though: the words Janzon will use in his defence will sound like a desire to collaborate, like kindness and support. Don't let yourself be misled, but let him finish. His story will focus on a mentally disturbed – he might employ that exact expression – employee who has fabricated evidence of alleged grotesque crimes. *Disturbed communications worker tilting at windmills.* But let me say this too: Janzon's way of speaking is smooth and brooks no disagreement, and, by the time he's done talking, his listeners will find themselves in a slightly different world.

As I mentioned, shit-talk concerns itself with a rhetorical atmosphere where a piece of information may be true or not – it doesn't matter, as long as the presentation is crowned by a polished assertion. That's the detail that stops lie detectors from picking up on shit-talk: it would be like attempting to check the outdoor temperature with a tape measure. Shit-talkers always bring a tape measure when it's time to get a sense of the weather. They've got razor-sharp opinions, a recipe for tostones, an account of yesterday's game or a video clip – always a clip on their screen – that's going to show you something absolutely amazing. No shit-talker is ever exposed; that's the nature of things, since there are, strictly speaking, no falsehoods to reveal. But when Weidar sat in that aeroplane and considered the detours the driver had taken around the city, perhaps to let the taximeter tick in peace, perhaps to extend the conversation, Weidar felt, from his no longer particularly mood-stabilised vantage point, that he could see straight through all the delightful crap that flowed incessantly from Janzon's mouth, those whispered promises about an uncomplicated world free of surprises.

Let me put it this way: if you try to catch a shit-talker in a lie – if you make the mistake of collapsing the two concepts – you'll find yourself pulled into a rhetorical epicycle so far from your initial comments that you'll no longer remember the original question, what inspired it or who was meant to answer. You get

Small Comfort

to a point where you just want to get out, leave, go home, be comfortable.

She was supposed to be waiting for him, *decades ago, everything is still the same*, but he landed early and Rebecca was neither in the arrivals hall nor outside it. The heat was a compact wall, his suit clung to his skin, and he considered getting a cab straight to his own hotel, then hop in the shower, eat something and call her. But then a car detached itself from the unmoving queue nearby and slowly rolled up alongside him. The man at the wheel parked, got out, opened the boot and pointed at Weidar's duffel on the pavement. When Weidar didn't react, the man picked up the bag, put it in the boot, closed it and returned to the driver's seat. Weidar, with Janzon's briefcase in hand, didn't move.

'Rebecca?' Weidar asked.

He held his hand out, palm up, and when he wiggled it he suddenly had the sense of impending disaster. The man nodded, smiled and tossed a fistful of peanuts into his mouth. It wasn't until half an hour later, when they had traversed both the slum that spread out around the airport and the suburbs in the valley, when they'd crossed the city in silence and parked in front of a villa concealed by a tall fence, that Weidar realised that this man would have nodded cheerfully no matter what Weidar had said, no matter who he'd asked for.

When the car stopped, the man reached behind the seats and calmly took the briefcase from Weidar's hand, locked the doors and went inside the building without a word. Weidar should have sensed something the moment he saw Janzon's suspicious gaze across the table at that dinner party, but it was too late now. It was too late when three other men came out of the building to bring him inside, and *it was all over before it had even begun.*

What are the workings of the world? I assume this is the kind of thing you arrange meetings about at the department, the kind of thing you discuss at the water cooler, go on retreats in order to study. You do get together at the conference to drink shots made of chaga and rosehip, right? You nod and smile, so I guess I'm correct on this point. I assume, then, that you're also familiar with the non-stabilised mood in which the conference ends, the way the throughlines you saw at the beginning, the robust graphs and tables – yes, the entire structure and all its symmetrical details – seem to fall apart around five o'clock in the afternoon. The way complications mount as armies of new parameters advance, the way the chokeberries in the fruit bowl appear to lose their potency, the way a certain despondency takes hold of the group and how someone will get a pot of coffee going and try to sum up the general disorder. *Just think, how little we can really know in the end.* For instance, we can only guess that Janzon took his phone out at some point, moved his thumb over the screen and set a few things in motion. That he made one, perhaps several, calls to someone, that this somebody got in touch with yet another person, who called the man who drove to the airport to get Weidar. But the hours in the windowless room in the building's basement – well, it's clear that the terrors of that darkness escapes imagination.

Fine. I know you don't have conferences any more, not even kick-offs. These days, you just get together at a rooftop bar downtown, right? You grab a few drinks beneath a fake palm tree, shove your grubby fingers into the bowl of peanuts like it's the twentieth century, and whenever you're on a sofa in someone's living room and the Jameson comes out you clear your throat to propose that a handful of irrational variables should be randomised into every prediction about the world.

Am I right or am I right? You nod and laugh, which indicates that you're no stranger to what comes next, and I'm glad, since more communiqués will arrive with material so substantial that you'll be able to start a process. A laborious process, granted, which could never be captured in six words, or even won, let alone make the world tangibly better. But let me put it this way: don't concern yourself with the identity of the sender. Just follow the laws of our land. Use what you know about lies and shit-talk; use your irrational instincts well. If Weidar used a crash into a ditch to get himself out of the back seat and flee, if he managed to locate Rebecca, if the results of their joint efforts are now beginning to disseminate – to you, to the relevant authorities, to the media – well, you could imagine him looking at his own reflection with a little smile. There's a crack of light here, and a smidgeon of love.

3

Speech at a Wedding

I'm an actor, and I'm here as a representative. This means I don't know you, dear bride and groom. I don't know any of the people at my table. My words are not mine; the words you now hear me speak are from a script I've learned by heart; it's been rehearsed, and since I'm a very experienced actor that's not difficult. You could wake me – me, the actor you see up here – at any point in the night in the next few weeks, and I would be able to recite the same speech with the same feeling. That is my job, you see; her job. Pardon me. Yes, even that throat-clearing is part of the manuscript. She fleetingly touches her dress as she speaks – like this, to signal nervousness. Shifts her weight to the other foot, her gaze darting around during the few seconds when her self becomes my self, when we, so to speak, swap places in the script. She lets her gaze grow steady again, a sign of acuity. An artful pause – like this – yes, you can already sense how the air has begun to vibrate. Everything you see, everything she says, all of it belongs to me. She's here because I couldn't make it today.

The words are mine alone, and I've chosen to convey them orally. The spoken word is superior: it's got claws and teeth; it hits you like inescapable weather. A written letter can be balled up and ignored, can be chased out of time in all kinds of ways. A production like this, though: it expands. There's no way around it. I can picture the scene, right now: yes, you're rapt, all of you. For the next half-hour, nobody will get up. Even the children at their child-sized table are glued to their chairs. The serving staff, the chefs out there – they've all lined up along the dining-hall wall.

The actor standing before you and I have never met. We've corresponded online for a few weeks. She familiarised herself with my cause in the first few days and decided to accept the job. Only then did I sit down to compose the script you're now hearing her recite. Later on, we selected her clothes, make-up, hair – and here she is. I'm quite pleased with the arrangement, if I may say so. The hair, the dress, her practised way of talking: she looks a lot like me, like the person I might be on a day like this. She's taking a risk being here in my stead, but there's a price for everything, right? For everyone. Don't you think? We've all got a price point where we can see eye to eye.

Small Comfort

I'll tell you a little bit about the actor's price point, which isn't primarily about currency – though you, of course, have no idea what currency her 200,000 comes in – but also time. The twelfth of April: what a great day for a wedding. Look at the woman speaking these words. Look into her eyes, which aren't only mine, but which also smoulder with something else. Ask yourselves: what might it be? You examine her. Some of you lean in and squint at her body, but no: everything is covered by make-up or clothes. The red, floor-length dress shows just enough arm and shoulders. At her collarbone is a gold necklace. She's perfect. Still, there's something about her gaze, isn't there? What is that glow? Could it be – death? Now that you've heard her speak the d in 'death' you know that it's true. Without this emphasis on the d, the word would be nothing. Death: the d reveals whether the speaker is familiar with its solemnity or not. I'll let her say it again: Death.

In its orbit, there's a price on everything. A fact familiar to anyone who takes cytostatic drugs and lives in the loop of six or eight infusions with three weeks in between each round. The final days right before a new cycle are essentially free of side-effects. Those are the patient's freest, most alive days. In a week, after the treatment starts up again on Monday, this actor won't be able to get out of bed. But today she's here, putting a spell on you. For those who have nothing to lose, there's always some kind of terminal justice. It's just a question of exchange rate, like I said, and time, the opportunity to leave something for your children.

Dear groom. As soon as I heard that you were planning an intimate, secret wedding with neither press nor security, I knew I had to be there. I mean, who else would tell your story? Your story, John. You've bent it to your desires. Managed the truth. Everyone here knows it – just see how they shift in their seats, how they move their hands, take a few quick sips. They avoid looking at the others. This is how stillness appears in a crowd: the listeners' silence is discrete and separate. A silent audience is made up of silent individuals, one by one, each on their own. Our individual freedom, our individual silence. There, you're looking at the groom again. There's a regal aspect to his figure, isn't there? His energy, his boyish eyes. How easy it is to be captivated by a man who commands a room just by entering it. His permanent magnetic field, his sharpness. He can do whatever he wants. Of course, let's not forget the explosive rage, of which I'm sure many of you have heard. Fist fights. But mere hours later you'll find him cooking a three-course dinner in a feminine apron. He buys chef's knives when he travels abroad.

Small Comfort

He dices onions. Perhaps you've heard tell of his methods, his business methods. The outbursts, the employees who quit. Investigations that are cancelled. Human rights groups, environmental law. Then you chat with him, or you see him on TV – his six crow's feet – and it's hard to imagine any violence coming from this man, isn't it? Not to mention the way he traverses the city by bike, the way he speaks with such insight about the triumphs of the women's football team. He knows his way around the left backs, who scored the goals, who should take over as head coach. All that's important in the world, all that's worth lingering on: there's always something trifling right next to it, and that's where we end up. That's where the whole world settles down, babbling. Why don't we pause right there? Listen to the uninhibited propulsion of that world: blah-blah-blah. It should give you an idea of how far we still have to go in this world. And if we could only be serious, for once.

In truth, it could only be someone like me standing here. We're usually interchangeable here on God's earth, but this is my place. I've got nothing to lose; I've already lost what I had. So here I am, at your intimate, secret wedding: eighty guests in a well-appointed banquet hall in the bride's hometown. Not a photographer in sight, and just one security guard at the door. I'm grateful to the toastmaster, who managed to fit me in right after the main course, but I politely declined the microphone used by the other speakers. The actor's voice is trained to easily reach every audience member in a big theatre, including those in the far back, even when she lowers her volume like this, to a near-whisper.

You can still hear her perfectly, right? As if the voice came from inside your own head. Indeed: who's talking, anyway? The actor up here is dissembling. That's her job, her task. She's working the night shift, a gig in the middle of her sick leave, one her employer at the theatre can't know about, a gig that could be her last. She's aware of the risks attached to the project, and she's put a price on her participation. We came to an agreement – in fact, we almost became friends. She lends me her voice, her body, her talents. She lets me crawl inside her, cut a hole for my eyes. I see you, dear wedding guests. Your impatience, the way you ask yourselves what I'm about to tell you. Your story, John. Everyone knows, and, still, everyone is waiting for it. That's why you're letting me continue. You'll let me go on, all the way up until the end. And at that point – well, I assume there will be a chase. That's why I've planned everything in such minute detail.

You must know that I weep at her stone every day. Nobody should live so close to their daughter's

Small Comfort

grave, but the thought of her, cold in a coffin in the lonely earth: no, I couldn't stand the thought of being far away from her. I moved as close as I could in order to keep everything else alive: the flowers, the little tree we planted next to it.

Even a grave ages – you should know that. It ages with the seasons, with darkness and light, with the years that go by. The inscription will lose its bright glow, flakes of paint will fall from the lettering as the dates for birth and death sink inwards and backwards in time. She's become part of the general hum that blankets all cemeteries. Those of us who spend a lot of time there are familiar with it. I am in it daily. All these days when singular people have died, days that slide deeper into the past. It's unbearable when you think of it, isn't it? That hum.

Let me tell you a bit about myself, the way I spend my weeks. Nowadays it's a small life. I do small things. I wake at seven and stay in bed for an hour, before Max arrives to get me up. He likes to turn on the radio, one of the talk channels, and though there's no music to sing along to, he still sings. He's always humming some melody. When I'm all washed up and ready, he rolls my chair to the window and asks what I want for breakfast. That's a joke, a little game we've got. He suggests different things every day: fried eggs and bacon, watermelon salad with white chocolate, hamburgers and French fries. This morning it was cake with butterscotch clouds. I don't know where he gets it all. Then he'll wash his hands and mix my real breakfast, shaking the powder into a creamy gruel and making sure there are no clumps before he twists on the port. Clumps give me a terrible stomach-ache. After the meal, he wraps a paper napkin round his index finger and – still singing – catches everything that, despite our best efforts, comes dribbling out of the corner of my mouth. I tend to spend this part of the day watching his good face. Because, if everyone were like Max, this world, what a world it would be! His singing patience.

I only had one child. Listen when she says that word again, listen to the bottomless diphthong in the word child, how lonely it sounds when we understand that life is played out in singular around this child. That singular diphthong, which must hold everything. An actor reveals themselves in the vowels, so I had the woman who stands in front of you send me a sound test. I'll tell you this: it was excellent. That's why she's here. That's why she's about to reach the point when she'd like to make a toast, though there's something else she needs to do, first. She is I; you need to see me in her. But she's also the guarantor for her children.

Small Comfort

Her children: the joy of saying these living words in plural.

Your hands, I thought of them today when Max left for his other jobs. Their violence, their fury, the way it spills over. Sadism, charm and how it's all mixed up in money. Exports and imports, profiles in the paper, wealthiest-people lists, most influential people. Nothing can get to a man whose face is in the international magazines. Nobody wants to ruin the pleasant atmosphere produced by a successful product. Who can be bothered to remember an old case of blunt violence now that the market is finally picking up again? That's right, nobody. Almost nobody, at least. Because some people do remember you: girlfriends, whores, those who've paid for their silence or been paid for it. They've told me what those hands of yours can do.

Let me cut to the chase and ask the question: do you even remember my daughter, John? She was no weaker than anyone else, she just had luck so bad it bled out. You consumed her because she was for sale, and I don't know what triggered your fury. That's what I find so odd about the world, the fact that you're still walking around in it, doing whatever you want. That you can shake hands on a landing strip next to your private jet, that you can be part of a delegation holding a press conference, with your relaxed, magnetic smile at the cameras. As if you were innocent.

Max works as an instructor at a gym, and also mans a store that sells powder to bodybuilders in enormous plastic buckets. Sometimes he tosses me over his shoulder like I'm a baby, but mostly he carries me in his arms like a sleeping child between the bed and the chair. If I have any strength in my arms that day, I like to wrap them round his neck, or put my hands on his enormous biceps. When the lift is broken, he'll carry me like that down three flights of stairs. I sit propped up on the landing while he gets the chair. Then we slowly walk through the park and up to the church, crossing the gravel path to get to the grave. We work for fifteen minutes, brushing the stone free from dust and picking rubbish out of the grass that surrounds it. At first, we tried to replace the flakes that fell from the letters, but these days we just take them on a fingertip, inspect them and let them float away on the wind. I guess that's why there are gravestones: so we can watch them age. In the beginning, I often heard her voice at the grave, my daughter's muffled screams, but it's stopped. Now there's only the hum that she's joined. The general, shapeless hum. The mass of dead people on earth grows at about the same pace as the mass of the living. You start out belonging to one flock, and next thing you know you've joined the hum of the other.

This is an actor. She's rehearsed the script she's reciting. She's very skilled. She's memorised far longer scripts than this over the course of her career; it's a craft of sorts. Her words are mine and only mine, but, then again, all you know about me is what she tells you. Who's speaking? As long as you're asking yourselves that question, you won't stop her. You look around; an audience is always comfortable in what it's doing when it's still, quiet. That's your role. History's most important role: an audience silently watching the events unfold.

When Gabriel comes at one, I'm usually reading or looking out of the window. Technically, it's a bit late for lunch, but he's got lectures all morning before he speeds through the city to get here. I always tell him not to rush, that a grey drink delivered through a subcutaneous port in the stomach doesn't warrant any stress, but he's still sweaty when he arrives. Gabriel is in law school, second year. He speaks incessantly, feverishly, and in this way he's like me, the person I used to be. He's less diligent than Max when it comes to shaking the powder, but better at distracting me from the stomach-ache that follows. He'll talk about human rights, environmental rights, prisoners of conscience, war crimes, free speech, whistleblowers, financial crime, international crime and the little guy who has no voice in this world. Whenever he gets fired up talking about everything he wants to do, I just lean back against my headrest and listen.

Before I hired him, I asked if he viewed me as a little guy with no voice, but he rejected the suggestion. A retired professor can never be a little guy in that sense, he told me. I was to be considered a person of stature in a little world. Since I can't speak well these days, Gabriel ended up making all the calls and visits. The larynx, the muscles of the vocal cords – not much works in that area. The vowels were the first to go: the meat of language, the very marrow of the words. What was left were the consonants, the skin. Until they went, too.

And during that process, which in my case took about four months, I gradually came to realise that the voice is the most beautiful gift bestowed upon humans. How strange it was to start loving something so heedlessly the very moment it was taken from me. So listen to this actor's voice. How it carries her through the space, into you, lodging itself in your memories forever.

Gabriel was my voice for half a year. He was my legs, my stubborn inquisitiveness. He is well versed in the art of staying put in a chair until someone can recall an event that happened many years ago. My daughter's circle of friends – well, not much is left of it. You see, heroin users don't tend to organise regular reunions and update each other on their new contact info. No – they just disappear. They die, they're buried, they're sucked into the psych wards and never heard from again. They end up behind bars, they're adopted by johns or pimps, they're abducted, they fall out of sight. They're tree-bark boats bobbing on the horizon: who could ever keep track of them?

I was already sick when I lost her. I still had my job at the university and I could still reach the back row in most lecture halls without a microphone, but I knew what my future held. After an MRI the year before, the neurologist ran his ballpoint pen along the white lines on the picture of my brain. 'Am I going to need crutches?' I asked. He angled his head this way, then that. A wheelchair? He shrugged and angled his head again. I told him I wasn't scared of catastrophes, but interested in knowing about them. I guess the catastrophe, he said, is exactly that. That we know nothing.

And then the catastrophe came. They spent twenty-four hours looking for her. Perhaps you think there's a difference between looking for a drug user and a real human being, a person who can actually get lost? Because a drug user could be anywhere, right? Underneath a table at some house party, in a ditch with a needle in their arm, in a shopping-centre bathroom, in a stolen car, shut inside a fitting room or the laundry room of a block of flats. They're sort of like quantum particles, their position knowable only in the moment you happen to lay your eyes on them. Can a drug user even disappear like a regular person can? Would it not be more true to say that they're out of sight for some time until they appear again, at a treatment home in a different part of the country, in a car, in a schoolyard, in a flat without a name on the post box. Death is proportionate to life, so you might believe that drug users, who don't seem to have real lives, can't have real deaths. That their death is but a natural extension of their already lifeless lives. Right? I see you shifting in your seats. It's uncomfortable, all this talk about the life and death of drug users. Of heroin addicts and whores. Almost as if they were human, right?

I'm a member of eight groups that organise parents like me, parents with dead children, but I have yet to come across one that organises for redress. Are you familiar with the true meaning of that word? Perhaps you're thinking about forgiveness, penance and reconciliation when you hear it. Do you confuse it with justice? Gabriel and I sometimes discuss this, and it often ends with him getting a little angry with me. He interrupts. I can only point at the first few words of a sentence before he understands what I'm about to say and moves to protest. He interrupts. He gets fired up. He argues his point while stomping about the room and waving his arms in front of me. The respect, I love it. He never looks at me with pity. When I think about this world: if everyone were like Gabriel. The way he gets angry.

How easy it is to dig up photos of successful people, pictures taken long ago. Portraits of a young man, a violent young man, a young client with particular desires. Those who encountered you back then remember. They remember your habits. I lean in closer to look at your bride, but no: I see no bruises or scars. She smiles, and I ask myself what kind of smile it is. You must have caressed her throat when the two of you slept with each other. Hesitated before you let your thumb linger, pushed it down, stopped only when she protested. Is this the type of smile you received then? Blurry, uneasy?

The starting point for all Gabriel's arguments is justice. It's a phenomenon he loves to discuss. I tell him that justice is nice but impossible. He tells me that justice must be the starting point. I tell him that justice is a fantasy. He tells me that it's the framework for every human encounter, for our gaze on the other. I tell him that justice is a metaphysical concept. He tells me that it's one hundred per cent real, that it's what the social contract is based on. I tell him that justice can be simulated through redress. That redress is another fantasy, but one that can be packaged as a spectacle and realised. I'm sure you have no trouble seeing how it's different. Gabriel is a future lawyer speaking of social contracts. I am a retired professor writing a script. Her death will never leave me. Her cold body in the earth and the aging stone, the priest's brief remarks during the funeral, the hum. None of it will leave me in peace. Gabriel says that when justice is impossible, all that remains is reconciliation. No, redress, I tell him. Redress is what remains. Gabriel, of course, has no idea what I'm doing tonight.

I did get to see her body, briefly, naked on a shiny table, and I immediately knew that I would never see anything again. What good are my eyes after that sight? My gaze, how could I ever direct it at anything else? There was an officer by my side with a canvas tote in hand. It contained my daughter's belongings: a few hairpins, underwear, a sponge bag with make-up and condoms. He was wearing plastic gloves, which he discarded after passing me the bag. I remember looking through the items, feverish and painstaking, over and over, hoping for some kind of clue. I wanted something I could trace all the way to the beginning, in order to find her somewhere and ferry her back. I wanted a solution that would unmake her death. As the police investigation unfolded and subsequently closed, I was called in to the precinct to pick up more objects. Her calendar was first. Then her jewellery. Then her wallet. Her diary. Transparent plastic bags, handed to me by the woman in the reception, with her pitying look at me and my crutches. There wasn't a lot of evidence, I told Gabriel when he first took an interest in the case. No witnesses had come forth; nobody had had anything to say. Gabriel was stubborn. His hubris keeps him from seeing obstacles. He made some calls, and unearthed what he called clues. I told him the police had probably already done everything they could and he looked at me and said, sure, the police probably did what they could, emphasis on *they*. As if he, Gabriel. As if I. That's how it started. That's how we found you, John.

I usually spend my afternoons doing administrative tasks, while Gabriel sits in the armchair with his tiny computer. He's currently writing a paper on imaginary property. We drink coffee at three, which is when he goes to the coffee machine, makes two espressos, and puts one of them on the table in front of me. That smell. He pulls out a chair and sits down, facing me. After a minute or so I'm ready, and I give him a nod. He sweeps his in one go as I close my eyes. It's my third cup of the day; it never fails to put me in a good mood.

Gabriel likes to say that people don't change – they just put on new clothes. I think he's quoting someone, and he's wrong, of course. We choose our history, each other. We choose what we remember and what we don't, what we hold and what we forget. We negotiate with ourselves. We manage our guilt. I'm sure you know who you are, John, and I'm sure everyone else in here knows too. And I'm thinking about the world and everyone who's like you. And about the rest of us, who keep silent.

The evening shift gets here around six. It's always two people, someone new every time. I assume they're part of some kind of part-time job pool. They clean, give me dinner, open the windows to freshen the air, do the dishes. If they've got time, we'll get the screen with the words and letters and spend some time chatting after dinner. My questions have to be specific to yield answers that interest me. Tell me about the country you're from. What did you do today? What kind of games did you play as a child? What do you think about your job? When they've transferred me to bed, they turn the TV on, adjust the volume and put the remote control in my hand. I've got fifty-two channels to choose from. But tonight, as this scene is playing out, my TV is off. I look at the ceiling and try to hear what's happening. The party is dead quiet now. Nobody moves. The guests' hands lie still on the tables. Their eyes are nailed to this actor who is speaking – almost whispering – to them. The staff are at attention along the wall; they've completely forgotten about the dessert they should be serving. The children are slack-jawed, frozen as they watch the spectacle. Is this what redress looks like? A life for a life. Do I feel the smallest hint of disappointment, even remorse? The O in remorse, oh, the vowel for all the hurt in this world. No, the remorse isn't mine. When this is over, you'll look at each other, stunned. You'll blame someone else, you were too far away, too close, too unarmed. You were too drunk, much too scared. You'll use many words to convince each other and yourselves, but when you lie down to sleep tonight there will be just one vowel left in you. O – oh, the sound for all that should be different.

Tomorrow I'll move to the other side of the city, leaving the flat and the hum behind, leaving her gravestone in peace. Perhaps Max and I will take the bus here every once in a while. Put a flower on the stone, brush off the debris. And, in case you're wondering: yes, redress does exist. What else could this be? Just look at how the actor opens her handbag, a small bag in brown leather with an oversized clasp. What is it that she's taking out, an object she needs two hands to hold? Hours upon hours with an instructor at her summer house have turned her into a skilled marksman. Look at me, John. I've waited so long for this. Look.

4
The Loser's Claustrophobia

Research Log

<u>10 April</u>
  Experiments 1–25
  Recruitment: Posters on campus bulletin boards
  Number of sign-ups: 94
  Selected: 50
  Groups: 25
  Median income: N/A
  Selection method: Randomised
  Time spent incl. instructions, surveys and games (average): 1 hour 5 mins
  Effective playing time (average): 35 min
  Number of cameras: Four
  Number of microphones: Four
  Position placement: Open random drawing by coinflip
  Tokens: 'Wealthy' – red luxury car; 'poor' – black shoe

Other equipment: Two chairs, one square table, one Monopoly board + two dice, bills in seven denominations and 18 chance cards

Present: Two participants, one experimenter/gamemaster, one technical support (in the adjacent room)

Follow-up: Survey (100%); in-depth interviews (20%)

Comment: For an in-depth description of the experiment, please see below.

Questions for Nicholas:

– Is the above sufficient to put together an initial application draft?

– Push deadline for second chapter? Need another five weeks for the remaining in-depth interviews.

– For the comprehensive description of the experiment, how long and exhaustive should it be?

– We need general definitions for the following terms:
- O Luck
- O Self-confidence
- O Empathy
- O Selflessness
- O Arrogance
- O Submission
- O Fairness

Notes to self

Sara, dear Sara, all scientists keep a log of their research, says Nicholas. Everyone needs a running document to jot down things that come up: drafts, ideas, questions, doubts. Maybe other things too, private things, personal notes. That spillage sometimes turns out to be the important stuff, he says, whatever that's supposed to mean. The important stuff sometimes ends up in the spillage? That's where I'm supposed to look? Twelve stops on the commuter train each way – at least I've got time to write. Make space for your own notes too, he says, random thoughts that enter your consciousness. His way of saying consciousness: vague, sibilant, exaggerated, solemn, over-sophisticated, enthusiastic, spiritual. I've promised to get a beer soon with him and some of the others at one of the pubs near campus.

Underline: 12 April

Experiments 26–50

Recruitment: Flyers at sites of employment (the parliament, tax authorities, computer shop, grocer, teacher's break room in primary school, hospital A&E, magazine publisher)

Number of sign-ups: 113

Attrition due to refusal to state income: 15

Selected: 50

Groups: 25
Selection method: Randomised
Time spent (average): 1 hour 5 mins
Effective playing time (average): 35 min
Number of cameras: Four
Number of microphones: Four
Other equipment: Two chairs, one round table, one Monopoly board + two dice, bills in seven denominations and 18 chance cards
Present: Two participants, one experimenter/gamemaster, one technical support (in room next door)
Follow-up: Survey (100%); in-depth interviews (25%)
Comment: For in-depth description of the experiment, see below.

Questions for Nicholas:
- How to compensate for attrition in round 2? Source income information from the tax registry? If income and wealth are parameters I assume we need that information?
- We need general definitions of these terms:
    o Imagined luck
    o Relative status
    o Imagined status/actual status
    o Equality
    o Warranted success

Small Comfort

I'm studying people who are given thirty minutes of wealth in a board game. This is my answer when a man at a party asks what I do. As for him, he makes computer programs that repair high-speed trains. We're basically equally uninterested in each other's jobs; he thinks of money as something he uses when he can and tries not to think of when there's nothing to use, though he never stops thinking about it entirely.

'I mean, nobody can forget about money, right?' he says, and looks at me.

'Probably not,' I tell him.

'Either way, wealth is a private matter,' he says in response to my question. I don't know if he's trying to provoke me or if he's actually questioning the foundation of my research, however he understands it. I ask if trains are a private matter too, if the travelling on them and the repair of them is a private matter. We keep smiling as we speak, fully knowing that we'll soon go home together and have sex, and he tells me that obviously trains aren't a private matter but a collective mode of transportation. I tell him that money in general also has the function of being a collective mode of transportation, and money belongs to the private sphere just as little as trains do. He gives me a long look. Maybe he thinks I'm trying to be provocative. Maybe I am trying to be provocative. The morning after, in my flat, he lingers in front of the social psychology bookshelf by my desk before leaving. He asks no more questions about my research.

15 April
More detailed description of the experiment
/draft one/

Wealth remains one of the singularly most potent variables that exist for human behaviour, and, nevertheless, the topic is more or less unexplored within experimental social psychology. TKTKTK about earlier research, etc.

Led by Professor Nicholas Strafford-Milou, the psychology department's research group has spent the last decade investigating the social-psychological aspects of the foundations of our monetary system. This study specifically intends to demarcate, interpret and understand the social interactions that appear around the distribution of property. Furthermore, this study intends to explore how cognitive conceptions of terms like justice and injustice vary with one's own position vis-à-vis the same, as well as, finally, surveying the mental processes that shape the sense of how important one's own effort is for individual financial success. Finally, the study intends to conceptualise some of the general ideas around why property is distributed the way it is, both within the confines of the experiment but also, hopefully, from a broader social perspective.

Aside from chess, Monopoly is the world's most popular board game. Hence, the selection of this game is motivated partly by the general public's pre-existing understanding of the game as such, and partly by the simple rules for winning and losing. Furthermore, the game's reputation as a simplified reflection of economic reality facilitates participants' transfer of ideas they may hold around concepts like wealth, justice and success to the experimental situation. In this way, the game is transparent in terms of values and social norms in the exact areas the study is intending to explore.

Based on the information provided during recruitment, all that participants know is that they will be playing a board game for a little less than an hour. The two people who participate in a round do not know each other; in most cases they haven't even met. They're introduced, but not given an opportunity to chat or get to know each other, and are immediately brought into a room furnished with a table and two chairs. On the table is the board game, chance cards, two dice, bills in seven denominations, and two tokens: the shoe and the luxury car. A brief introduction follows, after which the experimenter (a.k.a. 'the bank') flips a coin to determine the position held by each participant. Bills and tokens are distributed, and the game begins.

The brevity of the introduction is crucial: the fundamental inequality of this version of the game, described below, must be presented as an obvious, neutral, natural feature. It is important that the players are not allowed to reflect on the conditions together, since that could activate possible shared values. Equally important is that the participants cannot, during the course of the game, be given an opportunity to build any sort of relationship with each other that exceeds the experiment itself. The players, therefore, are given no time to consider the terms, and the game begins immediately after the instructions have been read. No opportunity is given to ask questions, seek out more information or discuss the terms.

Monopoly is normally played according to the following rules: all participants are given the same start-up capital by the bank, they use two dice and they move their piece over a board according to the dice. When both dice show the same number, the player may roll the dice again after having moved the piece. Purchases of streets are made along the board with the purpose of increasing one's own wealth by charging rent on any occupied streets and draining that of the opponents.

These streets are split into groups of three or two, distinguished by colour. When one player holds every street within any particular colour, they are given the opportunity to purchase homes and place them on one, or several, of the streets. A street with a house on it is more expensive for the opponent to land on, making real estate attractive. A player who manages to place houses on all properties within the same colour can make the opponents' stay on a street even more expensive by replacing a house with a hotel. The game is won by owning many streets and quickly building houses and hotels on them.

One of the board's corner tiles is a so-called 'jail', and the player who ends up there has to skip at least one turn, or can't leave until they have rolled a six or a one (various rules exist). The jail tile can also be activated by some of the chance cards, either by the player being sent to jail or receiving a card that allows the player to skip future jail time. Each time a player completes a round on the board, they receive a sum of money. Through so-called chance cards, the players can be made to skip a roll of the dice, give away or receive money and receive other advantages or disadvantages. It is up to the players themselves to decide whether or not they do business with each other, buy or sell properties or get-out-of-jail-free cards, take loans, delay repayments of debts or other transactions. Usually, collaborations between players and rent increases are not allowed. In most cases, the game takes two to three hours to play.

Previous research using Monopoly with ordinary rules (cf. appendix 1) has thoroughly surveyed the game's potential as a trigger for shifting emotional expressions, with aggression and schadenfreude being the most common outcomes. Other research has shown that in a third of the cases, the game's stipulated time span is not met with all players still participating. Instead, in one third of the cases, the game is interrupted or changed when one or several of the players prematurely abandon the game. Naturally, earlier research into Monopoly's potential as a trigger of values and emotions informs the choice of arena for this experiment.

Here, the game is manipulated in the following four ways in order to achieve a situation that is desirable to the study:

1) The person using the luxury-car token receives double the amount of money in start-up capital: £3,000 as compared to £1,500 for the person using the shoe token.

2) The person with the shoe token is allowed to use only one die, while the person with the luxury-car token can use two. This rule means that the player with the shoe never rolls twice, since an extra roll only follows two identical dice.
3) The person with the luxury-car token receives double the amount of money for each completed round: £400 as compared to the £200 received by the player with the shoe token.
4) The players draw their chance and community-chest cards from two separate stacks, where cards with the text 'go to jail' appear only in the stack intended for the player using the boot.

In half of the rounds of the experiment, the game is interrupted for a brief pause. During this pause, the loser – i.e. the player using the boot token – is brought to a separate room for a coaching session with the gamemaster. The other participant stays, without stimuli, at the table.

The game is documented by microphones and cameras that are visible to the players. Afterwards, a questionnaire is given to the two players, who respond independently and in silence. A third of the players are randomly selected for an in-depth interview conducted over the next day or two.

Questions for Nicholas:
- The survey: how long should it be? Different questions for winners vs losers?
- How to define the term 'justice'?

The papers report that Simmons is in some kind of coma after the attempted murder. The woman who shot him, and then leaped into a safety net stretched below the window, is still on the run. The cops are saying it was an interpersonal conflict, but nobody has been able to identify either the woman with the gun or those she must have collaborated with. Simmons was initially said to have been killed, though now it's been confirmed that he's in a coma. A medical expert said on TV that Simmons is essentially dead, that the state he's in is closer to death than life, since his consciousness has likely been snuffed out, which means he won't ever wake up again.

'Likely?' the reporter asked.

'Likely, yes,' the expert confirmed. 'There are no certainties in cases like this.'

'Wouldn't it be better to view him as essentially alive, then?' the reporter asked.

'If you prefer,' the expert said. 'But his state remains closer to death, and that is a medical truth complicated only by the fact that we don't know what death is, other than the absence of life as we know it,' the expert said.

I read an interview with Simmons a couple of years ago, a long piece about his business, his person, his methods and thoughts. That's how I had the idea for this study. I just skimmed the article on an aeroplane, but the words haunted me for months before I knew what to do with them: 'I have deserved every dollar I own.' Not *earned* every dollar, which I guess he has, but *deserved*, which is something altogether different. The smile that must have been on his face as he said it, the ease of those words. 'Deserved', is 'worthy of', the idea that every dollar that ended up in his hands belongs there and nowhere else.

<u>16 April</u>

SURVEY
/draft one/

Please circle the answer that best describes your experience. Pick only one answer to each question.

1. What was it like playing the game?
   Boring
   Neither boring nor fun
   Fun
   Very fun

2. What did you think of the terms of the game?
   Unfair
   Slightly unfair
   Neither fair nor unfair
   Fair

3. What did you think of the gamemaster?
   Partial to my opponent
   Neutral
   Partial to me

4. What determined your performance in the game?
   Skill/lack of skill only
   The terms of the game only
   Both skill/lack of skill and the terms of the game

5. Did you have luck at some point during the game?
   Many times
   Several times
   A few times
   Never

6. How skilled was your opponent?
   Very skilled
   Skilled
   Neither skilled nor unskilled
   Unskilled
   Very unskilled

Small Comfort

7. Generally speaking, how skilled are you at Monopoly and other board games with dice?
    Unskilled
    Neither unskilled nor skilled
    Skilled
    Very skilled

8. Generally speaking, how skilled do you think your opponent is at Monopoly and other board games with dice?
    Unskilled
    Neither unskilled nor skilled
    Skilled
    Very skilled

9. To what extent did you merit your win/loss in the game?
    To a great extent
    To a fair extent
    Not much
    Not at all

10. To what extent did your opponent merit their win/loss in the game?
    To a great extent
    To a fair extent
    Not much
    Not at all

11. How great would your chances be to win a game with the same rules next time?
    Non-existent
    Small
    Fairly large
    Large
    Very large

12. In your own words, explain why you won/lost the game.

13. In your own words, describe the main feeling you had while playing.

(14–17 to be answered only by coached participants.)

14. Did you feel that your chances of winning the game increased after the coaching session? Circle the best answer.
    Yes
    Somewhat
    No

15. Did the coaching session make you focus more on your own performance?
    Yes
    Somewhat
    No

16. Did you have a different experience of the game after the coaching session?
   Yes
   No

17. If yes, how? (You can select more than one)
   I was more inspired
   I played better
   I was luckier
   I played worse
   It was more fun
   It was more boring
   I realised that everything was up to me
   I thought more about the terms of the game
   I thought less about the terms of the game
   I felt more respect for my opponent's skill
   Other:

Questions for Nicholas:

– Should I write more about the game? Everyone knows the deal with Monopoly, right?

– How to word the study's purpose to avoid scaring funding bodies with potentially unconventional aspects of the approach?

– Do we need to formulate any theories about distributive justice, or are references enough?

At the pub last night, right before closing, the bartender had given me the bill and smiled one of those smiles – one that's arbitrarily compassionate rather than personalised and individually compassionate. Next thing I know, there she is, right next to me, looking at me, and it takes me no more than a second to recognise her. I rarely recognise participants – rarely or never. But her. Yeah, there's something about her. Beauty, I guess, that treacherous, obnoxious, in every way lovely trait. She might be nearing forty, maybe she's even past it. Her hair: dark brown, straight, medium length. Her eyes: narrow, dark, somewhat veiled, though that could be the darkness of night or the drinks I've had. There's a nineteenth-century novel and a pair of reading glasses on the bar in front of her. We don't talk at first, just hi. That was an interesting experiment, she says, finally. The subject interests me. Money? I ask. No, people, she tells me. Their behaviour. W not from here are you, and I say no, I'm not from here. A beat again before I continue since she doesn't say anything else, I'm here temporarily, maybe permanently, I'm here doing research. Ph.D., she asks, and I say yeah, that's the plan. It's hard to guess, she says, and I raise my eyebrows. I can barely hear it. That you're not from here. Only in the vowels, the diphthongs, and I say yes, those are hard to nail for someone who's not from here, that downward pitch

Small Comfort

to the consonants, it's tricky for an adult immigrant. They make me a stranger of sorts, don't they, I add, a moment later. She drinks, looks. No, she says, finally, not a stranger at all. The bartender clicks off the TV that's mounted above the shelves of bottles and I put my card on the bar and slide it in his direction. Next to me she does the same, turning the other way for a second, and I look at her skinny thighs, her arse in suit trousers on the stool's vinyl cushion. Black clothes, a viscose blouse. The way she moves makes everything around her seem clumsy and misplaced. There's a warm ease to her posture and I assume that my budding feeling in this moment is an amalgam – a feeling mixed with other things, a stranger's jealousy, the chubby woman's gaze on a skinny woman, I don't know – but suddenly I want her, I want to own her the way she owns herself. I ponder our exchange as she pays for her drink. Polite conversation, but there was something else too. What, though? I tell myself it's one of those things I'll never know. I'll wake up tomorrow morning with the reliable old sloshing in my head, dead thoughts rotting amid the bulrushes, amnesia at eight in the morning and the dry back road of my tongue, and I'll remember nothing other than the fact that I must have forgotten something. Instead, there she is again, with a note she wants to give me. It's outside the pub. She's standing in the rain when I exit. Her head is uncovered and there are raindrops on her forehead. She seems unbothered by the weather. Her phone number. The ballpoint pen is still in her hand. And the name, Ruth.

<u>18 April</u>
Addendum to more comprehensive description of the experiment
/draft one/

Wealth remains one of the singularly most potent variables that exist for human behaviour, and nevertheless, the topic is essentially unexplored within experimental social psychology. This is due to the fact that the subject has not traditionally been seen as part of social psychology, but rather a discipline within the field of economics. Past studies conducted in the behavioural sciences include, for instance, research into the motivation of entrepreneurs, as well as reports on altruistic charity's effects on health. But there have barely been any studies solely dedicated to understanding money's effect on human behaviour, and that is the lacuna this study is intended to fill. Its questions have been formulated over time, and have been adjusted based on previous studies observing actually wealthy people's behaviour. The results of this previous research, which are included in this application (cf. appendix 2–8), show that monetary wealth affects behaviour in a way most would characterise as negative in relation to the surroundings, with the degree of generosity standing in inverse proportion to the subject's actual, experienced capital. The difficulty of verifying a result such as this is highlighted by the question of what the true variable of the experiment is: the experienced wealth, or the relevant behaviour. Put differently: did research subject X become wealthy because X doesn't care about others, or is the fact that X doesn't care about others a consequence of X being wealthy? Did the lack of altruism and general empathy create the conditions that allow wealth to be built and maintained, or did the access to large amounts of money shield the research subject from other people and thus promote the emergence of selfish and fundamentally antisocial behaviour? The guidelines for the present study were drawn up based on these questions. The intention is to isolate wealth as an independent variable, which means it must be temporary.

The method, letting participants play a simple board game, has multiple advantages. A board game is easy to observe and interpret; the situation can be repeated in many conceivable environments, and can scale up greatly without a serious increase in cost. The game set-up also provides a relatively 'noiseless' experimental situation, where the players can easily pick up the compliance and obedience required by the experiment.

The intention is to create an experimental situation without basic fairness – where the uneven distribution between the participants is, so to speak, simply part of the game's premise. The new rules are presented as a normal version of the game, just as good as any other version, and are not subject to any further discussion. The participants are, however, allowed to discuss how to sit, whether or not to keep their shoes on, the camera's placement, the room's temperature and so on. The more attention given to irrelevant idiosyncrasies in the scenario, the better. The experimenter's role here is to encourage what are, in the context, immaterial discussions, and to draw the participants' attention to insignificant details surrounding the game. If the rules nevertheless do inspire comment or an exchange, it is the task of the experimenter to divert the conversation or to simply interrupt it. A preparatory study, which serves as the foundation for this study's final design, unequivocally shows that 1) the length of the participants' conversation prior to the experiment correlates to how they assess their own performance in relation to the other's, and 2) the number of values communicated around the term 'fairness' prior to the start of the game is in direct proportion to how the participants assess the rules' effect on the outcome after the game. In order to avoid any discussion of ethical underpinnings, the time between the presentation of the rules and the start of the game is reduced to barely four minutes, which includes the random assignment of tokens and seating arrangements.

The selection of Monopoly as the scene for the experiment's execution is partly based on TKTKTK.

Questions for Nicholas:

– How to introduce the selection of the game itself?

– When is my new deadline for this application?

– How can we explain/translate the concept of self-made luck?

I'm studying temporary wealth – what it does to people, I tell this woman I meet at a party. The host is one of the sophomore students I'm advising. His flat is unbelievably cramped, and he's invited so many people that you risk stepping on someone if you move at all. I guess it's a good illustration of the general conditions of this city. I immediately feel large, disproportionate, like I always do at crowded events, but the woman I'm speaking to is holding on for dear life. We're standing close to each other, and still people come and go in between us as we talk. Some of them pause and briefly join the conversation before continuing on. Have parties thrown by young people looked any other way at any point in human history? Are there alternatives to these crowds? The shoe piles of my home country don't exist here, since everyone keeps their shoes on everywhere, but the heap of jackets and bags with mobile phones dinging from the depths is the same, just like the smeared red puddles of wine on the floor, the rubbish bag that's overflowing under the sink, the flowerpots on the windowsill squeezed together to give people a place to sit, and the pleasant hubbub that slowly grows into shrill yelling as the night wears on. Temporary wealth? the woman asks. Half an hour, I tell her. That sounds interesting, she says, and reaches into a bowl of peanuts. They never serve food at parties in this city, just nuts and crisps, and the parties begin early and don't end until the morning when the sun's already up. They turn into arseholes, right? the woman says. Who? I ask. The people with money, she says. They turn into arseholes, right? The arsehole effect, it's famous, she says. It's more complicated than that, or we'd all be potential arseholes, I tell her, and look at her. I haven't been drinking that much, but apparently it's enough for something in my head to abandon control of my thoughts, and suddenly I realise that Ruth's face is a constant possibility in my mind. This speeding heart, this tension: I recognise the feeling. The woman yells anew: the arsehole effect, the arsehole effect. She keeps yelling, and I can tell by her accent that we're from the same country, but I don't want to get any more involved by pointing it out.

20 April
Addendum to more comprehensive description of experiment
/draft/

The choice of game is based partly on Monopoly's widespread popularity, i.e., the fact that most individuals are already familiar with and are likely to have played the game previously, and partly on the fact that it's an arena for money, which means that the currency is a given and does not need to be introduced. The game itself, however – and in contrast to its reputation – is not a good analogue to a Western market economy, at least not when using the ordinary rules. Monopoly was invented in the early twentieth century, and gained widespread popularity in the 1930s. Today, the game has sold more than 275 million copies and can be found in most countries, often with local streets represented. The board game is often used as a horrifying illustration of so-called 'avaricious capitalism' due to its competitive nature, the single-minded profit motive and the players' literal goal of bankrupting their opponents, but a closer look shows that most of Monopoly's core elements lack a corresponding factor in the modern market economy, and that far too many features of the capitalist system are missing for the game to be a useful parallel. This is true, for instance, if we consider that labour, a foundational element of the market economy, is entirely absent in Monopoly, and the fact that all capital in the game flows from rent and the sale of properties. Above all, however, it is the role of the bank that invalidates the parallel commonly drawn between Monopoly and our capitalist society. In the game, the bank acts as an impartial state guaranteeing formal justice, not as a profit-seeking actor. It also distributes a basic minimum income without demanding anything in return simply with the intention of creating baseline equality, thereby producing a situation where the dice and individual skill determine the outcome. The game's bank serves as a 'benevolent', impartial state apparatus, guaranteeing that each participant starts out with the same conditions; the bank is the feature that makes the board game fair and worth playing. The idea of an egalitarian starting point is so closely associated with the game that its terms can, in fact, be changed without the game's associations changing accordingly. The view that success is granted by the players' skill and luck holds even long after new rules have changed that aspect of the game, as is the case in our experiment. All the players in this study – even those who are disadvantaged – characterise the game's bank as primarily 'benevolent' and 'impartial' even when it distributes unequal basic income. Similarly, the dice are viewed as purveyors of good or back luck even if one player is allowed to roll two dice, while the other can roll only one die.

This study manipulates Monopoly to bring out pre-existing values and attitudes associated with financial wealth. Since our manipulated version of the game is closer to reality than a Monopoly game with regular rules, the results of the study are generalisable. The values revealed in the experiment – what 'happens' to people when they become 'wealthy' or 'poor', how they treat each other, how they view their own and each other's 'skill', as well as many of the incidental findings (see below) that emerge from the study are, in our view, easy to reproduce in similar studies, even in other fields. Furthermore, the values can be studied through the observation of real-life situations.

The participants enter the game with pre-existing ideas about certain baseline fairness, which means that TKTKTK.

<u>Questions for Nicholas:</u>
– What's my new deadline?
– In what order should the findings be presented?
– In what order should the secondary findings be presented?
– Is the phenomenon of 'the loser's claustrophobia' part of the study, or more of a secondary finding?

Yesterday, Nicholas and I were at the pub across from campus. Football on the screen in one corner, a biker gang in the other and a few of his colleagues sitting by the bar. He greets them before we sit down at a window table. They've got no handball in this country, he says, and points at the screen with his

Small Comfort

thumb. No, I say, but it's not a great spectator sport anyway. You don't even watch it any more, you don't follow the results? I follow my old team, that's it, I tell him. And football? he asks. Nope, I say. There's too many millionaires for my taste in that sport nowadays. Nicholas laughs; we order; plates and glasses arrive at our table.

The fries are way too big in this place, Nicholas says and holds one up for me to see. We're there to chat about the project in a slightly more relaxed setting than what's offered by the department's endless meetings, and I guess comments about the food's size and shape are part of that setting. Not crisp at all, I agree. Not enough salt, Nicholas says and reaches for the metal stand that holds condiments. One could almost say they fall outside of the definition. Yeah, Nicholas says. Sliced potatoes would be a more adequate description. We add salt, we chew, we take a few sips of our beers.

Then he asks me, for the first time, why. This subject, this angle, this weird idea. I've been doing this for over a year, I say, in your department, under your supervision, and this is the first time you think to ask. Your ideas have nothing to do with where your ideas come from, he responds. They don't? I say. They don't, he says. If I like an idea, I don't care how it came to you. Though sometimes I do wonder where certain bad ideas come from. There are lots of bad ideas, including in our department. People with complicated set-ups, spectacular houses of cards, pure madness. And I always wonder: how the hell did that idea come to them? A good idea, on the other hand, is a good idea, period. It's naked, he says. I don't believe that this idea is quite as naked as you'd like it to be, I tell him. Nicholas drinks and looks at me. When I was little, I say, and spin my glass. It wasn't exactly a life of excess. He nods. I suppose there's something I want to understand, I say, and I suppose that understanding would mean being free of it. It's good to bring your own experience, Nicholas says. It's not always the best motivation, but it's usually a good premise for science. He looks at me with a smile. Not all ideas are naked, I say. Nicholas shakes his head. Once they've been refined, once they've been turned into science and made the basis of evidence, when they can stand on their own – then they're naked, he says. In any case, you're doing a good job. Ambitious, long days, great applications, thorough descriptions. You'll do well.

Nicholas is easy to understand. In this country, nobody opens their mouth without announcing their background, their parents' position on the labour market, their political home, what currency their

Small Comfort

thoughts are thought in. The information is all there, neatly sorted between the vowels and the consonants, in the little snap when the k and the l hit the palate, in the ways they sometimes raise their voice at the end of a sentence and sometimes lower it. He votes left, but personally benefits from a right-wing government; he writes about immigrants, but knows very few of them; he's got an idiosyncratic way of pronouncing 'the working class', the object of many of his studies, in definite form, always definite form. We should include a picture of his perfect face with our grant applications, since nobody – absolutely nobody – can resist beauty as expressed in a symmetrical human face. He's got an easy, carefully considered style that's free of tics but marked by certain preferences: black, unpolished, seemingly random. Nicholas is the type of man who can wear a suit and still blend in at an underground music festival. I'd guess that he found his style in his late teens and it's been constant ever since, day after day, year after year. Since then, he's been the same weight and had the same types of garments in his closet, the same kind of car, the same kinds of neighbourhoods, the same kinds of girlfriends. The whiteboard over his desk has a picture of the son he sometimes sees on the weekends: a carbon copy of the father, with a straight nose, sharp eyebrows and ice-blue eyes. Nicholas saunters up to the bar and orders another round, then returns to our table with a smile. I'm halfway through my first. How long have you lived here now, he asks as he sits down. Two and a half years, I say. Almost three. Do you feel settled? No, not quite. So it doesn't feel like home yet, then, I take it. He takes a few big gulps, the foam sticking to his lip. No, I reply, it doesn't feel like home. Then again, home doesn't feel like home any more either, I say. Nicholas chuckles. I've read that it takes three years to feel at home anywhere, he says. People who are sent to work abroad for their company aren't allowed to stay longer than that. It's too hard for them to come back. You get de-integrated. I don't think that's true any more, I say, the world's become too small. You're probably right, Nicholas says. In any case, it might not be about the place, I say, but something else. The company, the environment. I travelled pretty far in my own country too. Nicholas looks at me. I see, he says, but I can tell that he doesn't. He says: All I'm saying is there's nothing to stop you from staying here. Even after your dissertation, I mean. I don't usually think that far into the future, I tell him. Why not? You're talented, you should plan ahead. Someone scores a goal on the TV in the corner and a bar patron slams his fist into the table. I don't know, I say. Either way, it doesn't matter, right? No matter how important a scientific finding is, it just flickers by. Nothing's going to change. People will read something in the news about it, move on to the next thing, and immediately forget about it. We live in a world that doesn't let itself be affected by the kind of research we do, since the only reasonable conclusion, if we really took our findings seriously, would be some kind of revolution. Nicholas sits up straight and puts his hand up, palm facing me in a stop sign. Not that word, he says. Never that word in this context. Never in an application, never in a conversation with prefects, the chair, the students. I understand what you mean, but you'll need to find a different expression. Radical reform? I ask. Nicholas takes a sip, puts down his glass, and burps through his nose. Too similar, he says. Complete overhaul? I suggest. No, Nicholas says. Radical revamp? I offer. Absolutely not, Nicholas laughs. Regeneration, improvement, evolution? I ask. That's closer. Evolution towards a just world? I ask. I'm not sure we should use that word either, Nicholas says. You mean 'justice'? Yes, that one, I'm not sure it's ideal. Do you have any other forbidden words? I ask. Tons, he says. Tons.

23 April
Addendum to comprehensive description of experiment results
/first draft/

The players come to the game with ideas about a type of basic fairness, and these contribute to upholding the feeling that parameters like good/bad luck and skill/lack of skill are the main drivers of the game's outcome, rather than the terms of the game. The level of attachment to these ideas varies between winners and losers, with the losers assessing their own efforts as less meaningful as the game wears on, while the winners maintain the same assessment about basic fairness throughout the game. Per the answers to the survey, the winners understand the rules of the game as 'fair', 'somewhat unfair' and 'neither fair nor unfair' (a deliberately vague formulation; see below), while assessing their own skill as 'relatively high'. The losers' understanding of the game's set-up falls between 'somewhat unfair' or 'completely unfair', and they put slightly less emphasis than the winners on their own skill and the outcome of the dice.

The phrasing 'neither fair nor unfair' in the survey's second question is deliberately vague in order to introduce and make space for a third attitude, which is that the dichotomy between fairness/unfairness is irrelevant. Since this stance is a value that isn't made explicit, i.e. a transparent value, it is difficult to bring it out without allowing the participants to use clearly irrational answers. A surprising number, around 20% of the respondents, selected this alternative, which can be interpreted to mean that for a fifth of the study's participants the question of fairness or unfairness is not a variable that factors into a preliminary assessment of the world around them – not even when the rules are explicitly unfair.

<u>Questions for Nicholas:</u>
- Should I attach an edited coaching script?
- Do I need to explain the term 'coach'?

The TV is on above the shelves of bottles. Do you know him, a voice asks, next to me. It's the same pub, the same woman. Ruth. She sits down on the stool next to mine at the bar. We haven't been in touch. The scrap of paper is on a chair in my hall. I slept in the morning after our encounter, her face melting into my dreams, and I haven't figured out a formally acceptable reason to dial her number. The brief spot about Simmons contains nothing new. No, I tell her, he's just a person I follow. Enthusiastically, she says. What do you mean, I say. Enthusiastically, you follow him enthusiastically. With a certain, I don't know, mania. Oh, I say. He's interesting, isn't he, I mean, as a phenomenon. He's on TV, we're all getting updates about his coma – it says something about the world, I say. Ah, and what does it say about the world, she asks. She emphasises the vowel sound in 'what', as if she were asking the question with absolute sincerity, for the first time. I'm not sure, I tell her. You're a scientist, I assume you've got some kind of analysis? I'm still in the fact-finding stages, I say. I'm not a real scientist yet. She laughs. White teeth, I want to own those as well. And what do the facts tell you, she asks. About what, I ask. Well, the subject in question. If you were to sketch a background for a project grant application. I clear my throat, and say, controversial businessman, forty-seven years old, often named as one of the world's most influential people. This, of course, is due not only to his wealth, but also his business models, his aggressive entry into new markets, his exploitation of new geographies in developing countries and his unconventional methods, including the way he promotes himself. And his persona, the person he's created that is Simmons: handsome, fit, tanned, intelligent, brutal, looks thirty-seven. According to recent rumours, he's considering getting into politics. Ruth looks at me and nods. I continue. Among the myths that surround him there is, of course, the one that says he started out with two empty hands, I tell her. The world loves a millionaire who started out with two empty hands. Admires, you mean, says Ruth. Isn't that what they feel, admiration? We might admire them, but above all we love them, I say. We love that they exist. And do you know why? She looks at me and shakes her head. I continue: We love millionaires who started out with two empty hands, because they allow us to keep believing. Believe what? Ruth asks. I don't know, I say, in fairness, maybe. A disadvantaged child who becomes a wealthy adult is proof that everything's in order, no? That's the kind of world we want to live in. And then it doesn't matter that fewer than one per cent of the world's millionaires were born poor. We hold them close, we love what they tell us about the world – in fact, we might not be able to bear it without them. And Simmons? Ruth asks. No, I say, I don't think he was born poor. There are strong indications that this story is exactly that: a story, a fairy tale. Like so much else that surrounds him. Without me noticing, Ruth has ordered us each a glass of transparent liquor, and now she sips and I sip and we look at each other. Okay, so a fairy tale, but in the news, she says. Exactly, I say. A real-life fairy tale, though it might be true. You got any more analyses? I laugh. It's not a question but something else, some kind of invitation. The bar is closing. The bartender takes our cards. Her bag bounces off my thigh when she puts her wallet back. You never called, she says. I was going to call, I say. A load of stuff came up. I see, she says. So I decided to wait, I say. Sure, she says. Until I had the chance, I say. Sure, sure, she says. She rubs the corner of her eye with her finger, catches a flake of mascara, studies it. So when will you have the chance, she says, and drops the flake on the floor between us. I don't know, maybe tomorrow, I say. Yeah, or what about now, says Ruth.

<u>28 April</u>
Addendum to more comprehensive experiment description
/draft one/

Coaching started in elite sports, and is a time-limited, supportive activity geared towards individuals or smaller groups. The original purpose was to help athletes reach one, or a select few, well-defined goals. In recent decades, the scope of the activity has broadened, and nowadays there are coaches in most contexts related to personal development, leadership and professional careers. The coaching itself is performed by individuals with various professional backgrounds who require no specific education in psychology, pedagogy or conversational therapy. Standards for knowledge, competence and potential-use cases appear to be set by the practitioners themselves.

Conversations between a professional facilitator and an individual in need is not a new phenomenon. Supportive or guiding conversations have long been part of the job description for professions like priest, psychologist, psychotherapist, therapist, careers officer, nurse, midwife, doctor and deacon, with the length, content and frequency of meeting shifting in accordance with the situation. These days, coaches exist in all these milieus, but what distinguishes a traditional supportive or guiding conversation from a coaching conversation is that the latter is brief, focused on the individual's own ability, and emphasises the benefits of positive thinking. In a coaching conversation, the structural, spiritual, material, psychological or social values of a traditional supportive dialogue are replaced by a focus on individual ability and positive thinking, which is why coaching sessions within widely divergent areas can appear identical to each other. Studies made of coaching sessions show that these often have a fortifying effect on the recipient (cf. appendix 9–10). For instance, unemployed individuals felt much better following a coaching session, assessing their ability to get a job as much higher than before. The coaching session did not, however, impact the person's ability to get a job, and it also contributed to a real reduction in the job-seeking individual's knowledge about the mechanisms of the labour market. For instance, following two sessions with the same coach, 40% of job-seekers rated structural reasons as less important when asked to name possible reasons for their own joblessness.

The purpose of giving 50% of the Monopoly game's 'losers' a coaching session is to study the effects of individualised positive thinking on assessments of structural unfairness. The coaching sessions unfold according to a generalised standard pattern, structured in accordance with existing coaching trainings (see appendix 11), whereby the participants are given ten to twelve assessments, pieces of advice and open questions. The tenor of the conversation is encouraging and supportive with an individualised subtext, where the focus is on an assumed 'potential'; a kind of hidden but present capacity that the subject is encouraged to bring out using various mental techniques. The participants are asked to name their negative mental frameworks around the game's set-up and outcome, and are encouraged to reframe these as their positive opposites. For instance, the thought

Small Comfort

'this isn't working' is swapped for the thought 'I can do this'. Armed with such personalised strategies, the players continue the game.

By referencing this imagined internal capacity and establishing it as a fact, other possible explanatory models that take into account factors outside of the individual are dismissed. The purpose of the coaching session is to activate a sense of individual responsibility for the game's outcome, and to underscore individual performance as central, regardless of the terms of the game. The players are encouraged to engage in 'positive thinking' about their own chances of winning the game, as opposed to 'realistic thinking' about these chances. This goal was met in every single case, and after less than ten minutes of coaching.

The coaching sessions had no effect whatsoever on the game's outcome, but afterwards, those who received coaching reported feeling encouraged and said that they believed, for a short time, that they could very well have turned the game around. On the other hand, they were less likely than those who had received no coaching to detect the reason for their major losses, and they state that in a potential later game with similar terms they would have a 'reasonable' chance of winning.

A week after the experiment, the long-term effects of the coaching sessions are examined using a survey for all 'losers', combined with twenty in-depth interviews with a group of participants where half received coaching during the game. Preliminary results indicate that the short-term effects of coaching on participants' ability to detect structural reasons for private defeat remain, and those who were coached link their loss to their own inability or bad luck, as opposed to the unfair rules of the game. The coaching sessions are experienced as 'a helpful kick in the butt' and participants who received coaching remember it as 'generally encouraging', stating that at times they've felt 'kind of like I want revenge'. The idea of participating in another round of the game (with the same rules) feels like 'an exciting challenge', and 55% believe that their chance of winning would be greater in the next round.

Questions for Nicholas:
 – Should I attach a full, transcribed, in-depth interview? Or excerpts?
 – Reference texts for coaching as concept? Can't find any relevant research outside sports medicine.
 – What about fairness section (not Rawls, right?).

How often do you do this? I ask. Bring people home from bars and keep them in your bedroom? It's the

Small Comfort

fifth day at Ruth's. We go our different ways in the morning and meet up at hers again a few hours later. I spend most of the time in my office on campus looking out of the window, forgetting the task at hand. I take naps on the breakroom sofa at lunch, and stand in front of the coffee machine reading the instructions over and over without understanding a thing. Never, Ruth says. There's art on the walls of her bedroom, a narrow bookshelf with paperbacks in three different languages, a bedside table with an open laptop on it, and an enormous bed without headboard or footboard. Our clothes are piled on an armchair and the window is open behind the curtains. It's late in the afternoon and still warm outside. So that's why I came to the city: to step into this, to slowly slip into Ruth's world, to unearth myself in her. How about you, she asks. Do you usually leave bars with women you don't know and set up camp in their bedroom? Not often, I tell her. At least not with women like you. I've been home once, to pick up clothes, and was left standing in my own living room for a long time, feeling claustrophobic, like a stranger, as if someone entirely different lived there, which was partly true. Ruth leaves the bedroom. I hear her steps vanish and be gone for a few minutes before they return. It must be an enormous flat. She brings me a robe, made from a weightless cloth and in a colour that immediately suits me. Then she goes into the kitchen, turns on the kettle, clatters with something and comes back with fresh tea and crackers on a little tray. Or would you prefer something more substantial? she asks. I shake my head and run a hand over the new robe. Whose is this? I ask. Nobody's, she says. So far it has been ownerless. So far it's been a piece of unclaimed property. But it's yours now.

2 May

Excerpt of transcript
In-depth interview 1

Woman, 29 years old, student. Shoe token, lost all her money in 27 minutes, five-minute coaching session midway through the game.

[. . .]

Experimenter (**E**): What did you think about the coaching?

Participant (**P**): What do you mean?

E: Well, in the middle. When we talked.

P: Ah, the peptalk?

E: The peptalk. Yes.

P: The peptalk was great. It made me get it. Like, I guess I felt pumped.

E: What did you feel?

Small Comfort

P: I felt pumped. I felt like, let's go get it. I can do this. I felt like it was up to me whether I'd win or not – nothing else mattered. Before the peptalk, I felt as if there was something wrong with the game, my opponent, but afterwards I was just like, okay, let's go.

E: Would you say that the coaching – I mean the peptalk – was a positive experience?

P: Definitely. Before that I was feeling really down. But then you really focused on my power, and that was great. You were supportive.

E: Supportive?

P: Yeah, you focused on my power, my potential. You said I had an innate power that I wasn't fully using.

E: And how did you feel about that?

P: I thought it was really well said. I still do, when I think about it. Like, really good, and also it's true for everything.

E: What do you mean?

P: I mean, it goes for everything. I'm fucking powerful, you know? As a person. It's in here, a force I'm not using fully. And when I home in on it, then, well . . .

E: Yeah?

P: Well, yeah, it makes me feel like I can do it. I feel my own power. In here.

E: In your chest?

P: Yeah. In my soul.

E: Okay. Can you compare the feeling you had about the set-up of the game before you were coached and after?

P: Oh, it was a huge difference. It felt more hopeless before. And after it was like, okay, I can do this. I didn't care about the circumstances, if that makes sense. I just focused on doing a good job. Since it was about my performance, and with your encouragement it was like I could focus on it.

E: And the circumstances?

P: What circumstances?

E: Well, like the rules of the game, for instance.

P: What about them?

E: The set-up. The way you received less money when you passed GO, for instance. That was one circumstance. One of the circumstances.

P: Sure, sure. But that's exactly the type of thing that stopped annoying me after the peptalk. I was able to focus on my own performance. Since that's what it was all about.

E: What was it all about?

P: The outcome of the game. Like, if I'd only pulled myself together better, I could have won. Or had a chance.

E: But you didn't get any hotels, and you only had two houses.

P: Sure.

Small Comfort

E: While your opponent bought, let's see... Right, he had Fenchurch Street, the Angel, Islington, Whitechapel, Marlborough Street, Coventry Street, Oxford Street and Mayfair after just three rounds. You had completed only one round, and had bought – ah... right, Piccadilly.

P: Right.

E: And after five rounds he had hotels on Park Lane and Mayfair.

P: Wasn't that when I bought Old Kent Road, though?

E: Yes. And then you were forced to swap Piccadilly for Fenchurch Street so he wouldn't bankrupt you. Then he built hotels on the yellow streets in the sixth round.

P: And I built a hotel on Old Kent Road.

E: No, a house.

P: Okay, a house.

E: But first you were in jail.

P: While he was building, right. I remember that – he was building and building.

E: But then we had the coaching session. The peptalk.

P: I know. Let's fucking go, that's what I thought. I remember thinking it was a kind of special treatment. A sort of advantage that he didn't have.

E: And what did that advantage lead to?

P: What do you mean?

E: Well, if it was a leg up, what did it lead to?

P: Does it have to lead to anything in particular?

E: Since you experienced the peptalk as an advantage. What did the leg up lead to, practically speaking, in the game?

P: I mean, I don't know if it had any practical results. But the way I experienced the whole thing, there was a difference there. I was more focused on the important stuff. That's an advantage, isn't it?

E: In the game, you mean?

P: Right. That's what I'm saying: that peptalk was great.

[...]

Excerpt of transcript
In-depth interview 2

Man, 28, student, luxury car, won in 22 minutes

[...]

E: How come you won?

P: What do you mean?

E: I'm asking why you won.

P: I won because I'm so fucking great, haha. No, seriously. I was really lucky too.

E: You were really lucky?

Small Comfort

P: Luck, skill – that's always the mix in board games, isn't it?

E: Would you say it was primarily luck or primarily skill?

P: It was probably a bit of both. But I was very strategic, I was. I focused on the expensive streets immediately, trying to build on them, focus my income there, so to speak. And I ignored the smaller streets, Old Kent Road or whatever they're called.

E: You owned both Old Kent Road and Fenchurch Street, though.

P: Sure, maybe I did. But I wasn't that focused on them at all. I've played a lot of Monopoly in my life. When I was little and all that – yeah, you know. With my family and so on. Christmas and summer breaks and so on. I think I've got a certain winner instinct from back then.

E: You'd win a lot when you were little?

P: As far as I remember. Yeah, I think so. I'm strategically inclined, got a good head for logic.

E: And the game you played the other day, was that mostly strategy, or mostly luck?

P: Like I said, there was probably a bit of both. Fifty–fifty maybe.

E: Half luck, half skill?

P: Something like it, yeah.

E: Were there any other factors in the mix?

P: What do you mean?

E: Was there anything else that shaped the outcome of the game?

P: I don't know.

E: I'm thinking about the rules, for instance. The way the rules were set up.

P: Yeah, they were kind of odd, I'd agree with that.

E: In what way were they odd?

P: We had different rules, me and the other player. I got more money every time I passed GO, if I remember correctly. And there was something else too.

E: Something with the dice? You had two of them?

P: Right. Though I don't know if that mattered much, I don't think it did.

E: Using two dice you'll get further, though. Plus, you were able to roll the dice again when they showed the same number.

P: I mean, I don't know if that's much of an advantage, to be honest.

E: By the time you'd completed three rounds and bought – let's see – seven streets and built three houses, your opponent was still on the first round.

P: Right, he was a bit of a slowpoke there in the beginning.

E: Do you think that might be because of the

dice? I mean, that you each rolled different numbers of dice?

P: It's possible. I don't know. I tend to be quick out the gate, though. I get things fast. I understand things easily. It's like that with everything, you know.

E: But the number of dice could affect the whole thing?

P: Like I said. I don't know, it's possible.

E: What do you think about the chance cards?

P: The fact that me and my opponent had different stacks?

E: Yeah. And you had certain cards and he had other ones.

P: I did notice that he had a bit of bad luck with his cards at times. That he had to go back to jail right after he was out of jail, stuff like that.

E: Does that have any impact on the game's outcome?

P: It's not like he's losing money being in jail.

E: Sure, but during that time you kept moving, building hotels and buying streets.

P: I even remember I helped him get out of jail once.

E: Yes, let's see. Right, you traded a card that let him out of jail in exchange for Marlborough Street. Is that the trade you're referring to?

P: I helped him, exactly. He was having a streak of bad luck, and I had a bunch of those cards.

E: But that trade gave you Marlborough Street.

P: Sure, sure.

E: You still think of it as helping him.

P: He got out of jail, didn't he?

E: And you got Marlborough Street?

P: Sure, I got Marlborough Street.

E: Was it a trade, or was it helping him?

P: Fine, let's call it a bit of both.

E: And considering that once you had Marlborough Street you were able to build houses and, soon enough, hotels on Bow Street, Vine Street and Marlborough Street, all the orange streets, it wasn't exactly a bad trade, right? Given what it would cost him, later, to end up on these streets?

P: It was a trade that helped us both – let's put it that way.

E: Did it help him in the long run, though?

P: Debatable, isn't it? Haha. That's certainly debatable.

E: When you made the trade, did you foresee the consequences?

P: I suppose it wasn't random that I wanted Marlborough Street from him. I already had Bow Street and Vine Street. Marlborough Street was the only one missing.

E: Did you feel smart?

P: I did.

Small Comfort

E: Or smarter?

P: How do you mean?

E: Well, when you traded a get-out-of-jail-free card for Marlborough Street, what did it make you think about your opponent's intelligence?

P: Uhm, I guess it was clear from the beginning that he wasn't the brightest. And that trade – let's just say it might have confirmed that understanding.

E: Now you're calling it a trade. Earlier you said you were helping him.

P: Trade, help, potato-potahto.

E: Could it even be said that it was a trade to your advantage?

P: In the long run it might have been to my benefit, sure. But he could have declined if he wanted.

E: He had to go to jail a lot, since his chance cards sent him there two times out of four. Did he really have a choice?

P: What do you mean, choice? Of course he had a choice. He could predict the consequences of the trade just as well as I could. Like, it's not poker.

E: I guess it was fun to get out on the board and move a little too, not just watch you build hotels.

P: Sure. But Marlborough Street, come on.

E: He didn't have any other streets.

P: No? Well, anyway.

E: Not the brightest?

P: That's one way of putting it.

E: Can you say a bit more about that?

P: What is there to say? We're different, us people on earth. We have different gifts of the mind, different talents. There are those who are intelligent, and those who are less intelligent. Maybe he falls into the latter category.

E: And you?

P: Me? I'm pretty smart when it comes to certain things.

E: What things?

P: I mean, in board games, at work, things like that. You can tell if someone is smart.

E: Who can tell if someone is smart?

P: Well, I think people who are smart can tell if someone else is not that smart. It's just obvious. You know, people who are smart do better.

E: In games like Monopoly, for instance?

P: Exactly. And in the labour market, in life, in society. Yeah. You know what I mean.

E: What if the rules had been the opposite, who would have won then?

P: I don't know. That's impossible to say.

E: You saw I flipped a coin, before the game started?

P: Yes?

E: What was that about? What was the coin toss for?

P: I think it was just about where we were sitting, wasn't it?

E: Nothing else?

P: What tokens we were going to use? I don't know.

E: The coin flip was to determine who would play according to what rules.

P: Fine, I get it, I get it. I might have benefited slightly, but I don't think that determined the game's outcome in any way.

E: What did?

P: Like I said, luck, skill, experience.

E: And the fact that your opponent wasn't the brightest?

P: Yeah, that could be part of it too.

[...]

Questions for Nicholas:

– Fairness, clinical definition? I'm stuck on that one.

– Random chance as explanatory model to legitimise undesired behaviours – is there a neurological model for this?

– The plan to study real-life wealthy people, what happened to that?

Yesterday Ruth told me she's moving this summer. She's got a similar flat across the Atlantic and regularly spends time there to take care of things related to her job. She might be away for six months, maybe a year. I still don't know what exactly she does for a living, but sometimes she gets out of bed and answers her vibrating phone, opens the computer with her phone pinned between ear and shoulder, gets her glasses out, and keeps talking as she scans numbers arranged in columns on the screen. Trust management, she says. Owning property is a job in and of itself. She likes me, but she's understood nothing about my desire, its character. Why don't you put me in a trust, I tell her, but what I mean is: eat me and keep me inside you.

I wake up alone in her home, drink tea in bed and flip between the channels on the TV that hangs on the opposite wall. After a while, I turn it off and go out onto the balcony. Ruth lives in the south-west of the city, among embassies and well-tended parks. I hadn't been to this neighbourhood before I met her, only read novels that describe the interiors. Most houses have been here since the late nineteenth century – at least those that weren't destroyed in the war. Ruth's balcony looks onto a little cul-de-sac, and across the street is the entrance to a park with tall chestnuts, leafy cherry trees and gravel paths. A low redbrick wall runs along the lawn, and when the street is quiet you can hear a fountain from somewhere

Small Comfort

inside the park. A wedding party is leaving through an opening in the wall, led by a photographer who walks backwards while calling out instructions. They all stop and arrange themselves in front of the park entrance, green filling the background of the picture. I watch them from the balcony. The bride's dress is ivory with long sleeves and embroidered pearls more pink in hue towards the waist; the groom is wearing a marine corps officer uniform with two squares crossing the epaulettes. Ten or so festively adorned people flutter around them with tall glasses in their hands. The photographer kneels and points with her hand; people switch places, smile for the camera, the groom puts his arm round the bride and kisses her cheek as the others cheer. Then the whole party starts walking again, like a live organism, onto the street and down the pavement beneath me. Snatches of conversation float up to me: they've got horse-drawn carriages waiting for them, a party to follow.

I walk through the flat, looking at everything. This furniture, this art, the books that lie open on a low table next to the sofa in one of the parlour rooms. One is about bridges, another about salt and another has photographs of old people from some furrowed indigenous population at the foot of a mountain. And then there's a door, a closet, which I enter. I walk through it and exit into another room, and the silky scent from in there follows me. Trouser suits and dress suits, mostly in black, and dresses in transparent plastic sheaths; rows of shoes on the shelves beneath; a small, curvy dresser full of underwear. I have no idea how big it is, her flat, just that its temperature and spaciousness and perfection correspond to Ruth in a way that's beyond anything I could ever learn by asking. It's useless to ask: where's that table from, and get the name of an auction house or a type of wood, cherry or walnut – or ask: what did that cost, and get a number. I know nothing about the make and provenance of these pieces, but I can picture the way hired hands brought them in under her watchful eye, how they were put in their right spots, how she leaned closer and passed her dry hand over their surfaces, looking for scratches. Her hands belong to the neighbourhood's cool satisfaction, including when they're on my body, and I am powerless before what she does. My own are ridiculous in comparison, incredibly clumsy and sweaty. She must notice, but it seems like she doesn't care. Big, clammy hands isn't a bad thing for a handball player and now that I'm sitting on the edge of Ruth's bed, studying them in the light of the open balcony door, now that I look at the glitter from the dew in the folds of my palm, I recall the exact feeling of a handball against my fingertips. I played every day for over a decade. No matter how many times my right hand holds Ruth, it will still have held a handball more times. She'll never catch up.

6 May

Addendum to more comprehensive description of the experiment
/draft one/

A number of accidental findings can be added to the study's preliminary results. Before the entirety of the results have been processed, it is difficult to ascertain whether these will ultimately be included in the main report, left out but inspire further study or discarded as irrelevant. Nevertheless, the results are significant enough to warrant mention in this application.

Many scientific advances emerge from mistakes. Mould on an abandoned bacterial culture led to the discovery of penicillin, setting sail in the wrong cardinal direction led to the discovery of new continents, and so on. Even in small, relatively marginal studies such as this one, an act of carelessness could lead to certain incidental findings which, in turn, can be scientifically interpreted.

During three of the introductory rounds of the game, a bowl containing seven cookies was accidentally left on the table when the experimenter and the participants entered the room, and to avoid stoking nerves or anxiety the bowl was left in place, without any comment. Afterwards, processing the video recording of these rounds – about 40 minutes each in length – two observations can be made concerning the consumption of these cookies. The first relates to the distribution of the cookies, and the other to the consumption behaviour. These incidental findings appear interesting enough for the bowl of cookies to be permanently included on the table and added to the list of observable behaviours.

Since the number of cookies (7) cannot be split evenly by the number of players (2), there is not an obvious fair distribution, immediately creating an interesting social-psychological situation. In brief, it can be said that the distribution of cookies that emerges is in direct proportion to the distribution of the board game's total properties.

Concerning the consumption technique, i.e. the eating behaviour as such, it can be noted, also in brief, that the grade of table manners is in inverse proportion to accumulated wealth. On average, 80% of the cookies are consumed by those who are doing well in the game, 10% are consumed by those doing badly, and the remaining 10% are left in the bowl.

How should this meaningful correlation be interpreted? Several other studies show similar results, and the 'generalised superiority' thesis is proven and well-established (see appendix 12). Per this thesis, a person who enjoys success within one area believes that this success can be generalised; a sort of universalised victory is attached to the victor, even if the original success was both random and temporary, creating a more self-satisfied attitude and drastically diminished empathy. Behaviour gets orientated towards self-satisfaction, while the most basic social rules are broken, often without the individual noticing.

The phenomenon of 'generalised superiority' can be psychologically explained by the way an experience in one area tends to spill over into other areas that are close in concept or time. As a consequence, the board game's winner does experience a genuine right to take the majority of the cookies from the bowl on the table, as long as the victory and the consumption of the cookies are proximate in time. This behaviour is based on the tendency to explain success using reasons that are related to the individual's own capacity, such that even random success (or, as in this case, wealth) is experienced as well-deserved. It's a pattern that makes success palatable to reason, even as it produces an overestimation of one's own ability, and an underestimation of other people's ability. Because success is viewed as well-deserved, the individual feels they deserve other benefits too, e.g. the majority of the cookies on a plate.

The correlation between temporary wealth and antisocial behaviour during the consumption of the cookies (e.g. chewing with an open mouth, reaching across the table without apology, commanding the other to pass the bowl) can be added to the previously outlined description of superiority, and is part of the overestimation of self that the game's winners express in the survey afterwards.

Questions for Nicholas:
– How to generalise wealth as predictor for rude behaviour?
– The concept of deserved bad luck (its psychological mechanisms): how should I lay this out?
– The concept of deserved luck, what do I do with that?

Ruth's question yesterday morning: your background. Yeah, I say. We're in bed. Satin sheets, Sunday, the balcony door cracked open, warm air. I can hear the fountain in the park. Your homeland, who were you back home? Someone else, I tell her. I wasn't anyone special, I sold reserve parts for office machines. I played handball, as you know. Were you good? Pretty good, Division Two, a few seasons in

Small Comfort

One. I was sturdy, which is an advantage in handball. And then what, Ruth says. What do you mean then what? Well, you're here now, so something must have happened. I discovered that I was good at thinking. I borrowed books from the library, non-fiction books in every subject I could think of. It was almost like a thirst. Then I went to university, left handball behind, moved here. It all happened pretty fast. And your family? Ruth asks. Are you the first? To study, yes, I tell her, but you already figured that out. Ruth smiles. She stretches and moves to get out of bed, but I pull her back. If I may ask, I say, how can you tell? She's resting her head in her hand, elbow on the sheet. Looks out of the window, looks at me. Maybe it's not what's visible, but what isn't. So what is it that isn't visible, then, I ask. I don't know, Ruth says. I don't know.

The texture of her speech: like coarse rubber. Every syllable has its own quality, the letters dry and perfectly placed in her mouth. I've never known anyone to handle language like this, as if the words have found a new meaning beyond their content, a tone that's behind the sound itself. When she speaks, I want to move closer, bite her lips, I want the sound inside my own body. It's struck me, the thought of carefully slicing her skin open so I can crawl in – so I can eat her breakfast, talk from inside of her, be the one giving those neutral directives to the male cleaner who comes on Tuesdays. Own those dry hands and the well-portioned movements, day after day. Yesterday, I found a new room in the flat. It's behind a door that looks like a closet and is, in fact, two rooms that have been combined into one, with its own balcony facing the park. There's a little desk by the wall, an armchair, a slender floor lamp and books from floor to ceiling, everywhere books, sorted from A to Z with fiction in one section, non-fiction in another, and reference works in a third. I pulled out a few of them at random and sat down in the chair.

11 May

Addendum to description of experiment
/draft one/

The loser's claustrophobia

The initial in-depth interviews are based on the answers given by participants in the last two questions of the survey, where they use their own words to explain why they won or lost the game, as well as to provide a brief account of their feelings over the course of the game.

Those participants who were randomly selected to be disadvantaged by the rules of the game invariably expressed a highly specific type of claustrophobia. They describe how, over the course of the game, they're increasingly aware of the small size of the room, the stale feeling of the air and the slow passage of time. They write that their clothes begin to feel tight, that a vague nausea overtakes them, that they fantasise about just getting up and leaving.

Accounts of claustrophobia recur in all in-depth interviews with 'losers' – even those who received a coaching session. The cognitive contents of this claustrophobic experience can be described as a combination of powerlessness and self-blaming mental constructs, and it primarily appears as if it is the sense of being responsible, combined with the inability to shape the game's outcome, that produces this deep discomfort. The fact that the game's fundamentally unfair rules were established as natural and not subject to change comes up again and again in the interview, though without any assignment of blame. Most evidence an astonishing level of acceptance of the rules and don't consider the consequences of the same. Instead, the subjects blame themselves for their loss: they 'should have been able to win anyway', they 'could have worked harder' and, even when the interviewer draws attention to the unfair rules, they still 'could have done better'. They deem the winning opponent 'more skilled', 'more strategic' and 'a little luckier with the dice and chance cards'. Even when the interviewer once again draws their attention to the rigged game, they explicate their own performance with reference to, primarily, a lack of skill, and, secondarily, a lack of luck. The unfair rules come only third in the ranking of explanations.

This individualised, or destructuralised, explanatory model could be one of the reasons for the loser's claustrophobia, since the frustration is directed inwards, at the self, rather than externalised at the rules that clearly benefit one player at the cost of the other.

The experiment reproduces the effect shown in multiple other studies: When structurally powerless participants are kept apart, they explain their situation by reference to themselves as individuals, a factor that is still within the realm of their own influence. A person with no power over their own situation does retain power over their own personality, which, consequently, becomes the primary arena for both blame and praise.

<u>Questions for Nicholas:</u>
– How should the results of the estimation of one's own intelligence quota before/after the experiment be presented? Table?

– How can the phenomenon 'loser's claustrophobia' be reproduced in other types of experiments? Parallel treadmills with different speeds?

Ruth leaves in less than a month, but we don't talk about it any more than we have to. How long is half a year in heartbeats? It will be winter here when she comes home, maybe spring or summer. Another thing we don't need to discuss.

Have you read everything in here? I'm in the library when she comes home. She sits down cross-legged on the floor by my armchair. No, she says. But almost all of it. When? I ask. When did you have time to read all this? I've been reading every day, all my life, ever since I was five. It's a habit, a hobby. For you too, no? Sure, I say. Well then, Ruth says. Then you know. But I won't ever catch up, I tell her. Catch up to what, she asks. I don't know, I say, because Ruth's question is an inverted question, an inverted rhetorical question. A rhetorical question is asked to show that the answer is given in advance, which makes it something totally different from a question. An inverted rhetorical question is posed to show that the answer is a shrug, which in its turn is meant to show that the question isn't valid. Catch up to what? Ruth asks, though she knows. Catch up to what, and I know the answer though I can't put words to it, and that exact inability is perhaps part of the answer. The day we can sort this out in any of our languages is the day when I've finally caught up, and that day will probably never come. Maybe it is this afternoon in her library that I understand the impossibility of our relationship. It's got nothing to do with my sweaty handball hands or the books or the money, just her way of asking that question and my inability to formulate an answer. Catch up to what?

But then she says something else. You could always come, she says. I live here, though, I say, in this city. Do you? she says. I'm tied to this place, I say, and think about my claustrophobic flat. Are you?

<u>17 May</u>

Addendum to description of the experiment
/draft one/

Embodied manifestations of material success

Over the course of the experiment, the subjective experience of wealth manifests spatially in several different ways. In practice, these manifestations mean that the body holds some of the success – expresses it, augments it, gives it meaning. Physically manifesting a subjective experience of success by, for instance, performing a victory gesture, is a way for the individual to confirm this experience in their social environment. If the success is based solely on luck and given advantages, as in this study, the embodied manifestations become a way for the winner to create contextual logic out of luck and provided advantages. The gesture turns objective luck into subjectively experienced, self-made success.

Success manifests in various victory gestures. The most common version, used at least once by 67% of the winning participants, entails raising the underarm to a vertical position. In 70% of these instances, the hand is briefly made into a fist before the arm is lowered again, and at other times the pointer and middle finger make a so-called V-sign. Around 50% of participants at some point also turn their entire arm into an erection, hand raised to the ceiling in either a fist or a V-sign. Additionally, almost 8% of the winners in a few instances make a two-armed victory gesture with both hands raised to the ceiling. A little over half the winners use only one type of victory gesture; 8% employ all three gestures. Only 5% of the winners refrain from victory gestures entirely. None of the losing participants make any gestures at all.

There is also a significant difference in soundscape between those who win and those who lose the game. The microphones are evenly distributed in the space to capture this aspect, and show no difference between the players in the first few minutes of the game. As time wears on, however, the frequency of loud sounds from the player with the luxury car increases. These sounds have multiple sources: a scraping chair, a fist on a table, different kinds of knocking with the knuckles, palms clapping together and various kinds of oral exclamations. What these sounds have in common is that they all increase in volume over the course of the game.

Making a claim on the audial space is a behaviour that's been well documented in social psychology. Studies have been conducted with various kinds of groups, like preschool children, celebrity athletes, homeless people and immigrant retirees (cf. appendix 13–15), and the results unambiguously show that social status (real or imagined) is the singularly most important factor in influencing this behaviour. Regardless of the basis (cultural, economic, functional) for this high status, and whether it is permanent or temporary, it appears to bring with it a claim to the larger audial space. This study, then, confirms previously known facts and adds further information about the effect of temporary wealth on audial behaviour.

Since the advantage is made obvious already when the gamemaster explains the rules and randomly assigns the game pieces, it would make sense for the victory gesture to appear at this point. That does not happen anywhere in the study, however; victory gestures begin to appear only when the winner starts buying streets and building houses, and they become more frequent as the game advances. Therefore, the victory gestures observed in this study can be interpreted as an expression of the human mind's desire to confer meaning onto the random advantage given to certain players. Studies of roulette (cf. appendix 16) have shown that people who win money will later claim that 'they could sense' that certain numbers would come up, that they had an intuition, heard a voice, or that the decision to play a certain number or colour was the result of an internal debate of some kind. The winners of this study provide a reason for their victory that isn't entirely random, and indicate that they deserved their luck through said intuition or hunch. In this way, luck is turned into a fortune a person deserves, not something that's randomly conferred. Similar studies have been conducted focusing on health and beauty (cf. appendix 17).

Random success, then, is interpreted in relation to logic, though no objective logic can be observed. The subjects' authentic feeling of being 'better', 'sharper' or 'a winner' is expressed in repeated victory gestures and audial domination. In such a situation, there is no space for solidarity with the player who drew the other lot; this person is, instead, generally viewed as a 'loser' in the sense of 'self-made loser'. In actual fact, the opponent's loss should be viewed as one of the preconditions for the 'winner's' gestures and audial expressions.

Studies conducted on players in dice games indicate that even situations where it is obvious that luck has a decisive role are interpreted into a context of meaning and consequence. The random positions of the dice are interpreted as signs of generalised success. Certain theories (cf. appendix 18–20) that are structured around such a view of luck as deserved or gained link this behaviour to the specifically Western, Calvinist version of Christianity. According to the Calvinist idea of predestination, God selects certain people for salvation, and the primary sign of having been chosen is success on earth. Here, success is not a question of chance or luck, but a sign of this chosen status. Success is predetermined. As many sociologists have shown (cf. appendix 21), Calvinism continues to shape the contemporary view on work, but it also shapes values around phenomena like luck, health, beauty, material success, chance and defeat. Today, these values have long been uncoupled from the religion itself, and could be associated,

Small Comfort

instead, with the economic system that characterises the world at large.

<u>Questions for Nicholas:</u>
– What would I need to do to take a break from the project?

We travel everywhere by taxi. Ruth hails the car from the pavement, and once it's come to a stop she'll walk to the other side so we slide into the back seat from opposite directions. She'll roll down her window a few inches, regardless of the weather, put her bag by her side, and give the driver our destination. Only after all that does she sink back into the seat and look at me. We edge towards the middle. Our fingers, our hands. Without letting go of mine she'll look out of the window while the car merges with traffic, but my gaze lingers on her for another minute. The situation is lovely, simple: she belongs to this place, but I am the one holding her hand, and I think to myself that this is all I need: to sit next to Ruth in a black, shining taxicab, watching her profile. There's no need to arrive anywhere; all we have to do is let someone transport us in this way, through a city like this one. If she gets a call, she turns her head to the window and speaks quietly into her earbuds; sometimes she opens her computer in her lap as she talks. I've never taken this many taxis, I tell her once when she hangs up. We're on our way to a restaurant in another neighbourhood for dinner with a few of her friends. Not ever in my life, I say. In total. I know, Ruth says, it doesn't matter. What do you mean? I ask her. I mean that it doesn't matter. I'm happy to introduce you. To the art of taxicab riding? Yes, among other things, she says. She puts a hand on my knee and continues: that's what love is about, introducing each other. Being the same or not the same, that doesn't mean anything. During the last few feet, as the car slows down and turns towards the kerb, we usually smile in some kind of mutual agreement. We've never discussed it; I've never started to rummage through my bag or dig in my pockets. I assume that she's as grateful as I am for this lack of theatre. She drops my hand, and while the car idles she slips a bill between the front seats and swaps a few polite words with the driver. I wait on the pavement, hands in my pockets. How long does it take, I ask. To be introduced to the art of riding a taxicab? When do I stop glancing at the taximeter? Ruth laughs at me. White teeth, I want to dive into her face and take up residence in there. She removes the glasses from her forehead, puts them in a case in her bag, and looks at me. It won't take long at all, she says. Then she hooks her arm in mine, and we walk the final block to the restaurant.

22 May
Addendum to description of experiment
/draft one/

This study describes a world where everyone reacts to money the same way. Individuals with actual wealth do not relate differently to the temporary wealth conferred by the game than individuals with a low or median income. Nor is there, among those who lose the game, any significant difference between wealthy and non-wealthy players when it comes to behaviour shown during the experiment or in the self-assessment afterwards. The attitudes described herein have the same temporality as the success itself. The behaviour, then, is a result of the property, just like the understanding that the person who wins deserves to win – despite the unequal rules that were openly communicated at the outset. In this sense, the game situation is very close to the 'context-free room' many social psychologists and other behavioural scientists strive to create in their experiments, a space where ordinary status is left outside, so that the participants enter the experiment free and 'pure'. It is probably money, or the holding of it, that creates this phenomenon. As Stanley Milgram and several other social psychologists have shown, all people seem to be capable of exhibiting behaviours like blind obedience and irresponsible submission; similarly, this study shows that monetary wealth, no matter how temporary, will cause people to fail in their compassion, shift their understanding of fairness and stumble in their ability to interpret reality correctly.

Many scientists research poverty, but there are surprisingly few contemporary studies on wealthy people. Other than statistical facts about lifestyle habits and consumption patterns, there is little information about this group's social behaviour and their attitudes to the world. Perhaps this study of temporarily wealthy people's behaviour and attitudes can serve as the basis for a future study of the chronically wealthy, with a focus on concepts like 'fairness', 'deserved success' and 'self-made luck'.

<u>Questions for Nicholas:</u>

– Should I cancel the applications, or wait until I'm back?

– How long can I be gone for?

We're back at the pub by the department. There's another game on in the corner. No fries this time, just a beer for each of us. Nicholas has his jacket on. I've disappointed him. It's just half a year, I tell him. We're losing you now, he says. Officially I'm still here, I say. We're losing you, since nobody else can run this project, he says. I'll be back, I tell him. In half a year, a year maybe, I'll be back to finish it all up. The final interviews, the groups. And maybe someone else can work on the administrative stuff in the meantime, I say. Nobody else can run this project, he says. Nobody else has your background, your vantage point. Few people do, and they tend to forget it real fast. Unfortunately, I have to say that you're unique on that point. Am I supposed to be flattered? I ask him. No, you're supposed to be ashamed, he says. You're supposed to blush. You're supposed to consider the facts and then change your mind. You're supposed to consider the importance of your research and tell her she'll have to go alone, he says. We laugh. He buys us another round. I can write while I'm away, I tell him when he returns. Apply for some grants, write a chapter or two. Sure, he says, feel free to tell yourself that you'll write. Me, I'll be glad if you manage to send us a postcard. We drink, he turns round when one of the teams scores a goal, watching the screen for a moment. Then he turns back, spins his glass. You know, love is love, he says. But what about the revolution? I have to do this, I tell him. I know, he says. I know.

5
Small Comfort

My name is Lars.

I have an ex-wife: Cilla. We've got two teens: Lukas and Nico. Cilla has another child, Molly, who's not mine. There is a new man in Cilla's life: Rainer, who is Molly's dad.

There is an ex-mother-in-law, who holds marriage in high regard.

There is an inheritance in the class of several millions; there is a summer house on an island off the southern part of the coast.

There is a weekend we just have to get through.

There is a play, a little annual production. It's about to begin.

My phone is next to me in bed when I wake up the first time. Notes/new post:

> Synopsis for crime novel: A man with a criminal past makes sure to disappear during a

natural disaster in a resort town. He's declared dead, but ten years later his widow hears the familiar sound of his bronchitis cough on a video recording of a play. She's watching TV, hears his cough and resolves to find him. She's assisted in this quest by a cop who is also looking for the man. The cop is at first infatuated with the 'widow', but eventually grows suspicious. Turns out the widow is the real criminal; the vanished husband has defrauded her and now she wants revenge. The cop: Chief Inspector Emmanuel Jancke, newly divorced, has a speech impediment and a nut allergy, recently moved in with his sickly father.

The dream when I wake up again a few hours later: a hodgepodge of irrelevance with no saving grace. Hills on fire and flooded streets. I run through those streets. I'm the danger and the prey at once. Worms crawl under my skin and the tigers step out of the wallpaper in the kids' room, and then there's the hand that reaches between the front seats, waiting for change. Waking up happens at the bottom of an exhale; I gasp for air. I haven't breathed with my belly in years, just panted with my gills, wagged my tail in the right direction while sober and other times slightly off-centre, which was the norm this summer. Slightly off-centre: what was the deal again yesterday? Did I tell Danjel that I'd finished the script?

'I mean, this is your chance,' he replied.

Danjel, my friend the TV middle-manager, a lunch lady dishing out work, monthly sustenance with salty terms and airy promises of more. 'Your chance': laughable words, since the jobs he gives me could be performed by any high-school graduate with half an ear for language. 'Your chance': as if I needed chances.

Then he corrected himself, specified:

'This is your last chance. I won't give you anything else if you don't meet the deadline this time.'

The last chance. We were on the balcony in Danjel's flat and he laughed as if he'd made a joke. His wife, Anna, who was bobbing around in an ironically colourful matching set, was celebrating her birthday, and their children as well as some other people's children were dominating the scene in the living room. The adults had squeezed into the kitchen, where they were discussing the benefits of teaching their kids Spanish during the summer holiday. They deliberated the utility of letting their kids study advanced maths, letting each of the s-sounds in 'study' and 'advanced' do victory laps round the world and then hook into each other even before the sentence ended. They discussed whether it was appropriate to submit photographs of their kids to a modelling agency. They listed the advantages of a histamine-free diet. They talked about the benefits of coal-fibre bike saddles. They chatted about their upcoming vacations. Danjel was about to return to the kitchen to show off his exclusive collection for anyone who wanted to see it.

It's been a long time since he gave me a project I found interesting, but maybe I'm getting sick of this business anyway, the grousing and cooing and fishing, the attention that slips over a shoulder on the lookout for somebody else, somebody more vital, younger. The tight turnarounds stipulated with a shrug, the pay nobody can live off. The jobs I've had this past year can be counted on one hand, and it requires enormous discipline each time to keep from laughing when Danjel describes them. Or crying. But he pairs every new project with a drop of hope that far bigger and more interesting jobs are on the horizon.

'We obviously know what you're capable of,' he likes to say – and the hope and humility contained in a line like that is enough to sate me for now. It's just a question of time.

I get up and fetch my glasses, which are slippery from last night's late and greasy meal. It's already

Small Comfort

nine. With my balls in one hand and my phone in the other I walk into the kitchen and turn off the radio that's been transmitting from in between two stations. The testicle: swollen, evil, perhaps a mechanical expression of the gap between erotic desire and reality's mortification, the body's way of saying hello, hello – sheepishly, of course. What else could be expected of the scrotum, that remotely situated old man, crooked and sensitive to the elements. The dick is noble, the scrotum embarrassing: such is the allocation of dignity down there. The balls have done their job – they've produced two polite boys in the early 2000s – and now one of them is a shrivelled peach pit past its prime, just one of all the other peach-pit has-beens I see in the public sauna, but one in a flock of greying old-man scrotums that rest on cotton towels in the heat. See, there's another inescapable humiliation everyone pretends doesn't exist.

I pull up a chair to the entryway mirror, sit on it and pull my knees up to my chin to explore the scrotum's backside in the reflection. Thirty or so millimetre-sized bumps cover the skin in a red band. When I squeeze one of them between my thumb and index finger, it crushes and scatters in smaller parts, like a Big Bang where the infinite new elements all emanate from an original, compact core. I wonder what these new units might cause.

Ia Genberg

Marriage: entered into on a high, ended in boredom. In between, muddied waters, just like in all marriages with offspring. The arrangement soon turned into a set of transactions, investments in time and chores, debt regulation through sex and favours, interest-carrying duties on a running tab. Nothing wrong with that; it's how it is for everyone. Still, most people prefer to turn a blind eye to the similarities between their own lives and the cuneiform tablets dug up by archaeologists. In contrast to what people thought these would speak of once deciphered – poetry, of course, or even truth; certainly they would contain some wise words about the gods and the meaning of everything – their message proved to be nothing more than laborious notes on debts accrued and settled. The oldest known document in human history is about money: saved, borrowed, held and soon to be recovered credit.

Marriage: a way to push one debt into the future and leave another behind, and then there's the conclusion that anyone who wants to be free of payments should choose solitude. A market is created as soon as the parties realise that their interests are distinct. Trade materialises, and the potatoes – so cheap at the time of harvest – are suddenly terribly expensive in springtime when the stores run dry. Lovers meet or walk side by side during a brief, interest-free forever, but sooner or later they'll find themselves at either side of the negotiating table. A shared currency emerges in the wake of the first gaze, and love's generosity, this primary foundation of the world, slowly turns into a commodity for sale. Happy marriages are just like all the others – just like the unhappy ones – but the currency is always specific. Mine and Cilla's market was standard in size: two kids, two adults. I spent a long time paying off an early infidelity and finally shed my debt by taking on most of the parental leave. The children stepped in as guarantors in their respective moments of birth, stabilising the course. Cilla brought an early offering that soon transformed into a means of unspoken blackmail: the future inheritance. My artistic talents fell in value as Cilla's career advanced, and was finally reduced to zero in the years after my parental leave, when I didn't achieve shit. This, in turn, created a debt, which I regulated using rents on larger projects in the home. Whenever the general mood fell, Cilla would introduce a stimulus by purchasing last-minute tickets to some sunny holiday spot; an accounting of the debt on my part, repayment on the part of Cilla and the kids, with new opportunities to explore the market's mechanisms as a result.

As long as time was the dominant currency, I held the advantage. The freedom granted by my employment provided me with certain merits: I could pick up the kids early, cook from scratch, clean out the attic home office. These were activities that brought me joy even as they filled up my account, and I found myself compulsively telling Cilla about each chore I had completed in the home. Cilla frequently seemed happy and grateful upon learning the details of my adventures with the dirt underneath the bathtub and the spontaneous outings with the kids to weekday-empty museums, but at times she looked a little concerned, or perhaps she seemed a little indebted – yes, somewhat mortgaged, even – as if her own contribution to our currency – the salary that fed the family – had been devalued into a few colourless bills in a wallet. It was a balance, a terror balance, and I held my positions as long as the currency remained intact. The expectations on my own professional achievements were kept low, as long as I dealt with the logistics around home and kids, but I still spent a few hours a day on some project or a scattering of small jobs from various employers. Then two things happened that turned the situation round in less than six months, at which the balance between time and money – which I had experienced as harmonious – was lost. The first event was the introduction of mandatory schooling also for our youngest son, Nico. No more days off, no more unstructured time; school and playdates with friends now colonised both children's lives. My market value as a stay-at-home parent was drastically devalued as the client base for my business vanished. The other event was that the rental flat that had been ours for nearly a decade was suddenly for sale. We were extended an offer to purchase our home at a reasonable price – though the offer wasn't an offer in any true sense, but, rather, a demand from a massive, ravenous flock of neighbours, and the price, to my mind, was anything but reasonable. The second we signed the mortgage with the bank, the balance between time and money transformed, and a different type of currency gained the upper hand: Cilla's currency, the previously colourless banknotes in her wallet.

Last night: an intense, emotional mood overtook the kitchen while Danjel demonstrated his collection of Japanese soda bottles. I realised that some of the men in there were fans themselves. They twisted their moustaches and shifted closer to Danjel, who took the bottles one by one from a box in the cupboard while speaking in the voice of an authoritative scientist. Someone shut the door on the rambunctious kids in the living room. Each bottle had its own individual personality and history. Some had a glass marble at the neck that blocked the contents when the bottle was tilted a certain way; others had narrowed necks that changed the position of your hand when drinking. These narrowed necks were a rarity, while the bottles with marbles had become more common, though it was still unusual to find ones with balls in a different colour from the bottle.

Only a few of the soda bottles were sold domestically, and most were purchased from other collectors. They bought, swapped, sold, and mailed these precious items between each other, wrapping them in enormous amounts of tissue paper and cardboard before placing them in little boxes that were outfitted with long rows of stamps. There were some that Danjel had purchased directly from a foreman at a factory on the outskirts of Kobe, a man who smuggled out bottles in order to sell them online. Others he'd found on the shelves of Asian grocery stores in southern Europe. Now he was showcasing his latest find, a small bottle of yellow glass with an artfully bent neck and a bright-red label that displayed the kanji for thirsty.

I had heard Danjel talk about his collection, but I'd never seen it before. I knew that it occupied one of the kitchen cupboards and that it was at times the subject of querulous negotiations with Anna. In total, it was made up of around fifty or so bottles, all without any soda in them. The cupboard also held a checked notebook, where Danjel logged each bottle in his possession. Duplicates were wrapped in tissue paper and stored in a separate box, in the wardrobe; he used these to swap for new bottles. For about a year now he had been part of a loose-knit group that tweeted pictures of their bottles and commented on each other's posts. It was an online community that was largely supportive, though Danjel had told me that there was some jealousy, even sabotage. For instance, his yellow bottle with the bright-red label had been the object of a significant number of resentful invectives.

'Interesting,' I said when we bumped into each other on the balcony again.

'I've been invited to the morning talk show. Did I tell you?'

'Yes.'

'They asked me to bring five bottles. I told them there's no way I could choose. My collection is to be viewed as a whole.'

'Ah.'

'So I negotiated up to ten.'

'Can't they show pictures of the rest?'

'They've already been over to film it.'

'Wow.'

'Yep.'

'And what does Anna think?'

'It's not a problem any more. She got a new vanity

with some of the money I got after Grandma passed. Gustavian legs. A deal of sorts; democratic decision-making. It's got two drawers in the front that open with latches on the side.'

> Synopsis for crime novel: Late nineties, Europe, a midsize, anonymous city. Junior high, four students bully a fifth so brutally that she ends up killing herself. Nobody is punished. The victim's mother never recovers, and twelve years later she goes after the bullies, one by one, to exact her revenge. It starts with a young body floating in the river outside the city. Police captain's name? Planck. He's got a helper, Philip, a closeted gay man who was bullied as a child. Cuts between police work and the mother's thoughts in italics. Flashbacks interwoven with contemporary narrative, etc.

I'm on my phone in the car when I spot Cilla approaching from the dock past the parking lot. We greet each other at a distance of five yards. She starts walking towards the boat and I follow. Once we're by the shore, she turns and looks at me.
'What's up with that?'
I run my fingers over my chin.

'Absolutely nothing at all. A beard rarely communicates anything.'

'Are you hung-over?'

'No. A little.'

'You look pale.'

'Been working for a few weeks.'

She raises her eyebrows.

'Just a script. A British children's book that's being made into a TV show. My role is to find words that match the characters' mouths.'

'Is it still that same guy doling out the jobs? Your buddy, whatever his name is.'

'Danjel. He's not exactly my friend, though. And, in any case, the job is basically done. Or I'm almost done, I'm going to finalise the last pieces this weekend.'

I pat the computer case that hangs from my shoulder.

'This weekend?'

'I mean, if there's time.'

Cilla sits in the stern, manning the outboard motor, and shouts something through the noise. I shrug and point at my ears. Cilla: in rubber boots from May through September, always ready for the great outdoors. A jacket for both forest and coastal weather, shorts with practical pockets, pockets with smaller pockets inside them. For a few years now, she's worn her auburn hair short, like a rug covering the skull, her curls a mere suggestion at the nape. When we lived together, that hair was so long that it attracted debris from the environment: pine needles and insects and sundry airborne rubbish. When it got wet, it took hours to dry, the hues shifting in gold and copper in a classical play I watched in secret for hundreds of hours in my front-row seat. When one of our sons mentioned that she'd cut it all off, I immediately pictured the brown-red battlefield by her feet at the hairdresser's, and I could not interpret this initiative as anything else than a slight directed at me. The hair was Cilla's, but also, to some extent, mine. That's how lawless ownership can be in a marriage.

In my first few years with Cilla, I thought of her as a practical person. This, however, was a view I came to adjust. Cilla is, first and foremost, a practician, and that's different: a practical person is practical, whereas the practician is engaged in practising a philosophy of life. When something is wrong it can be fixed, and when something else goes south, that, too, can be fixed – even if it means another piece of duct tape placed on top of the old one. Cilla never makes a theoretical retreat. She sees the solution long before I and the rest of humanity have even caught sight of the problem, and there's not a problem that could overwhelm her since no problem is a true problem; it is in the nature of life to give man problems along with one or two hidden solutions, and it is in the nature of Cilla to work out which one is the best of the two.

When we first met, she'd light a cigarette and squint at the ceiling; these days a lip balm will hover in the same general area, but the results are the same. After a while, she sits up in her chair, announces the solution and rolls up her sleeves. She's left behind the parts of our marriage that are over, and relates to what remains as the consummate practician she is. In preparation for the upcoming weekend, for instance – days that require an administrator – lists and schedules began to drip into my inbox as early as April. I noticed that Rainer was next to me in the to: field, an arrival that created a certain bond between us. We were lumbering along, side by side, behind Cilla, receiving her lists and admonitions. Maybe Rainer and I could swap jokes about it over the weekend. That remained to be seen.

Last night: I was watching the scene in the living room, some of the younger kids climbing on the sofa with their mouths full of crisps, the older ones hunkered down in the sofa with iPads and phones. The combined volume of their shrill voices was unbearable. I saw that this was yet another gathering that would never transform into an adult party, that I would probably never again attend an adult party with an intimate dance floor, heart-to-hearts in the kitchen and loud arguments about politics on the balcony. Danjel plucked a cherry from his glass and triumphantly held it between his thumb and index finger.

'Do you know how long I had to look?'

'For cherries?'

'Maraschino cherries.'

'Maraschino cherries?'

'Sour maraschino cherries, not the sweet kind. Not the regular, slimy ones they've got next to the crisps section. These are real berries, the ones used by the pros. The original berry. You know, there are the originals, and then there's the rest. A truth that holds for every aspect of life.'

'How long, then?'

'Three weeks. I had to comb through the city and the worldwide web. I was making calls from work, checking every online store you can imagine. There was one afternoon when I made fifteen calls. Same thing the next day.'

'Ah.'

'Some of them didn't even know what I was talking about.'

'Wow.'

'But I finally found a bar that does their own

Small Comfort

import. There are no wholesalers that deal in quality any more.'

'No?'

'It's a scandal, really, don't you think? A simple, classic product. How can it be so fucking hard to get hold of? I'm thinking of starting my own imports business. It wouldn't be that complex, actually, as long as I can get hold of a good supplier. I can keep the back office in my pocket. Most things can be done on this here.'

He hauled his big, flat phone and the headphones that dangled off it out of his pocket and held it up in front of me.

'Is there any demand, though?'

Danjel looked at me, put the berry in his mouth, and crushed it between his front teeth without dropping my gaze. He hummed approvingly.

'That's not really relevant,' he said while chewing. 'It wouldn't be for profit or anything. It's just because it's something I'm passionate about. When they serve you a gin fizz with a sad old regular cocktail cherry – it makes me dejected. Yes, sad. People have no eye for quality any more. They'll go for a drink, any drink at all, with a berry, any berry at all. It's awful. I really could make a difference in this space. Start small by selling to the bars in the neighbourhood, then find partners in the other big cities, slowly build up a network. Cultivate an awareness. The potential is there. People need to be jolted out of their slumber. High quality always wins in the long run.'

'Yeah, that makes sense. Sounds like a good idea,' I said.

'This too is activism.'

About an hour later, the kids convinced the hosts to organise a treasure hunt for sweets in the back garden, but I realised I was too drunk to participate with my dignity intact. Dignity: something I usually remember exists only by the time it's been lost. As everybody evacuated the flat, I walked between the rooms, studied the first-class stereo system, read the titles in their squat bookcase, swiped the bottom of the crisps bowls with my index finger. Then I went to the bathroom, but once I'd pulled down the zip I changed my mind and went into the kitchen, climbed onto a chair, took down the crate with Japanese soda bottles and pissed in the yellow one with the bright-red label. I carefully returned it to its place. Thirty-five centilitres: the volume of my bladder on this evening, apparently.

Marriage: there's always a winner and a loser, one who makes more withdrawals than deposits, one whose investments turn out to be wiser in the long term, who seems to constantly repay their debts right before the interest rate goes up. There's very little fungibility in my talent profile; most of my skills are specific and anchored in emotional values, while Cilla is the personification of today's most-requested design. Eff-eff-effective, with high demands and short contracts; she moves fast and at a slight forward angle, spurting verbs and crossed-off to-do-lists; she's got sixty-three minutes for every hour and more than four hundred days a year – at least – and she's the best cog in any machinery you can think of. Scratch that: she's a little machinery in and of herself, always running and with the kind of energy that vibrates even while she's asleep. I remember the way I would look at her then, when we'd just met, and I'd never seen anyone sleep so intensely before. The red shock of her hair, her eyes darting behind the eyelids, the breathing that carried her through the night. She woke up rested after six hours and began the day even before her feet had landed on the floor.

In preparation for every school field trip or bigger event there were flowcharts for bookings, table settings and planning tacked to the fridge with magnets; lists were written, updated, checked, discarded and replaced by new ones. The kids and I performed the discrete tasks delegated to us, but we rarely had any contact with the full picture because we trusted Cilla; everybody trusted Cilla, since the outcome was invariably perfect. The fact that she had once fallen in love with me was somewhat of a mystery to everyone, including me, and possibly even Cilla herself. Perhaps it was real love in the first, introductory years, a true love where the value of the goods is detached from the price and can, for a time, hover freely above the regulations of the marketplace, but this period did not shape the final bill. We never managed to find the synergy between our personalities, which meant that the investments we made did not lead to any mutual expansion.

At first, Cilla's energy was contagious and inspiring. We called around and organised picnics; we drove a VW bus to music festivals, buying tents on the way; we accrued new friends on every holiday. We moved as soon as something better turned up; we bought a boat and sold it and bought another; we bought a sewing machine, a canoe, an old camper. We arranged a three-day wedding and put up a tarp the size of a badminton court to ward off the rain; we made tomato soup for 150 guests. Cilla worked and studied at the same time; she paced out the route, set the direction and the speed, and I followed with great enthusiasm. I followed her enthusiastically for a good long while, until my enthusiasm faded and I began to experience her energy as increasingly aggressive and demanding.

Small Comfort

Meanwhile, Cilla changed. She was recruited to projects that required blazers. She flew domestic. She developed bags under her eyes. She worked some Saturdays. She practised yoga every morning and did shots of juice from centrifuged rutabagas. She stopped reading French novels. She drank her morning tea in brief, efficient sips. She squeezed her eyes shut when we had sex. She went to exercise classes on her lunch break. She stopped loving French movies. She stopped crying after our arguments. She remained the same but suddenly she was somebody else, and I viewed this process as a destruction of the original Cilla until I realised it was a question of refinement, that her character was being finessed as she came closer to her true self. Anything superfluous was peeled off; this was not a different Cilla, but the finalised, ultimate Cilla.

And today we wouldn't survive without her, the logistician who's made sure that both the engine and the reserve tank are filled with diesel, who's planned a discreet but delicious menu, who's written lists and delegated the purchases, who's looked up train timetables for her mother, bought the tickets and emailed them, who went to the cabin the weekend prior to clean and prepare it, who placed a bottle of Kir in the cabinet over the sink, who sent a message to Rainer and me with all the relevant details.

The trip across the sound that separates the island from the mainland takes about ten minutes. We've transported so many things in this exact boat, a bunch of things I've now forgotten, that I miss but also don't miss, that I don't remember but am reminded of here in my seat in the bow with my back to the wind and my hair in my face. I turn my head to see the island approach. I take my phone out.

Synopsis for crime novel: There is no body, no crime scene, no suspect and no victim. And yet the police keep receiving letters describing a crime in minute detail. The sender appears to know things that only the homicide division could reasonably know, describing details from ongoing investigations, etc. Finally, the crime described in these letters is committed, and the division sets off on a wild goose chase. Eventually, they understand that the sender has access to their internal network – but how? Answer: the perpetrator is a family member of someone in the division. The core group of investigators: Karen Berg, DA – brusque, divorced, five kids, type A. Mary Stinning – sort of broken, previously in drug enforcement but was transferred due to suspicion of using drugs herself. Aran Bjerkan – marathon runner, recently married, young kids, quick and nimble, the youngest member of the group. Mandus Blom – single, experienced, the group's oldest member.

Rainer comes to meet us on the dock, Molly on his hip. Disembarking, I feel the planks sag under my weight, a testament to the rotten beams. I offer Rainer my hand; he shakes it. Cilla takes Molly and Rainer picks up a few of the totes from the boat to bring them to the house. I follow him up the trail, taking my glasses off and cleaning them of splashes from the traverse. Rainer from behind: more scalp than last year, and in a sleeveless tank top as usual. He's flexing his triceps at me. Nico and Lukas are lounging in the canopy swing with a stack of cards on the pillow between them. My dark hair on both heads: all is well. They smile and wave when they notice me, and then they return to the game. I sit down next to them and watch Lukas diligently shuffle the cards. He's midway through an argument:

'My denial of cheating doesn't constitute a guarantee. Whether I speak or not about my cheating or non-cheating, it's impossible for you to know, right? The question, therefore, is pointless. So why even ask?'

'I ask if you're cheating because you are cheating,' Nico says.

I enter the house, put my bag in the hall and peer into each of the two tiny rooms, one somewhat bigger than the other, though darker and still with that disconcerting scent of damp that varies with the weather outside. The smaller room can only fit a bunkbed and a dresser under the window; the kitchen has space for a stove, a sink and a table for four. Why does memory always enlarge things that are too small? I remember the kitchen as tolerable in size, but now that I'm looking around in there, with my head touching the rafters when I get on my tiptoes, the kitchen is once again the smallest I've ever been in.

I head back to the garden and join my sons, putting an arm round Lukas.

'A father's embrace,' Lukas says.

'Are you protesting?'

'No, I'm just making an observation.'

'Is it true that you're cheating?'

'The question is an accusation in and of itself. I won't answer, since my answer can be nothing but apologetic.'

'Have you put the canoes in the water yet?'

'Last week,' Nico says.

'You paddled to the island? You went swimming?'

'Three times so far,' Nico says.

'Only eighteen degrees out there,' Lukas says.

Small Comfort

Cilla comes to sit on the other side of the table, with Molly in her lap.

'Okay, want to go over the whole thing?' she says. She looks for her SPF lip balm, applies it to her lips and begins to swipe one finger across her phone screen.

The cards are put away as everyone takes their position. Rainer shows up with a tray: cups for everyone, sparkling water, a big bowl of cherries. The sun beats down on my aching head. I rub my neck, squeezing the skin that covers the top vertebrae, feeling the subcutaneous fat that's collected in there. It's become increasingly saggy over the years. A roll of fat, ever-looser: the manifestation of slacking.

'When does she get here?' Nico asks.

'Afternoon time. Cilla goes to pick her up, and then we're off to the races,' Rainer says, and looks at Cilla.

Afternoon time. I ponder this word choice.

'Let's take it from the top,' Cilla says.

Lukas builds a little pyramid of four cherries on the table. I take off my glasses and rub my eyes with my knuckles.

'The three of us are going to get in the boat in a few hours,' Cilla says, and checks her watch. 'Molly, Rainer and me.'

'My car is in the parking lot,' I say. 'Same car as last year. Blue Fiat.'

I put my glasses on again, dig out the key from my front pocket and slide it across the table in Rainer's direction.

Rainer takes it and nods at me.

'You'll go to the city,' Cilla says, and nods at Rainer, 'while Molly and I pick her up from the train. We'll be back around five.'

'And then the weekend goes by without a hitch,' I say.

'Hopefully,' Cilla says.

A brief silence.

'I'll be back on Sunday. Three p.m.,' Rainer says. 'In Lars's car. I'll get groceries on the way, park and then I'll call you.'

'You will not call me,' Cilla says.

'I won't?'

'No. You'll wait. In the car. In the parking lot. When you see us getting into the other car you'll take the boat out here. I'll drive her to the train station. I might bring Molly with me. It won't take more than an hour, hour and a half.'

'And then I'll take the boat back again,' I say. 'To the mainland. We'll meet on the dock?'

I look at Cilla.

'Correct,' she says.

Small Comfort

'Easy-peasy,' I say.

'And you know the deal, right, boys?' Cilla says, and looks at Lukas and Nico.

They nod.

'Same procedure as last year,' Nico says.

'And the year before,' Lukas says. 'As well as the year before that, and so on.'

Everyone seems content. We look at each other. I take a cherry from the bowl and pop it in my mouth while rubbing my neck, massaging the top vertebrae. Perhaps a massage could revive the cells, help them heal somehow. I doubt that fat is supposed to collect in lumps like this.

'Did you tell Lars about our little complication?' Rainer says, and looks at Cilla.

I spit the pit into my hand, yearning for a coffee.

'Complication?'

'Molly,' Cilla says.

'She's talking,' Rainer says.

At this, the entire group looks to Molly, who is seated in Cilla's lap. She's one and a half. Terrified, the child stares at all the faces, her bottom lip quivering. She's got Rainer's strawberry-blond hair and green eyes.

'Only sometimes,' Nico says. 'A little.'

'What kinds of things does she say?' I ask.

'Mum, Dad, look, sometimes. Ico, Ukas.'

'It doesn't have to be a problem,' Cilla says.

'Not this year,' Rainer says. 'But next year, yeah. We might have a problem.'

'There won't necessarily be a next year,' Cilla says.

I wiggle my fingers at Molly.

'Say hi to your dada,' I say.

The child stares at me, mouth open. Rainer chuckles. Cilla takes the lip balm from her bag and runs it over her bottom lip.

'Like I said,' she says, while rubbing her lips against each other. 'It doesn't have to be a problem.'

Rainer clears his throat. I take a few more cherries.

'You guys are still deprived of coffee out here?'

'Free of coffee, you mean?' Rainer says. 'Non-toxic, is that what you're saying?' He laughs.

Cilla once again brings her lip balm to her lips and looks at me, straight on, face blank.

'Perhaps that is what I'm saying. Or perhaps I do mean deprived of coffee, in fact,' I say, and return Cilla's look. 'What if Annie wants a cup?'

'She's not had coffee in twenty years. Something about cardia. A hernia or some kind of cramp – I can't remember. Why would she want a cup all of a sudden?'

'I wouldn't be too sure,' I tell her.

'There might still be some in the pantry,' Rainer says. 'If you left any behind last year.'

'Coffee is perishable,' I say.

'Ah well, we definitely don't have any fresh coffee,' Rainer says with a smile.

'If you want fresh coffee, I suggest you bring fresh coffee,' Cilla says, and puts away the lip balm.

A remarkably amiable tone of voice.

My headache, the beating sun, this woman, the tone she uses with me and no other person in the entire world. It's hate without the emotional charge of hate, just an old, reflexive hate that her body automatically produces in my presence.

'How is she doing, then?' I ask.

'Annie?'

'Yes. My mother-in-law. I assume you've been in touch in the lead-up to this visit. How is her illness?'

'It's lying in wait, but it's a type she can live with as long as it doesn't become vascular.'

'Vascular?' I look at Rainer and Cilla. Rainer shrugs.

'Blood-based,' Lukas says.

'Yes,' Cilla says. 'Either way, she's not dying any more.'

'Oh, she's been dying?'

'That is unclear too.'

'She can be a woman of – ah, how do you call it?' says Rainer.

'Drama,' Cilla says. 'She's got a dramatic side, yes.'

'A restrained dramatic side,' I say.

'Fully reined in,' Cilla says.

'But what are the symptoms?'

'I don't know that, either. We haven't seen each other since last summer. She likes it down there. We talk on the phone. We email sometimes. We email more than we talk and we almost never email, so I'm pretty out of the loop. And as you know, she's only here in the summers.'

'We can thank our lucky stars for that,' says Rainer. 'That she doesn't come for Christmas too. Considering the arrangement.'

'The inconvenience,' I say.

'Yes, Jesus,' Cilla says.

We look at each other. We agree, because despite everything we're comrades, three investments in a little house of cards that sits on top of this exact weekend in July.

Synopsis: A former intelligence officer comes across a few news items about a bunch of people killed in a chemical-plant explosion in a remote, impoverished country, and immediately realises that their deaths are due not to a chemical-plant explosion, but, rather, an incident in a chemical-weapons research project, a space where he himself was active during his

Small Comfort

enlistment. A group within the military has secretly been working on this for many years, and the ex-officer decides to leak the case to the press. He calls a reporter at an evening paper, and they make a plan to meet at a café an hour later. On the way there, the ex-officer is run down by a car and dies. Everybody thinks it's a hit-and-run, but the reporter has a hunch and sets off to find the murderers. A large conspiracy is revealed, entangling even the minister of defence. The reporter: Viktor Abel – has a pacemaker, an unhappy marriage and a hysterical teenage daughter. His assistant, Benedikte – young, hot, single, difficulties with intimacy.

Rainer: I assumed he was wealthy at first, since he used to play professional tennis. To my mind, 'the tennis circuit' oozes prize money and lucrative sponsor deals, but it turns out he was just a regular tennis serf among thousands of other tennis serfs who were all tooling around pretty far beneath the top layer. Rainer was part of the filler meat in his circuit and spent his career scratching by, waiting for some kind of breakthrough. By the time his knees were ruined and the last pro-level match was done, the balance of his savings account was near zero, and a new, tottering career as a trainer began. Dating Cilla meant starting over with everything: a new country, a new language, new jobs in a new city. At one point, Cilla laughed and told me that Rainer was as useless an investment as I had been; he, like me, needed to be provided for now and then and didn't mind it. Molly often skipped daycare to spend all day playing with Rainer, and when Cilla came home at seven dinner might be ready and the flat clean – but Rainer hadn't called a single one of the tennis schools on his list to offer his services. Once or twice, Cilla has hinted at how weary it makes her to carry the entire financial burden year after year and with husband after husband. This has increased my sympathy for Rainer.

A drawer – the top one – needs to be emptied and filled, because I can't keep my clothes in a bag on the floor. Rainer and I squeeze into the tiny bedroom, our necks bent and our heads grazing the ceiling, looking at each other's garments. He transfers his socks, underwear and a number of carefully folded cotton vest tops to a suitcase, shuts it and puts it standing on one side in a corner. Cilla appears in the doorway, Molly on her hip.

'Oh no, no, no.'

She points at the bag.

'That works fine, doesn't it?' says Rainer.

Small Comfort

'Oh no. Oh no, no. You know what she's like. She snoops and sniffs around everywhere, poking at things. You know the way she moves. Opens cabinets, drawers, checks the flower beds. Everything gets an inspection. This place is still hers, right? Rigorous checks.'

'A suitcase, though,' I say. 'What's the worst that could happen?'

'Precisely, a suitcase. In a corner. Why is there a suitcase in a corner? Who put it there, and why? Annie sees it, she picks it up, she reads the luggage tag, she might even open it. Whose clothes are those? One whiff of suspicion and it's over. She's not blind. She's stingy and awful in lots of ways, but she sees everything. Like a hawk. Don't you remember last summer?'

I do remember last summer.

'When she got her hands on the toiletry bag you left behind,' Cilla says, pointing a finger at Rainer.

She is employing her shrill voice.

'Right,' Rainer says.

'With your toothbrush, with your imported toothpaste. She thinks of snooping as her right, which means we need to be careful,' Cilla says.

'So where do we put it?' I ask.

'The suitcase? I have no clue,' Cilla says. 'Just get it out of sight. Out, out.'

She leaves the room with Molly.

'What about the attic,' I suggest.

I stuff my clothes into Rainer's dresser and walk out with my empty gym bag in hand.

The hatch comes down, the ladder unfolds. We climb up, each of us with a bag in hand. Up there, everything looks the same as last time I was there, the same as it's looked all these years. Rainer is by my side. The back of his vest has dark patches of sweat on it.

'It would be easy to finish the attic,' he says. 'Create a bedroom up here, take out a wall down there.'

'All you need is a bit of insulation,' I say.

'And a good floor.'

We're silent, looking around. It smells of wood and old dust.

'A hundred in total, maybe?' I say.

'More like two. If we do it ourselves. We've done the sums.'

'And?'

'Yeah, about two hundred thousand. Then again.'

Rainer lugs his suitcase to the wall and sets it down next to a couple of paper bags full of empty glass bottles. I follow his lead with my bag.

'Yes?'

'Then again, we could expand the first floor

instead. Tack another room onto the back, take out the walls to the kitchen, make it so everyone can fit in there. And a new patio, or a deck with wide planks. That might be a better use of the dosh. Though it would be a bigger project, of course.'

The way he says dosh: almost with a t-sound. Tosh.

'Three hundred?'

'About that. A little more. Depends on how much we do ourselves.'

'Right, of course.'

'Then again.'

'Yes?'

Rainer looks at me, his hands on his hips.

'We don't spend enough time here for the investment to make sense, though at the same time the reason we don't spend time here is because it's so small. So if we made the investment we might be here more often, all of us. Then again, it would be a summer of hard work on the attic, finishing it. Then again, the flat in the city needs the money too, a new floor, a load of shit. The drain in the bathroom, that shower that leans in the wrong direction.'

'So you'll have to see, in other words.'

'That's right – we'll have to see. Then again.'

'Yes?'

'Then again we could just not, right? We could wait, and buy something new later. Or build something. Or do whatever's needed on this house, just let the contractors work until its done. We'd wait for the tosh to come in first.'

'The inheritance, you mean. When it comes.'

'Yeah, that is what I mean. Not that it's something I think about. Though naturally it would solve certain things.'

'Indeed,' I say.

'The house would become ours for real. We could expand, renovate, do what's required to be able to spend time here. For real, I mean.'

'Yes, of course.'

'You too, I assume?' Rainer says, and points at me.

'What do you mean?'

'It would solve a few things for you too, wouldn't it?'

I look around. If we'd had the money from the beginning, the tosh. The space we could have made for ourselves. A roomy home, a roomy marriage.

'Yeah. It would bring a bit of respite.'

'You're still driving?'

'Yep. On nights when I don't have the kids.'

'Yeah, so it's only right.'

'What is?'

'Well, your share. The reason you're game for this ... what should we call it?'

'The performance,' I say.

'Yes, the performance. You've said twenty-five?'

'The share?'

'Yes.'

'Yeah, twenty-five per cent. Of Cilla's share, that is.'

'All in a lump sum?'

'All in a lump sum.'

'A fairly substantial lump.'

'Hopefully, yes. Though time will tell, of course.'

'Indeed, time will tell.'

Rainer walks up and puts his palm against the slanted ceiling, runs his hand over the wood, knocks on it with his knuckles. I tilt my face towards the dirty skylight and its piece of blue. Yes, I do love this concept, unconditionally: a lump sum, an indivisible lump, the smallest indivisible lump in the universe, rough stacks of smooth bills in a mountain at my feet, mercy after all these years. Finally. I've got a thirst that can only be slaked with a lump sum.

'You never wavered?' asks Rainer. 'I mean, it's got to be tempting to just up and leave. Say fuck it.'

He paces on the creaking floor, hands on his hips.

'Getting an offer you can't refuse, and then refusing?'

'It must be tempting,' Rainer says.

'Of course it was. For five minutes, until I came to my senses.'

'Yes, it's just a formality. Papers sent to the government, no greater significance.'

'A few days of this every summer. A ring slipped on a finger. No big deal.'

'Exactly,' Rainer says. 'Do you still have yours, or do you need to borrow?'

He demonstrates his left hand, wiggling the engagement ring with his thumb.

'I've still got my old one, actually,' I say, and dig through my front pocket.

When I first met Annie, her husband, Karl-Axel, was still alive. Cilla's dad, the source of the money, a man who sailed in the summers, spent winters skiing in the mountains and played tennis every Friday until the Friday he had a transmural heart attack on his way to the net after a serve in the second set, sixty-two years old. He is believed to have been dead before his opponent's return smashed into the fence behind him. Karl Axel's wealth was the old kind, derived from industries in the country's southern parts, mixed with some inherited real estate and funds that had been squirrelled away and that subsequently swelled in the second half of the twentieth century, after which it was invested in more properties and stocks, which, in turn, grew into something that immediately became a flash point between his former business partner and Annie, the widow.

Five lawyers were involved and the world followed the process in the financial pages. Ultimately, Annie was forced to give up her stake in the companies, but she was generously compensated and invested her liquid assets with the help of a panel of experts. A move to Minnesota, where parts of her family lived, followed. She was gone for three years, returning for a visit back home every Christmas, increasingly strange in disposition and increasingly stingy, and never did any of what Karl-Axel had left behind trickle down to us. Never, ever, did Annie lift as much as a buttock to release a minimal contribution, no matter how we contorted ourselves, no matter how lavishly we decorated the home for Christmas.

Annie's strong voice and conservative values were reinforced during her years in exile. Take marriage: holy far beyond religion's sacrament, possibly instituted by God, but above all created by man for man's benefit and for the continuation of civilisation. When Cilla and I finally got married, with Lukas as our flower boy and Nico in utero, Annie waited to clarify her terms until mere moments before the wedding dinner, when she herded us into the kitchen, closed the door and gave a little speech. This was eight years after Karl-Axel's death, and Annie had the sharpness and oratorial gifts of an evangelical minister. She began by posing a series of rhetorical questions, intended to have the kind of long-term effect on us that truth is assumed to have: did we want a stable society or an unstable one? Was stability created by calm, faithful people, or people jumping from bed to bed, always looking for something better? Were they happy, those who put the cyclones of lust behind them in order to sail at a steady clip, or were they happy, those who bucked the minute the wind began to still? The message was crystal-clear: marry, and thou shalt remain married. Annie's speech contained one clause I didn't catch, but which Cilla immediately apprehended and relayed to me the next morning, a clause with many zeroes. In the time since, Annie has retired and was, later on, lured to the Mediterranean by a favourable real-estate deal and charitable interest rates, but the terms remained unchanged for Cilla and her sister: marry, and thou shalt remain married.

> Synopsis: A woman brings home a one-night stand, and after he leaves in the morning she stumbles on a bag he's left behind. It contains workout clothes, a squash racquet, five kilograms of cocaine and a machine gun. She goes to the police, but since she's a foreigner with limited grasp of the language, she finds herself jailed as a suspect. Through her lawyer, she learns that the man was killed as part of a settlement in the criminal world, his body

Small Comfort

found in a gravel pit. There's nobody who can verify her story, and it's only three weeks until the trial. She gets in touch with a female private detective, Minea Schubert, who throws herself into the underworld looking for a solution. Schubert – single, frustrated, bipolar, excessively intelligent.

I cross the lawn with my sons trailing after me.

'We'll do something later,' I turn round to tell them.

Why do kids always walk behind? When did they stop walking by my side?

'Later as in this afternoon, or later as in after this weekend? Or later-later, as in a few years?' Lukas asks.

'Later as in after the weekend. You'll be staying with me then.'

'Obviously we'll do something. Everyone is always doing something, even people who aren't doing anything, since they're doing nothing. A human being can't exist in the absence of at least one verb.'

'Can we go sailing?' Nico asks.

'A subject and a verb. Though there are those who claim the subject is unnecessary,' Lukas says.

'We can go sailing,' I tell them. 'I just need to find a boat.'

'And a captain, perhaps,' Lukas says.

'And a captain, perhaps. Sure.'

'Considering the last time we went sailing.'

'I know. We could also get tickets to somewhere.'

'This is beginning to sound like later in the sense of later-later. A later that never really comes into fruition,' Lukas says.

'Where?' Nico asks.

'We'll get discount tickets to somewhere. What do you think, Lukas? To travel, does that feel like a nice verb?'

'Nice feels like an appropriate adjective,' Lukas says.

The location is splendid, when you think of it: a piece of land on an island facing the sun, shaped like a face with the house on a hill atop the chin, overlooking the bay. The plot is large and above the house there's a parcel of sparse forest with big, flat rocks, a few mature birches, raspberry brambles and wildflowers. Below the house, on the other side of the garden, is the beginning of the path that leads through a grove and to the water. The lawn in front of the house is enormous, but there's also the Incline, a steep hill that takes up half the land and which begins thirty feet below one gable and continues down to the grove. For some incomprehensible

Small Comfort

reason, it feels steeper every summer. I don't know how many soccer balls we've lost to the thicket only to find them again next summer, essentially decayed. It would have been easy to fix the Incline and make the garden flat with a few loads of gravel, a tiller, and some new grass, but every year Annie shook her head with a sceptical smile as soon as we broached the subject. There was no reason to change anything, neither in the house nor in the garden, or the world at large, since that would be in opposition to life's fundamental principle, which is that everything is fine as it is.

There are just four other houses on the island. A football player in the twilight of his career tried to buy all of it a few summers ago, but was immediately thwarted. There was something improper about his enquiry, which arrived by way of a lawyer, this signal that the entire island needed to be evacuated, that this man required the whole island for himself, and that the land would likely be developed with new-money tastelessness. The current owners all rejected the offer without talking to each other, and whenever I see the football player on TV running around in the penalty box, I wonder what exactly it is about his activities that lets him do this kind of business. He scores a penalty goal and sprints down the right touchline. He kicks a ball to another millionaire, who also uses an attorney to buy up all the most beautiful land on the coast.

The fact that this property tilts shrinks its useable area. The cabin limps along, summer after summer, and its state, combined with its size, meant that Cilla and I rarely managed to hold out for an entire holiday. Sooner or later, the clouds would come with the rain, and the card games would dry up, as did the radio serials, and next the fire would falter in the hearth and put an end to the cosy atmosphere. Eventually one of us would sigh and shake our head, sometimes a week before the date we'd set, sometimes two – even three, every once in a while – because no matter how often we told ourselves that thirty-one square metres was bigger than what the median family had at their disposal globally, year-round, for the entirety of their lives, our Western bodies were not able to keep the peace in those small rooms for an entire summer. A few days of rain made everything wet and brought the smell of mould out of the sink. It would lodge itself in my nose and didn't go away no matter where I went. I wanted to excavate and dehumidify, or drain, or, even better, redo the foundations, or, ideally, tear down the house and build a new one. Annie disapproved of all my ideas. Karl-Axel had bought the land with the cabin on it as a romantic gesture more than a half-century ago, back when neither electricity nor fresh water was available on the island. In the mid-eighties she agreed to a few updates, but she still felt that the original state was ideal. Hence, the cabin's size remained the same year after year, as did the incline of the lawn, the smells from the sink, the height of the ceilings, the tiny rooms, the broken apple tree, the rotten beam in the dock.

Cilla: queen of logistics, master of administration, the boss of every conceivable type of planning and structure. If the Earth's crust needs to be stabilised: Cilla will structure the workflow. If all people on two continents are to switch places with each other: Cilla will deal with the logistics. If every single grain of sand must be counted and sorted according to size: Cilla will take the lead on the project. Her job is to organise things, logisticate, hold space, guide, shake loose, resolve and undo impossible knots in the body politic. She is regularly headhunted for various projects in departments, corporations and governmental authorities. Last summer she coordinated the merger of three newspapers in one part of the country, making the whole thing look simple. Now, I've got no idea.

'We need to get up to speed,' I tell her. 'Rehearse.'

'I know.'

'In case she asks. Since we're married and all.'

'I know, I know,' Cilla says.

She's doing the dishes. Molly is in the high chair stirring a pile of grated apple with her index finger. They need to head to the boat soon. Cilla lets the dish brush slide into the water and turns to look at me.

'She's going to ask,' I say.

'Yes. She'll control and compare our versions. As if she knows.'

'Yes.'

'Okay,' she says. 'You start.'

Cilla takes a seat at the table.

'I'm forty-four years old,' I begin.

'I'm not an idiot. I know how old you are.'

'I'm forty-four years old, I freelance as a TV writer and sometimes I drive a taxi in the evenings.'

'No, you don't.'

'I don't?'

'No, you're a writer. No taxi, she hates loser shit like that. Spending the nights driving a taxi when you want to write. No, we can't have that.'

'Okay. I'm a writer.'

'Good. You're a writer.'

'For TV. Things are going well. Lots of scripts, new projects all the time.'

'That's good,' Cilla says. 'She can't check that. She doesn't know how to look up stuff like that.'

Small Comfort

'I'm currently working on a script for children's TV, coordinating the lines for a mouse and a few other characters.'

'No.'

'Why not?'

'Too loser-y. Sounds like the last project an employer gives someone who's on their way out.'

'You think?'

'Let's move on.'

'I play badminton every Friday.'

'Still?'

'Yeah, why not. It sounds good, doesn't it?'

'It sounds great.'

'At four o'clock. Then I go home and make dinner for the whole family. Starter, main course and dessert. I drink a Belgian Trappist. On Saturdays, the boys and I like to go see a movie while you go swimming.'

'If I'm not working.'

'If you're not working. On Sundays, we clean the flat together. Then I go and buy us cinnamon buns.'

'You definitely do not.'

'No, I don't. I buy an assortment of fruits and nuts.'

'No, you don't buy anything. We clean on the weekends. We go to the movies and to the pool.

Sometimes we go out for dinner. We see our friends. We're normal. The kids are at their friends', they play computer games, stuff like that. If she asks anything, just pretend we're normal. Don't make up any details that aren't normal. And don't say anything spectacular if you find yourself alone with her, things she could verify with me later.'

'I get it. Your turn. I don't know where you're working right now, for instance.'

'I'm overseeing the merger of two departments.'

'Which ones?'

'Agriculture and environment. Everyone's furious. But they'll be smiling by the time it's done – that's my job. All the pencils will be newly sharpened and face the same direction, everyone will have a coffee mug they like, every computer will be connected to a nearby printer, the decision tree will be as straight as a ruler and everyone will understand it. That's my job.'

'How big is your own staff?'

'There are eight of us.'

'Lots to do.'

'An awful lot.'

'But we go out for lunch sometimes, don't we?'

'We do?'

'Yes, we do. Sometimes, you've got time for a long lunch with your husband, in the midst of it all.'

Small Comfort

'I do?'

'Usually on Wednesdays. We head down to some nice restaurant with table service in the city centre.'

'Oh?'

'Gives us a chance to really talk. About the kids, about our work. Right?'

'I'm not sure about this.'

'Married couples need to take some time for themselves, a sort of respite in the chaos. A little break.'

'But not every Wednesday. That's impossible. I would never have time for that.'

'Every other, though?'

'Okay. Every other Wednesday.'

'That's good. That works.'

'We can go to that Indian place. Where we used to go.'

'That's still there?'

'Yes,' Cilla says. 'I eat there sometimes.'

'Okay. But we need more details. Are we happy in our flat, for instance?'

'Of course.'

'Though I'm getting a little curious about buying a house, right?'

'No, you're not. We're not talking about any houses,' she says.

'Why not?'

'She'll just think we're asking for an early inheritance.'

'Are we not?'

'No. We're not. We're happy in our flat. It's the perfect size, it's close to the kids' schools and Molly's daycare, we've got a parking spot in the garage.'

'Who went alongside her the first days of daycare?' I ask.

'You.'

'That's right, it was me.'

'Took five days until she was fine being there alone.'

'Right.'

'And the staff is wonderful. The kids are outdoors almost all day, year-round.'

'Bright-red cheeks sometimes when I pick her up, right?'

'Exactly.'

We're silent for a moment. Molly looks at us sleepily from her high chair. Cilla gets up and fills a sippy cup with water, then puts it on the table in front of the child.

'I cook most of the time,' I say.

'I take care of the laundry,' Cilla says.

'I vacuum.'

'I help with their maths homework. Always.'

'I deal with Swedish and English.'

Small Comfort

'French is mine.'

'We split everything else,' I say.

'Yes. We take one thing at a time.'

'We're thinking about getting a cat.'

'We definitely are not,' Cilla says.

'Dog? Rabbit?'

'No pets. We do have a cleaner, though.'

'No,' I say. 'Never.'

'How did I know you'd say that?'

'How did I know you'd suggest it? Do we have a car?'

'We have the car she's riding in today,' Cilla says.

'We don't have two cars?'

'We live in the city. Absolutely unnecessary, terrible for the environment, expensive.'

'I don't have my own car?'

'No. I don't have my own car; you don't have your own car. We've got a communal car, the family's big people-carrier, the one she will see this afternoon. Why would we each have a car of our own?'

'Wealthy people have two cars.'

'No, people who feel that they need two cars have two cars. People who travel to two different jobs that are far from where they live.'

'Okay. I bike to my office. I've got an office, right?'

'Sure. You've got an office.'

'Good.'

'I also bike to work. When I don't walk.'

'We use the car on the weekends when we're going somewhere, and in the summers when we come here,' I say.

'Exactly.'

'What consoles do we have?'

'Xbox. The kids are only allowed to play on the weekends. But they play a lot of games on their computers too.'

'Sounds good. Pocket money?'

'A monthly stipend. Two hundred and fifty kronor, plus phones.'

'Sounds good,' I say.

'It is good. It's normal. Do you have the ring?'

I show her my left ring finger. Cilla coaxes her and Rainer's engagement ring off her own, opens a kitchen cabinet and puts it on a shelf behind the coffee cups. Then she gets her purse from the handbag in the hall, sits down at the table, opens the coin pocket, and takes out the ring I gave her one May day in the previous century. She puts it on her finger. Wide, white gold, dulled from wear.

'Perfect,' I say. 'Still fits you.'

'Anything else we need to touch base on?'

'That's it. Now we know everything about each other. As becomes a married couple.'

Cilla looks at me, twisting the ring.

'And how are you?' she asks.
'How am I or how *am* I?'
'How *are* you.'
'I might pick up a hobby.'
'Like what?'
'Collecting something. That's the new thing, haven't you heard?'
'I know nothing about the new things. We live sort of different lives, you and I,' she says, and nods in Molly's direction.
'And how are you? How *are* you.'
'Today I feel somewhat fatigued,' she says. 'Look. Came in this morning.'
Cilla reaches for her phone, sweeps over the screen a few times and puts it on the table in front of me. I remove my glasses to look at the screen. It's an email from Annie, addressed to Cilla and her sister and with a list of organisations in the body. Some of them I recognise, others I don't.
'Ah, a little reminder,' I say. 'With a few new additions.'
'Yes, a conservative cultural organisation in Minnesota, for instance.'
'Just think how grateful they'll be. Your entire legal-right share in their coffers. And your sister's.'
'It's possible that everything is already in their account. All our efforts for nought.'

'No,' I tell her. 'She's just reminding you that she can give it all away whenever she wants. A little demonstration of her power, that's all. A warning that she can create issues for the inheritance.'

'Enormous processes.'

'Lawyers, law cases. Trials.'

Cilla looks at me. I wonder how often the thought of the lump strikes her, how often it creaks under her feet on her way to work. If it's on her mind while she pays her bills online, when she pulls out her card at the petrol station, when she digs through her coin compartment at the grocer's on the square during her Saturday stroll. I wonder: is it a living thing for her, like it is for me? Does it follow her into the day and out again? Is it like a pet? Does it gaze up at her like it does at me, promising her the world?

'And no surprises this year,' Cilla says, 'when you talk to Annie. No surprises.'

'Definitely not.'

'Last year you told her that we were thinking about more kids, that we were planning to buy a boat and sail around the world together, that we were going to ride some fucking railway to China. All kinds of things.'

'I did? You're right, maybe I did.'

'You did, and I had to sit there and refute and make a fuss. It didn't exactly sound like we were a

Small Comfort

harmonious couple in a well-functioning marriage with good communication.'

'Those are actually all things I've thought about us doing.'

'Us?'

'A little fantasy, that's all. A joke.'

'Yeah, and it wasn't a funny joke. I'm begging you. Please, Lars. You know the terms and conditions, you know what's in the goddamn pot. We just need to get through this weekend. That's the sole objective.'

Cilla stands, scrapes up what's left of the grated apple and throws it in the trash. Molly is sleeping with her chin to her chest. Cilla removes the bib and coaxes her daughter out of the high chair before she heads to the garden, child in her arms. I follow them.

Annie: she always tilts her head a few degrees clockwise when she looks at me, an angle inherited from generations of nobility, an instinct lodged in her bone marrow, just like the throat-clearing and that scoffing smile through her nose, the scoffing-nose smile brought on by an encounter with a suspected parvenu. That angle: ten degrees, not more, and only ever when I'm speaking. The head is righted as soon as Cilla or somebody else talks. Over the years I've learned to expect her silence, watching her head's automatic operations as I open my mouth, a remote control in my voice that sets off these subconscious movements in her vertebrae, nudging them clockwise. Modern society compels Annie to interact with me as if we were equals, standing side by side, as if we were sitting at the same table, but there are protected spaces no social change can reach, little hidden crevices in the body politic. The cervical vertebrae are just one example. Other stashes: the look that passes between the vendor of Christmas trees and his buyer in the more well-appointed city squares the moment the bills swap hands; the lack of price tags at the market off said square; the cars that stop and the cars that don't stop at the pedestrian crossing on the street that leads to said square.

Rainer has thrown on a button-down shirt over his vest and changed the shorts for jeans, the slippers for trainers. The three of us are standing in the kitchen, our bodies taking up the entirety of the small space between the table and the sink. He slides the slippers my way. In the room next door, the boys are on their phones in the top bunk. Molly is asleep in her pram in the garden. Tentatively, I put on the slippers, which are black leather with a worn rubber sole.

'They're more comfortable than they look,' Rainer says.

Small Comfort

'They're incredibly comfortable,' I say. 'I remember them.'

'You do?'

'Or do I have it wrong?' I look at Cilla.

She nods.

'You're right,' she says. 'Dad's slippers. They've always lived here. They come with the house. Just like the robe in the bathroom.'

'I remember that one too.'

Cilla bends down and pulls the rubbish bag from the bucket under the sink, ties the flaps and gives it to Rainer.

'Could you take this and toss it on the mainland, please?'

'We've got a rubbish bin here,' Rainer says. 'The waste-collection boat comes next week.'

'The bin can't be too full. That would look strange. She doesn't like waste. It would seem weird if the bin is beginning to spill over. And it might smell.'

'You want me to keep this in the car?'

Rainer holds the bag aloft for us to see.

'Just stick it in the boot and toss it in the first bin you see. How hard can it be?' Cilla says.

Rainer, still holding the bag, looks at me. I open my palms and shrug before I leave the kitchen and step out onto the porch. I hear Rainer and Cilla mumbling in there and after a while Rainer comes out, bag still in his hand. We head down to the boat. The heels of the slippers make a dry, scraping sound when they drag on the ground, a sound I'd forgotten but which is so familiar that it's beginning to feel as if it's got a home inside me, these exact slippers on this specific dirt trail, heels that never leave the ground but get towed with every step, producing a gentle, creaking sound. That sound: timeless, priceless. I might be too hung-over, too strained by lack of sleep and financial need, too overworked and distressed and harassed by advanced age and a dearth of ideas and bosses with a superiority complex in an era of my life when I myself should be a boss with a superiority complex, because it's been no more than a minute of walking on the path in these slippers when the sound has me close to tears. Rainer is still chatting away down ahead.

'Don't you think?' he says.

He stops and looks at me inquisitively. I scratch the corner of my eye.

'Sorry?'

'I'm thinking this could be the last summer,' Rainer says.

'Yeah, maybe it is.'

'Of course I don't want to hope that it's the last summer, of course not. But it could be the last summer – let's put it that way.'

Small Comfort

'It could be the last summer. It very well could be. Though I feel like we had that thought last year too. And the year before that.'

Rainer doesn't move. 'Something wrong?'

'No. I – what can I say? I'm suddenly a tad nostalgic, I guess. This island, this trail to the dock.' I look at my feet.

'I know,' Rainer says. 'It's credibly beautiful out here.'

'Incredibly beautiful,' I say. 'Incredibly.'

'Yes, credibly beautiful. I can see how you'd miss it.'

'I don't really miss it, though. I never long to come here or anything like that. I rarely think about the place. In my memory, we spent most of the time out here having arguments. It was raining and we had fights and we were on top of each other until we went back home. Nostalgia is weird in that way. I suppose it's just the price I'm paying.'

'For the deal?'

'For the deal. And it might be worth it.'

Rainer spins round and keeps walking. The water soon expands before us, grey and mild to our left, where the horizon is broken only by a few islands; to the right is the mainland with its green forest and boat masts. When we get to the dock, Rainer drops the trash bag between his feet, puts his hands on his hips, and looks across the water.

'You know, you can always come.'

'What do you mean?'

'Just that – even if this is the last summer, you're still welcome. The place will be here. I can't imagine we'd sell. We might tear something down or add an extension or do some renovations. But it will still be here.'

'Ah, we'll see,' I say.

'You don't have a summer house of your own, do you?'

'No, you're right. I don't. At least not yet.'

'So it could be nice to come out for a few days in the summer, or for Midsummer. And when we've finished the extension it will be more spacious. A cabin for you and the boys. A guesthouse, I mean.'

'Sounds nice. But I imagine I'll buy something of my own in time.'

'In time?'

'Yeah, later.'

'You mean when the money – when the money comes in?'

'Yeah. Something closer to the city, where I can write.'

'No more taxi, then?'

'Perhaps. We'll see.'

The sound is oddly still. A hundred and fifty feet

Small Comfort

from land, an optimist dinghy is bobbing around without any discernible propulsion.

'I imagine it doesn't pay much?' Rainer says with a glance at me.

'Not these days. There's more competition. Too many cars. A bunch of private companies that operate outside the law. People will do whatever, drive without taximeter, without a light on the roof. Customers pay on their phones in transactions the government will never see.'

'Good for the passengers.'

'But not us drivers.'

'How much do you make in a night? A thousand?'

'If I'm lucky.'

'I can imagine it's inspiring in some ways, though? All the people you meet, all those characters. I mean, you've got to overhear some stuff you can use in your writing.'

'I get to hear all kinds of things. To be honest, I hear way too much. After a night of driving, I've got no love left for the human species. After a week, I'm fully at peace with the idea of the end of the world. Whatever it is that comes after us, it will be better.'

'That bad, huh?'

'That bad.'

We laugh and turn to face the water again.

'Still, the situation can be viewed as temporary, right?'

'Yes. It's just that the situation has been temporary for so damn long now. A temporary situation can't go on for too long if we're going to keep calling it temporary. There is a point in time when what is temporary transforms and stops being temporary. I suspect I've already passed this point in time without noticing.'

'Nobody notices those points.'

'Perhaps not.'

Rainer spits into the water.

'Either way. Can't be long now,' he says.

'You're referring to the tosh.'

'Yes. One day it will be ours.'

Cilla appears in the glade, coming our way. Molly is sleeping in a carrier on her back.

'Train's here in half an hour. Get in the boat.'

I shake hands with Rainer and untie the ropes on the runabout. Once they're seated and have the engine going, I toss the ropes on the flooring in the bow and wave before making my way back to the cabin.

> Synopsis for crime novel: A male prison chaplain takes on a case of what truly does seem to be wrongful conviction. The chaplain starts

digging through the convict's past, and it turns out that the man is an undercover cop who's been abandoned by his bosses. When the chaplain goes to visit the man in prison, he's no longer there, transferred to another unit and accused of attempting to kill a guard. Investigating the case, the chaplain learns that the police unit the man used to work for no longer exists and has left no trace behind. The chaplain is friendly with a high-ranking police officer and goes to him for more information, but his buddy has nothing to say. When the friend briefly leaves him alone to get them coffee, the chaplain spots a document with the imprisoned former undercover cop's name on it, and now he knows he's on the right track. Name of the chaplain: Thomas Hartmann – progressive, sometimes wavers in his faith, overweight, stomach issues, single.

Danjel and Anna: I was the one who introduced them back in the day, but the goodwill I earned in making the connection is beginning to dry up. The value of any service will diminish, thoughtlessly forgotten in the river of time. The two met at one of my parties ten years ago, when old and new acquaintances were invited to mingle and imbibe on my dime. Anna was a friend from some university course, Danjel worked in my industry, and I introduced them to each other in the kitchen. They chatted, drank, danced and eventually went home together. They were in touch the following week, soon became a couple and within a few years they had a flat, a car, a summer house and two kids together. There were a few months of couple's therapy after their second child, but they kept at it: they mounted black tiles in the kitchen, went on a long family holiday and found a way to make it all work again. It's a perfect match: they're equally frivolous and disinterested in reading books longer than a hundred pages, and nevertheless they both deliver proclamations like: 'the project of modernity has played out its role' or 'we have to stop thinking in fossils – that's what it's all about right now'. Whenever I mention a book – a thick new American novel or a thick old European novel, or some buzzy thick East African novel, Danjel grins with something like embarrassment, and as the conversation wears on it always seems to shift to TV shows and movies, Japanese soda bottles, the advantage of socks with individual sections for every toe, the world's hottest chilli, a torch with infra-red frequency that reveals plaque left on your teeth after brushing, a computer case with a built-in charger that he's bought. All you gotta do is charge the case occasionally.

And I sit there, stunned into silence as I stare at the exquisite wrinkles in his clothes. Sometimes, he and I will go for a beer or two, or we'll hang out on his balcony with a few of his colleagues, and when he's next to me yapping about all the things he yaps about he appears impeccably placed in time and space, as if a conversation couldn't possibly be about anything but these exact things: the many uses of coconut oil, the benefits of intermittent fasting, the technique for regularly rinsing one's rectum with apple cider vinegar, the technique for cutting apart conjoined twins, a child born with fish scales instead of skin, the world's hottest hot dog, a speaker he's bought that's smaller than a thimble, an app that tracks your blood sugar.

And then there's this situation with the mouse's mouth.

Hello: a cooperative word, similar in many languages. A greeting phrase with two syllables, one open and the other closed, that fits the mouth of an animated mouse.

Bye, however, is a whole other story, with the *hejdå* of Swedish. If a monosyllabic original is translated using a word with a two-syllable lip movement, the mouse has to speak with a closed mouth during the first or second syllable. No matter how I solve the problem it's all wrong, which is to say: no matter how I solve the problem, I don't. The problem is unsolvable.

Look: equally unsolvable, since it's *titta* in Swedish.

Numerals: only three and six work.

I spend an hour in the canopy swing with the film clips and an open text document until the boys appear next to the table.

'You're interrupting,' I say, and close my laptop. 'Welcome.'

Lukas is dressed in a pair of cut-off jeans and a tank top; Nico is wearing shorts, socks, and nothing on his upper body. The unbothered movement of his muscles is visible under the skin of his torso; his bellybutton is an oval on the horizon, a young, healthy eye with an unbroken view. For some time now my own belly button has belonged in the category of sunken indentations, invisible in most positions. I move my hand to my waist and press where I recently discovered a hard lump. It's still there, though it's moved down an inch or so. Things in the body that move are less dangerous than those that stay in one place; this is a well-known fact. Though it's also a well-known fact that lumps that don't hurt can be more dangerous than those that do, and that lumps that remain hard month after month, with unstable coordinates – as if they can't decide where to take root and sprout – are exactly the type of phenomena that makes a primary-care doctor pick up her phone to schedule an emergency X-ray. An aging male body is full of unstable objects nobody knows anything about. I picture the lump's insides as a milky liquid on the verge of something, like a yolk that is about to curdle in warm milk: a process of sorts, a possibility teetering on the edge.

'When will she be here?' Nico asks.

'Annie? In an hour, maybe.'

'I've got an idea,' Lukas says.

'Can we eat first?' Nico says.

'And you're not going to like it,' Lukas says.

'We'll have a snack,' I say. 'Okay, you've got an idea?'

'Yeah, listen: we'll tell her everything. The law is on our side.'

Lukas holds up his phone with an article from some family-law website. He's been doing research.

'The law is actually complicated on that point,' I tell him. 'It's a slow process, and we won't get it all back. Maybe not even half, maybe not ever a fourth. People are legally able to give away a lot of their wealth before it constitutes a breach of inheritance law.'

'And the truth?'

'What about it?'

'Doesn't the truth have a value in and of itself?'

Lukas remains on his feet, ready for a rhetorical excursion, a Kantian struggle where the one with the best starting position inevitably emerges victorious, since there is technically nothing that can get at this introductory assertion. The truth is true, period. It's a sly strategy, partly since truth's defender is always the one who sets the rules of the game, and partly because only he is free to move his positions. All the loser can do is change the character of his disadvantage. It's impossible to explain to someone in their late teens that the truth can be both slippery and relative. That it can be discoloured, unpleasant. That it tends to be banged up already when you take it out of its package. That it often ends up being small comfort. Few parents succeed; most give up halfway, perhaps right where I am now, side by side with Kant and next to the demanding ethics that marinate the brains of an eighteen-year-old in unbearable hubris.

'No,' I say.

Lukas immediately inhales for his next attack, already smiling and not unlike his mother, but I get there first.

'Think about it. Who benefits from what? And what about the long run? You know, potentially. If two parents have a financial windfall, where does that leave their offspring? Any guesses there?'

Lukas looks at me with scepticism.

'Are you trying to bribe me?'

'You and your brother.'

'Do you think I'm for sale?'

'You don't need to put it so dramatically. Just tell me what you want.'

Synopsis for a damn good crime novel: A hospice nurse hears a dying man's final confession: a two-figure number, a pause, another two-figure number. She writes down the numbers but doesn't have the chance to ask any questions before the patient's family enters the room. The next morning, the man is dead. She ponders the numbers for a few days before realising, by chance, what they mean: they represent a geographic location, longitude and latitude. This position turns out to be in the middle of a forest, and the nurse decides to go take a look, bringing her ex-husband, an archaeologist. Upon arrival, they find a homemade cross, and when they start digging they come across a buried human skull. They leave the forest to get mobile-phone reception, and when the cops finally arrive, the skull, the wooden cross and the grave are all gone. The nurse and her ex-husband start investigating, and it turns out that the man she cared for on his deathbed killed a neighbour who spent years abusing his daughter without legal consequences. It's the daughter (who is aware that her father killed their neighbour) who followed the pair to the forest and took the skull before the cops could pick up the scent. The nurse – smart, likes sudoku, riddles, crosswords and trivia; under-stimulated, lovesick. The ex-husband – in early retirement due to arthritis, binge-drinker. They have a grown-up, highly successful son together.

And finally there's Annie on the lawn. It feels just like last year: the same outfit, the same hair, the same little tilted smile when she lays eyes on us in the canopy swing. And just like last year: Cilla just a few steps behind, with Molly in a harness on her chest.

'Ah, déjà vu,' says Lukas.

'That's not what this is,' Nico says. 'This is just a regular old recurrence.'

'Collective déjà vu,' Lukas says. 'What do you call these moments of momentarily collapsed consciousnesses again? Oh right, mass hysteria. We're a little community who share a delusion.'

Small Comfort

I am fully dependent on my kids for this type of priceless entertainment.

Annie leisurely makes her way to us. I see that she's writing everything down as she walks, a fountain pen scratching in the little notebook in her head, and I'm suddenly aware of my slouchy position in the swing, of Nico wearing socks in the grass, and the excessive number of glasses and cups on the table. All this gets entered into a column in my mother-in-law's mind, and will, when the time is right, be used against me. I can tell that Cilla has the same thought and she does a little swerve round Annie to get to the table before she does, picking up some of the cups and glasses before she goes into the house.

'Get it together,' she hisses.

The boys get up and give Annie the cheek kisses that have become praxis since her move south. I follow their lead and feel her bony fingers squeeze my biceps. There's a scent of some perfume I recognise but can't place. I pull out a chair and she sits down, launching into her annual quiz of the boys while I bring the rest of the glasses into the kitchen. The school, what they do in their free time, their hobbies, all of it gets ticked off, and then it's back to school again: their grades, the length of their school days, future prospects. Cilla is rummaging through the fridge.

'The same dress,' I say. 'How's it possible?'

'For a person who owns no more than three or four dresses, the odds aren't that high.'

She takes out a plastic bottle of sparkling water and puts it on a tray.

'Doesn't it look like she's lost some weight since last year?'

'Perhaps,' Cilla says. 'But she says she's doing well, that she's in good health.'

'So you asked.'

'I asked about her health. A friendly, polite question from a daughter.'

'And she denies her illness?'

'What illness?'

'I thought you said she was dying earlier.'

'How should I know? Bring the strawberries, will you.'

She points at the gleaming berries sitting in a sieve in the sink and leaves the kitchen.

The rest of the evening is painless. I make a lamb stew and Annie goes to bed after dinner, while the boys and I go for an evening swim from the dock. After an hour of hopeless work on the mouth of the mouse – which needs to be saying some version of the Swedish word *'bra'* for 'good' even though the mouth is shaped like a narrow pout – I tuck in next to Cilla who is already asleep in the queen-size bed.

Small Comfort

Synopsis for crime novel: There's a serial killer in town. The common denominator for all the victims is that they've dated the same woman. The men she sleeps with, whether at her place or theirs, are found dead the next day. Naturally, she's a suspect, and no new murders occur during the two weeks she's in jail. She's released for lack of evidence, starts dating again and the first man she meets is murdered. The case is assigned to a special police unit, and they decide to tail the woman (who won't collaborate with the police after being arrested on unclear grounds). No murders take place while they watch her, and they realise that their cover's been blown. Changing tack, one of the detectives starts to date her. After a few dates, she sleeps over at his house. Soon after she leaves, the murderer shows up and is arrested. But the man won't speak, and his identity seems impossible to crack. When they confront the woman, she, too, refuses to say much, though it's clear that she knows him. Digging through her past (orphanage, foster homes, etc.), the special unit finally learns that the man is her twin brother. The two had a terrible childhood together and grew more intimate than is appropriate. The investigative unit: Edgar Forster – lead detective for the case, older, uses chewing tobacco that he spits everywhere, constantly quotes from literature. Merit Heskinen – young, intelligent, attempts to control her weight using various methods. Bert Hempe – a rural cop who wants to leave. José Morales – climbing the career ladder. May Müller – former canteen worker who switched careers after her son died of a drug overdose.

Cilla's breakfast: made with ingredients that change according to trends, company and international health science. Wheat bran came and went, as did filbunke, dried fruit and eggs – initially over-easy, then poached, then boiled, and then, on second thoughts, omitted from breakfast altogether. Centrifuged root vegetables were abandoned for thicker smoothies with all kinds of greens. The present spelting, berrying and herbing arrived on our kids' plates about a year or so ago. It entered my home as well, sending me to the organics section in preparation for the weeks they were staying with me, and there I stood, touching the unbleached packages with seed and nut mixes and grains and flakes and chips and tiny dried berries from the other side of the world. Sandwiches are yesterday's news, just like chocolate milk and scrambled eggs with bacon on the weekends and the little sausages I used to

Small Comfort

buy at the deli counter and then sliced and fried and put on their plates next to toasted bread as white as sin, as white as death itself. My sons no longer eat breakfast on my planet.

I watch my family. The coordinated army of spoons that transport perfectly proportioned amounts of almond milk, fruit and nuts to their mouths, the masticating harmony that follows. Their hands: each pair enclosing a steaming cup with a stringed label for some Himalayan bush. A reasonable morning, a nice day, a good year, a meaningful life, a well-functioning universe: it all starts with a well-designed breakfast. It is, in fact, more than a meal – it's an ideology, a paradigm, the stipulation for being a good person, the foundation for a good life in an evil world. And the evil world? Well, since you ask: here I am with my coffee. I found a crumpled purple bag of it in the far recesses of the pantry. It's strikingly easy to be a rebel in this family: all you have to do is drink a smooth cup of coffee for breakfast. All you have to do is smoke a cig. In fact, the mere thought of a cigarette is enough – the mention of a cigarette. Dark, French, terrible tobacco.

'What's that?'

'Gitanes.'

'You can't be serious,' Cilla says.

'I'm always serious. Why not smoke the best if I'm going to smoke?'

I allow the unlit cigarette to caress the skin between my lip and my nose.

'You're like a child. A baby. Ah, I've turned forty, what can I do? Life feels kind of empty. I think I'll start smoking again.'

Cilla puts on the raspy voice she often employs to imitate me, pulling her chin back and lowering her eyebrows. Most likely she's not even aware of this pantomime. I look at her while I spin the unfiltered cigarette between my fingers. A bit of tobacco falls to the table.

'Honestly, though – why not? Better than therapy. Cheaper too.'

'But more dangerous,' Nico says, and looks at the flakes.

'Son, it's not dangerous to smoke,' I say.

Everyone looks at me. Cilla smiles, most likely gearing up for a new croaky imitation of me having lost it, because her chin returns to her chest as she pulls in air.

'Smoking isn't dangerous as long as you don't light the cigarette,' I say, and slip one end of the cigarette between my lips, pull in my cheeks, fill my lungs, and take it out again. I let it rest in the most perfect of its many perfect positions: Bogart's tender grip between thumb and pointer finger.

'See? So safe,' I tell them, and blow some air towards the ceiling.

Small Comfort

I place the cigarette behind my ear and look at them. Lukas and Nico return to their plates and Cilla regards me without interest.

'Research,' I say. 'I have to get into it. Some murderers simply must be smokers.'

'So there's a murderer now?'

'Is there not always a murderer?' I say.

'Who smokes tobacco? Sounds like a cliché to me.'

'Clichés are useful if you just know what you're doing.'

'I thought you were working on a script for a children's movie,' Cilla says.

'A TV show for kids. It's about a mouse and her pals, the butterfly and the crocodile. Geared towards kids aged two to four. The translated lines in their mouths – that's where I enter the picture. It's not easy – I can tell you that.'

'That stuff never turns out well,' Nico says. 'The mouth is always mismatched. It just looks silly.'

'That's why it's one of the most thankless jobs in the biz. Awfully difficult, awfully thankless. It's rare that I even get my name in the credits.'

'And who's the smoker?' Cilla asks. 'The crocodile?'

Everyone around the table laughs. We look at each other. These gorgeous moments, the banter that pulls everyone in, the effervescent sound of family: perhaps the reason human beings exist.

'The day I strike out and write a crime novel, the murderer is going to have to smoke Gitanes. Way too few murderers smoke Gitanes these days.'

Annie coughs in her room. Nico has offered up the bottom bunk and sleeps on a mattress on the floor next to mine and Cilla's bed in the master bedroom. Lukas spent the night on a mattress in the kitchen. Is she getting up already? We listen in focused silence, but no more sounds come from the room.

'Go grab a plate,' Cilla hisses, and points at my coffee mug.

'Why?'

'It's implausible that you wouldn't eat breakfast with the rest of us.'

'Why can't I skip breakfast?'

'In a family everyone eats breakfast at the same time. This looks strange, that you're just sitting here with this cup of coffee.'

'Okay?'

'While the rest of us – well, while the rest of us are actually eating. Grab a piece of bread at least. And toss that cigarette, please.'

> Synopsis (good!): An imam and his son are murdered in broad daylight in a big city, and the cops immediately suspect a right-wing

extremist organisation that's previously threatened the congregation and the imam. The imam was a radical himself, controversial in his own community for his views on women and homosexuals, and a frequent voice in the media. The other victim, the imam's nineteen-year-old son, doesn't get much attention at first. But Beatrice Albons, who leads the investigation, takes an interest in the son's activities leading up to the attack. It turns out that he had an affair with the wife of a famous businessman, and that this businessman ordered the assassination. He's a handsome but slimy guy. Smokes Gitanes, has a criminal past.

A few weeks ago, Danjel slid into my back seat, followed by a co-worker. I had stopped for a red light downtown with the entire miserable night in front of me, heavy and wet with rain, and me chained to the wheel, to this horrid service job, so far from the life I'd imagined for myself. He gave me the address while he put on his seatbelt and without meeting my gaze in the rear-view mirror, then returned to the conversation with his co-worker, who I recognised from a TV party. I pulled down my beanie to cover my forehead and hair, and adjusted the mirror. My face is quite indistinct when my hair and most of my forehead are covered by a black hat – a round, smooth moon face that could belong to anyone. I still don't know if I'd hoped to pick up some kind of useful information from the back seat – whatever that would be – or if I was humiliated by the age-old hierarchy that exists between the driver of the carriage and his customers, and pulled my hat down for that reason. It was a long drive waiting for Danjel to put a hand on my shoulder and exclaim: 'Lars, is that you? I had no idea.' But when I stopped outside the nightclub there was just a discreet hand passing a credit card in between the front seats while the conversation in the back went on, uninterrupted. I returned the card with his receipt and got a twenty-kronor tip; Danjel and his co-worker kept chatting as they left the car and shut the doors. The topics discussed in the back seat: the uses of a mandolin on broccoli stalks; the uses of a mandolin on carrots; the uses of a mandolin on Jerusalem artichokes; the uses of a mandolin on apples, pears and frozen bananas. The dangers of putting a mandolin in the dishwasher. An upcoming documentary about Hitler's dogs, all of them German shepherds except a Scottish terrier – black and polite – and most of them females, who were replaced as soon as any of them died. Several were named Blondi, including the one found with him in the bunker. They discussed the dogs of other dictators. Afterwards, at another red light, I thought about the project he'd given me a few months prior on which I'd procrastinated. It was hard to muster much interest in this group of friends wandering around a placid little town, counting clouds in the sky, hiding from each other, losing their teddy bears and getting their shirts spotted by raindrops, and when I sat down the next morning to look at the lips of this animated mouse, rummaging through the most basic building blocks of language, rifling through words like 'no', 'stop', 'look' and 'here', and thinking about the sum I would invoice for my efforts – at most five kronor for every 'hello' and 'yay' – and added to this the knowledge that these jobs only lead to more jobs in the same category, I sank into an empty, wordless amnesia. That put an end to my work for that day. The word 'work': closely linked to the word for 'slavery' in so many languages.

And the word for my present condition, what's that? She's got money, Annie, and they didn't, my parents – these days they're but a few kilograms of ash in two anonymous containers below ground – but what about me? What am I, Lars? What do you call that? What is that word? What is the term for one who is not rich and has never been poor, who lives his life in the slow-moving mulch in between, among all the others in this enormous span? That word doesn't exist in my language – I've looked it up. Which means there are millions, perhaps billions, of people in this world who live in a financial reality with no name. Most likely all these people are able to define their own situation. They know what sets them apart from the wealthy and what separates them from the poor, and their feelings are global, the chagrin of not being wealthy and the gratitude for not being poor, the itch that belongs to that nameless state in the middle. It should have a name. What am I? What's it called, the space between rich and poor? What's the word for the state there in the middle? What's that word? The word!

Breakfast is over and Lukas and I are looking down at the wilted vegetable plot. Annie is still sleeping, Molly is eating in her chair by the kitchen table, Cilla is doing the dishes and Nico is drying them.

'There's no way that Jesus could make himself heard if he came back now,' says Lukas.

'You mean, theoretically?'

'I'm saying, how would he do it? Concretely, how would he go about it?'

'Let me think about it,' I say.

'Let's put it this way: you're Jesus, son of God, and you've been sent back to this world to mend it. We can assume that a whole bunch of people would listen as soon as they understood that you're actually Jesus. But how would you do it? I mean, initially. Would you go yell on some street corner? There are already thousands of people in this world who stand in various town squares and scream that they're Jesus. Most of them eventually get locked up in some kind of institution.' Lukas looks at me with a frown.

'Right, the majority of those who go around yelling that they're Jesus ultimately do end up in some kind of institution,' I say. 'In-patient, out-patient.'

'Exactly. They go to various adult day-care centres, they sleep outside, nobody listens to what they've got to say.'

'They pick up treatment-resistant skin infections. Terrible diet. Bad teeth.'

'Nobody listens. Nobody looks. That's how he would end up.'

'Most likely, yeah. I think you're right about this. Maybe he already came and went. One morning when they open the door to his room in in-patient ward fourteen, it's empty. He's gone. Brought back home. Project failed. They need to regroup.'

'Exactly. So what would he do to get the right sort of attention?'

'Maybe he could perform one of his tricks,' I suggest. 'The fish and the bread, that stuff. Walk on water.'

'Everyone does magic these days. The whole internet is full of tricks.'

'True.'

'The world is overrun with tricks. Nobody can prove anything, neither this nor that. A person who tells the truth has to prove he's not lying, and what would that look like? Hey, guys, I'm Jesus. Listen up. Everyone's like, BS.'

'BS?'

'Bullshit.'

'If I were Jesus, I'd want to make sure I had a platform before I arrived. It shouldn't be impossible to figure that out ahead of time.'

'It doesn't work that way,' Lukas says.

'No?'

'In this thought experiment, it needs to be sandals and poverty. A pared-down life. And even if he were a leader, people would stop listening the second he said he was Jesus. He'd be shot. And do you know why?'

'No.'

'Because scepticism is our new religion. It's the only thing we believe in.'

'Is that so?'

'These days everyone wants to look behind the curtain.'

Small Comfort

I think about the little bumps from this morning. Lukas continues:

'Doubt is our true north.'

'Someone would believe him, though. If he came back and got on a soapbox. Someone would believe him. Someone would listen. The message would spread. There would be organising, factions, popular movements, awakenings. Social media. People joining in.'

'Nuh-uh. Maybe his case manager would believe him. She'd come to visit the psych ward. Bring a couple of cinnamon buns from the cafeteria for the coffee break in the day room.'

'What if he took the buns and used them to feed the whole ward?'

'The buns?'

'Yes.'

'There are weirdos like that everywhere. Though the staff would appreciate the buns, of course. He'd become a popular patient, but that's all,' Lukas says.

'It makes the ward a nicer place. More family comes to visit, there are buns for everyone, the other patients feel happier, they can taper down on their medication dosage, the nurses whistle on their commute to work. All of which would be a tangible contribution by the guy, don't you think?'

'A hyper-local contribution. And I don't think that's the idea.'

'What if that's where it starts, though? His return. Perhaps, in this very moment, there's a guy in inpatient care who's sharing cinnamon buns with everyone, brightening moods. A guy who, it seems, has a never-ending supply of buns.'

For the first time in this conversation, Lukas smiles.

'Maybe. But working yourself up to an international saviour position from there? No, that's insurmountable.'

'Even for Jesus?'

'For anyone.'

The garden smells of soil, iron, decay. Singular rotting beet shoots poke out of one of the grey furrows. Some of the trenches are covered in grass, others are just a hardening crust of mud; a lonely, craggy hill in a moon landscape. A decade has passed since I last kneeled in this plot of dirt, digging in the loam, putting down seeds and tender plants, pulling out weeds and adding sticks for the sweet peas to climb on. The garden was my domain, the destination for the first and last walk of the day, a place of quiet order and control. I get bored with most things, but here, in the garden, I was always alive. For a few summers Cilla kept planting new seeds and caring

Small Comfort

for my perennials when she was on the island alone with the kids, but when Rainer entered the picture, she got too busy for gardening. They went abroad on vacation, travelled to see his siblings in various parts of the world, rented a bigger countryside cabin that would fit them and all the kids. For years now, the garden has laid fallow, its face to the sky in some kind of anticipation. We're all waiting for the future. I crouch and touch the soil. It breaks with a cracking sound when I push harder. Some vague idea about organic links, growing and harvesting, made me steer mine and Lukas's walk this way, but now I can't recall what I wanted to say. I stand back up and put my hand to my belly, trying to localise the vague pain that's ravaging unchecked in there, looking for any undiscovered lumps that might be the origin, the source of the ache. It's quite likely that it all derives from the peripatetic hard lump that is presently in the area around my bellybutton. I take off my glasses, wipe them with my shirt, and turn to Lukas.

'A miracle is necessarily a surprise, right?' I tell him, and put my glasses back on again.

'I've a hard time believing that,' he says.

'Exactly. A miracle, by definition, surpasses our understanding of what is possible. You think you know everything, that you've found every opening. Then there's the miracle, and it hits you in a way you hadn't expected. We know what we know, but we don't know what we don't know, what we don't yet have a conception of. Nobody can count on a miracle.'

'What would the miracle even be?'

'I can see that you're quite open to miracles, actually. You've got the right sceptical mindset,' I tell him, and put an arm round his slender shoulders as we walk back up to the house.

Synopsis for crime novel: A group of women, seven of them, gather for a two-day hen party on an island. One of them is Sara Flinck, a young police officer. The bride-to-be often refers to her colourful past, but without any details. One morning, she's disappeared along with one of the others, and Sara Flinck recalls a strange conversation she overheard between the two of them the night before. She shares this with the police investigating the case, though they don't give much weight to her testimony, assuming that the bride got cold feet and is trying to run away from her own wedding. Sara starts her own investigation with the help of another of the women on the island, who is an assistant judge. They learn that the bride-to-be used to date the leader of a drug cartel and was given an assumed identity after testifying against several of the cartel's members. The person who ordered the kidnapping of the bride-to-be is the cartel's leader, her former boyfriend Liam Hantz. Sara Flinck – short hair, former hurdler, philatelist, loves Baileys. The assistant judge – Malou von Bandau, quick-witted, intellectual, hungry for love. Keeps having affairs with various defence lawyers.

'What are you doing on your phone all the time? Texting?'

'I got tired of always having to look for a pen and paper whenever I had an idea. The phone makes everything easier. It never runs out of space and everything's in the cloud.'

We're sitting at the outdoor table. Over the years, Cilla has developed a special face for me, an expression I've never seen her direct at anyone else. One corner of her mouth pulled up in the initial stages of disgust, her eyes half closed in a sign of boredom, nostrils vibrating in tempered aggression. And then there's her body: sort of leaning forward in an act of accusation, her breathing audible and bored, first looking at me, then through me and finally past me, looking ages past me in a reminder that no, no indeed, I shouldn't be here. I often find myself wanting to lift my phone to take a picture of this face and show it to her, ask about the real ingredients, what's truly behind this hackled irritation.

'Ideas for a thick novel?'

The corner of her mouth lifts; her expression has transformed into one of mocking sarcasm. Over the course of our marriage, I started work on twenty or so different novels. I smile, return my phone to my shirt pocket, cross one leg over the other and put my hands in my lap.

'That particular genre I've abandoned, actually. Nobody reads thick novels these days, not even those who identify as readers who read thick novels. Not even librarians whose job it is to read and recommend thick novels read thick novels these days. Not even literary critics read thick novels these days. They watch TV shows all night. People don't care about thick novels. They'll just catch the movie later. Everyone will watch the movie instead, or the TV show if there is one. The only people who read thick novels are the scriptwriters who make the movies or TV shows based on the thick novels, in multiple seasons and with characters and events that aren't even in the novel. Once the movie or show is released, it's a banging success and everyone involved gets rich as hell aside from the author of the original thick novel that everything is based on. Nobody remembers the author any more, the name is barely even in the credits and the thick novel is relegated to the library, one copy that soon goes missing and nobody even asks for it. And if somebody, against all odds, were to stumble on the thick novel behind the radiator in the basement of a used bookstore that's going out of business, they'd think that the thick novel has stolen its plot from that amazing movie or TV show.'

Cilla is rummaging through her bag, apparently forgetting that we're in the midst of a conversation. Then all of a sudden she looks up, running a sunscreen stick over her nose ridge.

'Speaking of TV. Did you see the one with the mannequins who wake up in a deserted world?'

'Spare me.'

'I'm joking.'

'I spent several hours on a balcony in the city yesterday, listening to people talk about TV shows I haven't seen. Impassioned analyses, details that couldn't be dissected closely enough, characters referred to as if they were real people. Intricate speculations about what might happen in the next season. It made me want to jump, honestly. Everyone was talking about how well the shows represented the real world, but nobody was interested in talking about the real world.'

'Why didn't you go inside?'

'The living room was a kids' party. The kitchen was all about bike saddles and the benefits of goat liver oil. As long as it's wild, at least. The goat.'

'Wild goats?'

'Apparently, they've got them on Kilimanjaro.'

'And why didn't you go home?'

'It was at Danjel's. I guess I thought a project might materialise. That he'd suddenly feel like giving me some kind of freelance gig.'

'And?'

'No. But I did leave, eventually. I pissed in one of his bottles and left.'

'His bottles?'

'Japanese soda bottles. Danjel is a collector of everything that's important in this world.'

Cilla moves her chair next to mine and touches my cheek.

'It's going to work out, I promise. One day, we'll wake up and everything will be just like we planned it.'

'She might live for another hundred years.'

'This is the final summer.'

'You said that last year too.'

'Maybe I did. But this time I mean it.'

Small Comfort

Synopsis for crime novel: A recently retired cop who's been diagnosed with brain cancer is on a week-long cruise when a man he's chatted with the night before suddenly disappears. Believing he's been murdered, the man's desperate wife reaches out to the retired cop, who fights headaches and dizzy spells as he works to solve the mystery. He begins to hear and see things, confusing the symptoms of his tumour for real events. The missing person is a businessman in the chemical industry, and from conversations with his wife, the retired cop understands that his dealings might not always have been above board. It turns out that he's wanted by an international cartel, and the retired cop discovers that the ship is carrying lethal cargo. The retired cop – Halvar Mase, single, lifelong workaholic, remembers every case he's been involved in. His brain is like a library.

I get up to check on the boys, who are sitting in separate chairs in the shade, pecking at their phones. The apple tree leans heavily on the stick I propped against the trunk a decade ago; the lawn tilts and everything tilts with it. And there's Cilla, wielding her phone.

'You know what to do,' she says.

'I do?'

'As soon as she wakes up.'

'Is this another thing on one of your lists?'

Instead of replying, she keeps flicking her thumb across the screen and goes to the boys. Everyone must be activated before Annie wakes up; everyone must look busy with some kind of project related to the property; there must be the impression that we love the cabin and tend to it lovingly now that Annie can't. I really did love this house once. The quiet of the garden, the sense of freedom on the dock with the archipelago and the sea right there. I loved sawing that pole that props up the apple tree so it doesn't collapse, a temporary solution until we could get hold of an arborist to help us; I repaired the roof with roofing felt, smeared sealant around the pipes in the kitchen when they leaked from the fittings, spackled the rowboat's hull where the surface had cracked, painted the façade red where it was peeling, and researched draining and regrading lawns. And when it became impossible to ignore that these temporary solutions were permanent, I shrugged and figured that we'd remodel most of it soon anyway, extend out and regrade the whole goddamn incline.

The boys grumble but still slide out of their chairs and join me. We head to the tool shed. I open the door

Small Comfort

and wait a second in order to air out the first stale puff of mould and dust. Then we enter the darkness. I flip the switch and nothing happens. Nico whimpers when he stumbles on something and Lukas mumbles, spins round and leaves through the door. After a minute or so, he's back with a torch, painting the room with the beam.

It's big for a shed, perhaps sixty square feet or even more, and I remember how pleased I used to be with its size and everything we could store in there, everything we'd hauled to the island and never returned to the mainland. Lukas methodically illuminates the short wall of the shed, pausing at every object as if to identify it before he continues his search. Our attention follows the light: dirty garden tools in an old milk crate, a stack of board games, a soil auger, a pressure washer and tree clippers sharing a paper bag, a pile of kid-size rubber boots under a stool and on top of the stool a baking machine and a table fan with the cord in a knot next to it. By the stool are two additional paper bags holding comic books and, on top of them, children's rakes, children's shovels and a children's lawnmower in red plastic. The shed's long wall is lined with hooks from which hang hand nets, life vests, fishing rods and nets in blue nylon, and under these hooks are black plastic bags full of clothes, a bag of mortar, stacked tiles in some bumpy kind of stone, a transparent plastic bag stuffed with empty cans, a children's bike with stabilisers, a box that's got parts of a car track poking out of it, a rubbish bin with rolled-up posters in it, a low bookcase that holds paperback crime novels and an incomplete encyclopaedia, a few folding chairs, a rusty pitchfork, a partially inflated sea monster, a toolbox and a number of crates.

Lukas shines his torch into the crate, revealing perhaps fifty records, two speakers, a record player, an amp and an old typewriter I don't remember ever using. Nico grumbles behind me, Lukas hums some melody, the light continues its journey. On the other short wall there's a small, inflatable canoe leaning next to a red stove made from particle board, and a beer crate full of toy cars. Next to it stand paper bags with gossip magazines, another rubbish bin, an unopened pack of toilet paper, a couple of empty glass frames, a three-legged kitchen chair and two oars. The beam lingers on a yellow truck in plastic that a child can ride by kicking the ground with their feet.

'I remember that one,' Lukas says. 'I rode down the Incline on it.'

'And I caught you before you crashed into the bushes,' I tell him.

'Here,' Nico says.

Small Comfort

He's got two rakes in his hands. Lukas grabs one, hands me the torch and leaves. I shine the light into one of the corners. There it is, all the way in the back, behind stacked kitchen chairs and a folded tarp. We bought it second-hand on the mainland and took it out in the boat. Driving across the bay, Cilla and I sat in the aft and looked at the enormous object in the bow, convinced the boat would sink unless we sat completely still. The gas canister stands next to it. I move some things around to make a path through the disorder, grab the canister, and roll the machine into the sun. I get a rag from the kitchen to clean the dust and oil off the chassis. The boys are both leaning on their rakes and watching me.

'We're going to wait until she wakes up,' I say.

'We know,' Nico says.

'The minute she's up, though.'

'That's when we get going. We know,' Nico says.

'Are we supposed to put on our happy faces?' Lukas asks.

He contorts his narrow face into a smile and I'm suddenly aware of how serious he always looks, as if he's perpetually trying to solve a complex riddle.

'I don't think our faces are a parameter in her assessment,' I say. 'But feel free.'

'You're telling me I'm free to dispose of my own face as I see fit?'

'I think we should stick to a standard range of faces. Though I imagine that's a pretty broad range.'

'And at dinner tonight?'

'In a more intimate setting, the facial expression has a greater impact. That narrows the interval.'

I open the fuel cap and fill the tank. Cilla comes walking, Molly on her hip, phone in hand.

'She asked me to wake her at ten. So it would be appropriate if you could start at five past. Over there. No need to be right at her bedroom window, considering the fumes.'

Cilla points at the Incline.

'Sure,' I tell her.

We wait. It's a warm day, cirrus clouds and a chorus of thrushes and finches. After I popped the biggest bump yesterday, the itch has expanded its territory on my balls, taking on the character of an invasion. There's no suitable mirror in the house and no privacy at all, so I won't be able to do a more thorough inspection during the day. I consider the possibility of locking myself inside the bathroom to photograph the back.

'There's a route,' Lukas says, after a while.

'A route?'

'Along the west coast. Route 66. We'll rent a car at the airport. Three weeks.'

Small Comfort

'This is the bribe that you're talking about?'

'Or four, so we can shake the jetlag and see everything we want to see. Roadside diners, motels with balconies, the ocean.'

'The ocean, naturally. Beach, a bit of sun,' I say.

'Motel rooms with bloodstained carpeting.'

'Corpses in the tub.'

'Not quite dissolved in nitric acid.'

'The cops came and the murderer didn't have time to conceal all his evidence.'

'I'm in,' Nico says.

'Everyone's in,' I say. 'The three of us are in. I promise.'

Synopsis: A forensic psychologist is brought to a cave on a touristy island in the Mediterranean. A whole family has been murdered in there, and the bodies have been arranged in a strange, highly symbolic manner where every victim's placement and position appears to tell its own story. The psychologist is asked to interpret the patterns and provide a picture of the murderer's psyche. The bodies indicate a tragic childhood marked by violence, abuse, monotony and loneliness. Initially, the choice of victims appears random, but over time details emerge that make the psychologist believe that the family's father and the murderer knew each other. Alongside a string of jobs in politics, the father has been running a chain of badly functioning residential treatment facilities, turning a handsome profit. The murderer is among those who've had the bad luck of ending up in one of these institutions. The forensic psychologist: Jakop Mendel – prostate cancer, issues with his own masculinity, makes swift psych assessments of everyone he meets, is secretly in love with the colleague assisting him. Said colleague – Amanda Ranje, intuitive, former professional gymnast, happily married.

Five minutes past ten I drag the machine to the top of the Incline, pull up the choke and grab the choke lever with my index and middle finger. There I am, the little plastic piece in my hand and gas fumes in my nose, memories rising and sinking along my spine. The many summers with this colossus on the hill, in recent years solely for Annie's satisfaction. And then the tug, so hard it's as if my elbow is going to crack, a rotating cough from inside, and another tug, more forceful this time. My sons are watching. I hear Cilla on the porch. Another tug and there's just a sad wheeze from the inside, and yet another, now with no result at all. I grab the choke with both hands, put one foot against the chassis and pull from the bottom of myself. I hear one of the boys chortle, but avoid looking their way, cognisant of the sun burning my neck and the bad footing I have in my father-in-law's slippers. They're not made for labour, these slippers. They're made for gin drinks on the veranda, cigars and quiet, a leisurely stroll on the trail down to the water. They're made to wait on the dock while their master goes for a swim. I hear Cilla say something and I tug again so I won't have to listen, pull from the depths of my body, this working-class body, this working-class body that hates physical labour, that hates all kinds of labour, and I remind myself that this is the last summer and that next summer I'll have my own place, where a self-driving robotic lawnmower run by remote control will mow the lawn all day. I tug again, for the last summer, in a prayer that this is the last summer, and the engine rattles and coughs into action. I straighten my back, give the boys a thumbs-up and start pushing the roaring colossus down the Incline. The boys come after with their rakes.

Going down, the incline of the Incline helps the work. All that's required is a strong grip on the handle so the machine doesn't roll down the hill too fast. Going up, however. I can't remember how I attacked the slope last time, or how I usually do it. The first time I push it in front of me, early Sisyphus-style, with glasses fogging up with perspiration and my arms and shoulders going numb from the effort by the time I reach the summit. I don't want to risk turning off the engine so I stand in the roar and shake my arms while looking at my sons who lazily scratch through the islands of grass that have formed in my wake.

Next time I go uphill, I pull the machine after me, walking backwards up the incline, and this must be the approach Sisyphus would ultimately have chosen if he could, providing optimum dividends from the muscular exertion. The slippers have become sticky from mud and grass and I worry I'll slip and drop the machine right down the hill. I consider going to the shed for a pair of boots, but I don't want to turn the engine off. Nor can I let the machine stand there and drone while I run to the shed and look, and trying to reach either of the boys with a request in this noise seems hopeless. The slippers will have to do. It's probably the last summer I'll wear them, the last summer these slippers will exist at all. They are likely to disappear when Rainer and Cilla move on the remodel. They'll be gone just like the bathrobe and the stinking sink, the apple tree and the attic, the dock and the rubble in the shed and all the rest of it and this lawn and the ancient hulk I am now, for the fourth time, dragging up the Incline.

An hour later, Cilla waves at me from the porch. I've finished work on the Incline and have transitioned to the lawn's flatter parts. There's a pile of fresh grass three feet tall next to the apple tree. My sons have abandoned their rakes and returned to the recliners in the shade. Exhaust fumes cover the garden like a fog. I turn off the machine and go up to her. She's looking at Molly, who is falling asleep in the stroller.

'That colossus, huh,' she says.

'Weighs a ton.'

'We should have got a new one ages ago.'

'A ton, two tons.'

'And the fumes.'

'She's up?'

'Breakfasted and ready. She was watching you guys through the window. Looked impressed.'

'Did she say anything?'

'No. But it created a good atmosphere. This desire to make things look nice. She likes it when the family collaborates.'

Cilla seems relaxed too. Her face is smooth when she looks at me, no angry lines, no narrowing ironies, nothing sharp.

'And now?'

'The annual inspection.'

Annie is scanning the kitchen. She stops and looks at a wall, puts a hand against it as if to assess its structure and durability. Then she probes the floor with her cane, walks to the sink and loudly pulls air into her nose.

'No, there's no smell of mould here.'

'Not now, no,' I say. 'It's only when it rains.'

Cilla looks at me and puts a pointer and middle finger to her mouth. I look back, quizzical. The boys follow our gazes. I pick up my phone and start moving my thumb across the screen; Cilla shakes her head again, so I put it back in my shirt pocket. Annie opens the cupboards over the sink and inspects every shelf, moving what's in there so she can get a look behind. She opens the pantry, the bottom kitchen cabinets and the chest that doubles as kitchen seating, takes out a bowl and turns it in her hands before putting it back down. She mutters something, pulls out a creaking drawer and looks.

'You've kept the silverware.'

'Yes,' Cilla says. 'Why would we change it?'

Cilla's voice: as if she's on stage, trying to make herself into someone else, another daughter than the one she is. The person Cilla now plays is constructed from soft malleable plastic that she's wrapped around Annie's opinions and impulses. This person is attentive to every nuance of Annie's voice and ready to fulfil the smallest hint of a wish. I've got enough tenderness for Cilla to have empathy for the acrobatics she's forced to perform, but not so much that I can't see the humour in this situation. There might even be a role for me to play here, now that I think about it.

'We're thinking about buying new silverware, though,' I say.

Cilla glares at me and Lukas chortles through his nose.

'Why would you do that?' Annie says, and tilts her head.

'Well, this set has been here since the seventies. Or even longer. What do I know?'

'Yes?'

'Sixties? Seventies?'

Everyone in the room is looking at me. Annie with her head tilted, Cilla with a frown, the boys with anticipation. I have no idea what I'm going to say or why I even opened my mouth to talk about the cutlery at all, but standing in the middle of this stuffy kitchen I have a lovely feeling of vertigo, a feeling that I could jeopardise everything by saying just a few words, that I've created a choice for myself, an opportunity to risk it all. During a few seconds of clarity, I consider the situation. Perhaps this is where the horror of my life begins, on a pleasant Saturday in July, with a former mother-in-law performing an inspection of a house and a marriage and a little uppity obstruction around the silverware.

'I mean, we were planning to buy a new set, but then we concluded that this lovely silverware will do just fine for a few summers more. It was actually hard to find anything as good to buy. The design on those is classic – you might even say timeless,' I say.

Cilla shakes her head, digs in her shirt pocket and finds a lip balm. Nico smiles; Lukas studies my face with interest. Annie closes the drawer. The situation and its set of possible outcomes recede, and we move on.

Annie inspects every room, every drawer in every dresser. She pulls her cane over the floor planks, she sits on the sofa and immediately stands up again, she pokes her head into the outhouse, raps the trunk of the apple tree with her knuckles, then stops at the open door of the tool shed. Here she looks at Cilla with an expectant expression.

'That's this summer's big project,' Cilla says. 'Right, Lars?'

'That's right. The boys and I are going to get started the minute we're done with the garden.'

'And paint it too,' Cilla says.

'Spackle first, then paint,' I say.

Small Comfort

Annie leaves the shed without a word. She wanders across the half-mowed lawn and stands on the edge of the Incline, inspecting it for a while, then walks back to the porch. We follow.

Molly is awake in the stroller, eyes darting around.

Annie looks at the child, then up at us. 'Does she talk yet?'

'A few select words,' Cilla says.

'When she wants to,' I say.

Annie looks down at the child again.

'I suppose a bit of variety never hurt,' she says.

'A girl, right. That's kind of new,' Cilla says.

'Right,' I say. 'A daughter. What else can a man hope for in life?'

'I mean the look of her,' Annie says. 'She's got something entirely her own going on, doesn't she? If you compare.'

Annie gestures at the boys, who are standing next to each other with their hands behind their backs. Aside from what distinguishes them, they're identical, with my thick, dark curls and eyebrows.

'Yeah, she seems to have picked up a different set of genes,' Cilla says, and looks at me with an urging expression.

'My mother was pretty blonde,' I add.

'Yeah,' Cilla says. 'We think that's where it comes

from, her light hair. Genes, you know, they're a real lottery.'

I lift Molly from the stroller with one hand under her back and one under the diaper. But she's too heavy, so I have to change my grip and hold her with both hands around the torso instead. She's wearing a green romper with clouds on it, white socks and a yellow sun hat. She looks at me with a trembling lip and I hear Cilla inhale sharply next to me.

'Come to Daddy,' I say and place Molly with her face against my shoulder. I bounce her gently while I look at the others. Lukas has turned round to stifle laughter, Nico looks at Molly and me with narrow eyes and Cilla has her lip balm again, eyes glued to the patio floor as she smears it over her lips. Annie steps closer to me and puts her hand to the child's cheek.

'It is indeed a real gamble,' she says. 'Genes. A true lottery.'

She caresses Molly's cheeks and nose, then moves her fingers over her blonde, wavy hair. I hear Molly gather her voice in a complaint and pass her to Cilla.

Annie leaves the porch and enters the house. There's the sound of the electric kettle turning on.

'I think I'm going to head to the mainland for a couple of things,' I say.

Small Comfort

I put my hand out to Cilla. She looks at it. A delicious moment.

'What do you want?'

I smile and tilt my head.

'Do you not have any?' she asks.

'My card isn't working.'

'Well, I guess that's just something you'll have to fix.'

'Now?'

I keep my hand extended to her, and smile.

'Doesn't matter from which wallet the money comes,' I say, 'right?'

Cilla shuts her eyes for a brief moment and breathes through her nose. Then she puts Molly back on her hip, enters the cabin and comes back with a card in her hand and a sticky note with the pin code. I look at the card.

'Mastercard. New?'

'A year, two years.'

'Last year you had something else.'

'Could be.'

'This is some kind of platinum, or what?'

The card gleams when I hold it up to the light.

'It's an absolutely normal credit card. I thought you said you were going?'

Annie comes out with a teacup in her hand.

'Anything you want, Annie?'

'What would that be?'

'Oh, I don't know. Some kind of particular chocolate. Crispbread. Anything.'

'Thank you, no need.'

The angle of her neck and the gaze on my feet in the soiled slippers before she turns around and disappears into the cabin again.

Cilla looks at the slippers.

'Those aren't some fucking farmwork shoes,' she hisses.

'No. And I'm no farm boy.'

'I've come to understand as much, thank you very much. Clean them and put them by the stairs. So everyone can see that they've been cleaned.'

Synopsis for crime novel: Late nineties, a helicopter downed in Murmansk, two little pink pills in the throat of a dead canary bird in Åhus, tiny swastikas etched into the nails of a legendary Jewish CEO when he wakes up one Christmas morning from a lethal injection in the back of his knee. How are these things related? In the final minutes of World War Two, a group of guards in a Nazi concentration camp swapped identities with Jewish prisoners, pretended to be saved and subsequently

Small Comfort

absconded. One of the young ex-guards started a business and made a name for himself without anybody knowing his secret. Now, however, history is catching up with him, as he understands when he wakes up with the swastikas on his nails. His wife and grown grandchildren (proud grandchildren of a Holocaust survivor) don't understand why he doesn't want to call the police. He feels the poison work in his body. The day prior, a helicopter was downed – and another Holocaust survivor was supposed to have been onboard the craft, assaying new gas fields. This man decided to stay back, following an intuition that surprised even him. Just a feeling, he told his daughter, a well-known media personality. Inspectors Cresson and Turner look down at the canary with two cyanide capsules in its mouth, brought to the precinct by its confused owner. Who were they meant for? Could it be the bird's owner, a female retiree whose biggest hobby was attending the funerals of people she didn't know? Or her terminally ill husband, a Holocaust survivor? Inspector Cresson – single, with children all over the village and a number of angry ex-wives, charming curls, witty, drinks too much. Turner – ex-evangelical, has a wife and a daughter. The two inspectors are always talking about something else while they discuss the case they're working on.

I walk the trail down to the boat with the boys in tow; I stop and wait until they're on either side of me before I keep walking.

'Why are kids always walking behind their parents? Toddlers will hold your hand, but soon enough this strolling-behind takes over,' I say.

'It starts around the age of five or six. That's when the kids realise,' Lukas says.

'Realise what?'

'That they're involved in a towing project.'

'Towing?'

'What groceries are we getting?' Nico asks.

'Chocolate. Cinnamon buns. Coffee. Everything that's delicious in this world,' I say.

'It would be great if you got a divorce soon,' Lukas says.

'We will, we will. It's going to happen,' I say. 'Very soon.'

RAISING READERS
Books Build Bright Futures

Dear Reader,

We'd love your attention for one more page to tell you about the crisis in children's reading, and what we can all do.

Studies have shown that reading for fun is the **single biggest predictor of a child's future life chances** – more than family circumstance, parents' educational background or income. It improves academic results, mental health, wealth, communication skills, ambition and happiness.[1]

The number of children reading for fun is in rapid decline. Young people have a lot of competition for their time. In 2024, 1 in 10 children and young people in the UK aged 5 to 18 did not own a single book at home.[2]

Hachette works extensively with schools, libraries and literacy charities, but here are some ways we can all raise more readers:

- Reading to children for just 10 minutes a day makes a difference
- Don't give up if children aren't regular readers – there will be books for them!
- Visit bookshops and libraries to get recommendations
- Encourage them to listen to audiobooks
- Support school libraries
- Give books as gifts

There's a lot more information about how to encourage children to read on our website: **www.RaisingReaders.co.uk**

Thank you for reading.

hachette UK

---

[1] OECD, '21st-Century Readers: Developing Literacy Skills in a Digital World', 2021, https://www.oecd.org/en/publications/21st-century-readers_a83d84cb-en.html

[2] National Literacy Trust, 'Book Ownership in 2024', November 2024, https://literacytrust.org.uk/research-services/research-reports/book-ownership-in-2024